To Tina,

be

ADEN *to* ZANZIBAR

R DAVID

The first of the *Plain Sight* novels

Published in the UK in 2020 by Athan Press

ISBN 978-1-8380825-0-5

Cover design and typeset by Spiffing Covers

For Gill

For my Father and *Sohrab and Rustum*

Contents

Chapter One

Aden, Australia, Bahamas, Barbados…

Jack's earliest memories were jumbled fragments, he didn't know which was first and it didn't really matter. There was Auntie Nesta coming down the road from the bus stop with a packet of hake; the smell of Gwyn the Milk; the night his brother was born; running with the wind on Rest Bay with his coat held up like a sail; fireworks in next door's garden; Uncle Idris watching the rugby and crying during the anthem; hearing the pop lorry beeping its horn and running out to catch it with his friend Huw – always Huw. But it was on the day the boy from school disappeared that Jack's memories sprang together like iron filings around a magnet.

When he came down in the morning, his father was sitting with Gwyn the Milk talking about it. Gwyn's hat was on the table and he was filling the kitchen with the smell of cows. His rusty old van was in the drive, covered in mud, where it had clinked with milk bottles and grunted to a stop. Jack heard him every morning because he used their house as a delivery depot for the rest of the street and he always came in for tea. *The Herald* was spread out between them. It had a thick, black headline and a picture. His father was saying, 'I'm going to take him up to Jean's aunties' in Porth.'

'I would, Alan,' said Gwyn. 'It won't do for him to stay here if you can help it. It won't do for any of them. I don't know what the school's going to do, do you? But I'm sure they're not going to object to you taking Jack away for bit.'

'I wasn't going to ask them, Gwyn.'

'No, no. I'll be interested to see how many of the children will be in today. I'll be down there later. I might see Mr Tanner.' He looked at the paper and shook his head. 'I wouldn't be at all surprised if there wasn't any school, would you? No, not surprised at all.' He shook his head again.

'Jack?' His father saw him standing in the doorway. 'I didn't hear you come down. Where's your mum?'

'She's upstairs with Aled.' Jack was still sleepy, but now on tiptoe, trying to see whose picture it was in the paper.

His father closed the paper and folded it. He looked at Gwyn, 'You take this,' he said.

Gwyn heaved his tummy off his knees. 'I must be going, I'll see you later, Alan. You behave now, young Jack,' but he didn't smile as he left.

Outside, Jack heard the rattle of milk crates and the creak-slam of his van door.

Up, up and when they reached Trebanog and came over the top of the mountain, he had to put his legs out to stop himself sliding off the backseat of the car as they started down the other side. It was raining. The terraced houses were piled on top of each other ready to tumble into the Rhondda Valley and the grey, lifeless river far below. Halfway down, they got to the shop and parked opposite at the Beinon Arms. His father called, 'Wait, Jack.' It was too late, but he remembered to look both ways. He ran across the road, banged open the door and went straight to the sweet counter, watched by one of his uncles in his brown shop coat standing next to the bacon slicer. Another uncle was sitting on a high stool in front of the till, smoking a cigarette between the tip of his thumb and forefinger. He had small, round glasses.

The shop had three uncles, Emlyn, Howell and Idris, and two aunties, Delia and Nesta, who ruled. There were two staircases, middle and back; seven bedrooms off a big square landing, with a cast-iron safe in the inner corner; and it took up two terraced houses at the end of a row. As well as sweets, it sold groceries.

He had other uncles, aunties and cousins scattered in identical houses all the way down to Porth. He couldn't remember who they all were, or how they were related, but they all knew him as Jean's boy. He did remember being shy and thinking, 'Which one is this?' They loved him because of who he was, every one of them.

Jack lay on the floor and slowly turned the heavy, stiff pages of Idris' album of stamps of the Empire. It was a wonder, with the stamps laid out like tiny beds of summer flowers from faraway, exotic places: *Aden, Australia, Bahamas, Barbados…* pastel windows to scenes of palm trees, blue, blue seas and one or two as much as ten shillings. He went to those places as the windows streamed with rain and mountains and the granite fist of Nelson's Rock.

Idris, painstakingly precise, had written under each stamp in black fountain pen (*always* black), *Perf. Wmk.* (whatever that meant, it was complicated) and, where there was a fault, a tiny, sticky red arrow pointed to it with a note at the flight end explaining what it was.

The album was so heavy Jack couldn't pick it up and, because it was precious, he only tried to once. Idris kept it in a glass-fronted bookcase in his bedroom (the second on the right off the landing). Jack asked to see it whenever Idris wasn't working in the shop.

In the dead of night, when he was cwtched under the satin eiderdown of his auntie's bed, Jack went to those places as he listened to the Western Welsh buses grinding their way out of the depths of the valley, vibrating the bricks and bedposts with the strain. In the morning, curled up in the chair in the back room watching Auntie Delia light the fire, he imagined the sun rising over the white, white beaches but the warmth only crept and the butter on the hearth didn't even begin to soften for half an hour.

After Nesta had swept the pavement outside and talked to the neighbours in their flowery house coats doing the same, Jack sat behind the counter in the shop as the customers came and went. The uncles spent more time talking than serving. Delia came in and asked them if they wanted peeled or unpeeled tinned tomatoes with their lunch. The uncles pondered and had a vote but Emlyn couldn't make up his mind, so they left the deciding vote to Jack. 'I like peeled tomatoes,' said Idris. 'Don't you, Jack?'

'I like peeled tomatoes, too,' he told Delia and she took a tin off the shelf and went through to the back.

At 1pm (there was a big, wooden clock on the wall), they locked the doors and let him turn the *Open* sign around to *Closed*. He had lunch with his aunties and uncles around the table that folded out, with the bowl of wax fruit moved to the windowsill and, afterwards, he helped with the washing up. He didn't drop any plates and stood on a chair over the sink to soap them down. Then they sat in front of the fire until it was time to reopen the shop. Every day the same and he loved it (except the cold in the mornings when he had to run down from bed to pull the rug over his knees and wait for the fire). He forgot about school and wanted to stay at the shop forever. But, after a week, his father came to fetch him. One of the uncles gave him a half crown, the other two a shilling each. Nesta said, 'He's been good as gold, Alan,' (she always said that) and they left the drizzle-filled Rhondda for the drizzle-swept spaces of Bridgend.

His grandfather, John, was there when they got back. 'Come on boy,' he said. Jack was always 'boy' to him, never

Jack or John (except to his mother – *sometimes* – and two Johns was confusing). 'Let's go for a walk.'

He knew where because his grandfather often took him for long walks on the dunes – long for little legs – over the hidden rooftops of the lost city of Kenfig, buried beneath the sand, with only one crumbling pillar of stones proud above the marram grass and brambles, defiant like the standard of a beaten army. They always stopped there, as if it was an altar to pay their respects, but it also let his grandfather catch his breath.

In the distance, ten miles down the coast, huge clouds of steam, lit by a flickering orange light, rolled out of the steelworks at Port Talbot and flames on masts flapped slowly as they burned gas from the oil refinery. 'Can you smell the sulphur, boy? There's nothing between here and there, no roads, no paths, only Sker, the loneliest beach in Wales and dunes and dunes and the river where it comes into the sea. I've only ever been there once. Too late now, I won't go there again, but you can, boy, one day.' He bent his ear toward the sand. 'How many people are down there, do you think?'

Jack got down on his hands and knees and listened but all he could hear was the rustling grass in the wind. Then, Sam, his grandfather's labrador, stuck his curious nose in Jack's face and snuffled. He pushed him away.

'What do you hear, boy? Can't you hear their voices?'

'Are they down there, Grandpa? Go away, Sam.'

'Of course they are, can't you hear them?'

'No.'

'Maybe they don't want you to hear them? Maybe you're not old enough yet.'

'How old will I have to be to hear them?'

'Ohhh, ten at least.'

'*Ten*?' That was impossibly grown up and an impossibly long time to wait. 'Will they let me hear them just a little bit?'

'We'll see on the way back. If you're nice to them they might let you or perhaps they won't, who knows?'

'Can't they let me hear them just once, just for a second?'

'They've stopped talking, now, boy. I can't hear them either. Maybe on the way back?' Jack got up and Sam bounded away to the top of a dune and started barking at something. 'What's the matter with that dog? *Sam, Sam*, come away, boy.' Sam was 'boy' now too.

His grandfather had been a miner, a pit sinker who lined the shafts with bricks and his hands were clawed with arthritis. He said that falling bricks had broken every bone in both hands and the lasting damage of years underground was obvious to everyone. Jack grew up with old men who had blue scars and no puff where every son was told the same: 'You don't want to go underground. In my day, there wasn't a choice, except the army. You've got your whole life ahead of you. Get a job where you don't have to take your jacket off, boy.' He walked slowly, stooping, planting a wooden stick with a bulb-like head, with his flat cap (never without it) shading his eyes, and grey curls springing out over his neck. He had been a big man but, now, he was gaunt and his skin was yellowing; there were liver spots on the backs of his crippled hands, blotching over blue veins and a taut, uneven fan of whitish bones. A long time afterwards, when time didn't matter, he told Jack about his life from beginning to end. He said he had been ill for years, 'As so many of us were.'

When they got to Kenfig Pool, a glassy lake like a hidden oasis, his grandfather said, 'Don't ever swim in there, boy, *never*,' because almost every summer, a swimmer got caught in the weed and drowned. He shook his head, 'Why won't they stay out of the water?' but he wasn't asking because Jack would have told him it wasn't the weed but the people from the lost city grabbing them and pulling them down.

Jack chattered more questions about the people in the sand and, after a while, his grandfather stopped trying to make up answers in his hoarse voice and laughed, 'Do you have any more difficult questions, boy? Wait until we get there, will you?'

There was a place where they stopped to sit on a log and Sam ran ahead to lie in the grass, with his head between his paws and his tongue hanging out, watching them intently as they approached. His grandfather sat down carefully with his hands on his knees and legs apart to open his lungs and do a contemplative battle of remembrance with the dust, mouth open, chest rising painfully and falling. A full moon was rising, round and pale. 'A spring tide, boy,' he said quietly, almost to himself. 'Did you know there are four tides each day? Two low and two high. Do you know what a spring tide is, boy?'

Jack sat with him for a while, swinging his legs, forgetting the question, but he was soon bored and jumped down as Sam jumped up to chase him along the bank.

They listened for the voices again next to the pillar of stones. His grandfather watched as Jack ran his hands over them, put his ear against them and then lay flat on the dune amongst the grass and crawling tendrils of brambles. 'Can you hear them, boy?' he asked, leaning on his stick. 'They're keeping quiet, I think they must be listening to us. Ask them, boy, go on, ask them.'

Jack put his mouth as close to the sand as he could. Sam's head appeared over his shoulder and panted into his face. '*Shhh*, Sam,' he told him, and Sam swivelled his head to look him directly in the eyes. He pushed him away and Sam ran off, barking at something invisible. '*Shhh*, Sam,' Jack hissed after him, sitting up and slapping the tops of his thighs with annoyance. '*Shhh*.'

'He can hear them, boy, that's why he's barking. Go on, ask them.'

Jack put his mouth to the sand again. 'Hello, hello? Are you there?' and listened hard. 'Are you there? Please answer? *Please*?' But Sam was barking.

'I don't think they're going to, boy, not this time. They can be awkward. Next time, we'll ask them, next time we're here.'

'What's he looking at, Grandpa?' Sam was standing very still with one paw raised, staring at an empty patch of sky above the dune, as if someone was standing there.

'That *dog*. What can he see, I wonder?' He hobbled up to the top of the dune and looked over. 'Nothing. What's the matter with you, boy? Rabbits? Come on, we can't stay here all day.' He turned to Jack. 'They're not talking today, boy. Ice cream?' and he came sideways down the slope, stick first.

Sam perked to life and rushed past them, barking again, and disappeared.

It was uphill back to the car and Jack could hear his grandfather wheezing as Sam ran in every direction, following his nose, sneezing into the sand.

They stopped twice, the second time for minutes, because his grandfather was struggling. 'Don't go underground,' he gasped, 'you don't want to end up like this, do you?'

When they got to the car, he bent over and rested with his hands against the roof. His eyes were squeezed shut as all his effort went into sucking air deep enough into himself. A drop of sweat dripped from his chin. Then he blew out his cheeks and stood straight. 'Come on, boy. Sam?' He fished the keys out of his pocket and Sam jumped in.

On the way into Porthcawl, Jack dropped one of the shillings through the metal grille in the dashboard. He tried to see down the slit.

'What have you done, boy?'

'It's gone down there.'

'What has?'

'One of my shillings.'

'It'll be in the road or stuck in the engine. Do you want to stop to look for it?' They pulled over onto the verge. 'Stay there, Sam. Traffic.' But there wasn't any. It was a quiet country lane bordering the fields and dunes with the sea beyond – and the growing moon. They searched. 'Let me get the bonnet up.' His grandfather looked into the engine. 'It's not in there, boy, there's nowhere for it to catch. Keep looking.'

'I hope it hasn't gone into the grass, Grandpa, we'll never find it if it has.'

'It has to be here somewhere, boy. Do you remember what we were passing when you dropped it?'

Jack looked down the featureless verge: there was no hedge, no trees. 'No.'

'Well, keep looking then. Are you sure you dropped it? It's not still in your pocket is it?'

Jack took out the half crown and remaining shilling. 'No.' His eyes filled with tears.

His grandfather brushed back Jack's hair. 'Come on, boy, we'll find it and, if we don't, I'll have to give you another one before we go for the ice cream.' They carried on looking. Then his grandfather stopped and pointed with his stick. 'What's that, then, boy?' And there it was, standing on its edge, lodged between blades of grass. 'No wonder we couldn't find it. It must have rolled in there.'

Sam was watching curiously through the rear window of the car as they went back. Jack was happy again. 'I need a cup of tea,' said his grandfather.

Alphonsi's made the best ice cream Jack had ever tasted or ever would taste but he couldn't say 'Alphonsi' properly so he called it Porthcawl ice cream and everyone knew what he meant. His grandfather told him he had known Mr Alphonsi for thirty years. 'Interesting time, the war,' he said, and added (mysteriously, to Jack's ears), 'he was interred at Island Farm but they still let him out for three days a week to make the ice cream. No one wanted to stop him doing that.' Now the café was run by Mr Alphonsi's son and daughter-in-law. They had two children who were a bit older than Jack.

When they went in, Mr Alphonsi was sitting at his usual table drinking coffee from a tiny cup and reading the newspaper. 'We don't serve your type,' he said.

'You've got no choice,' answered his grandfather, sliding onto the red leather bench opposite him. Jack climbed up beside him. They both laughed. Jack had to kneel to get his elbows onto the table.

'Ice cream, Jack?' asked Mr Alphonsi.

'Yes please.'

'Emma,' he called to his daughter-in-law. 'Ice cream for this young rascal and tea for the old bugger.'

Jack looked at his grandfather.

'Don't you repeat that in front of your mum,' he said, 'she'll never let me take you out again.'

Mr Alphonsi folded the newspaper and placed the sugar dispenser on top so it was out of bounds. 'Dreadful business, dreadful,' he said.

'He's been up in Porth since… with Jean's family.'

'Ah, the ice cream,' exclaimed Mr Alphonsi, seeing Emma approaching with a dish with three white domes and a wafer stuck in each one.

'Raspberry, chocolate or *both*, Jack?' asked Emma, glancing at his grandfather. 'Whisper to me,' and she bent close.

'Both please.'

She squirted the sauce in circles all over the ice cream. 'Here's your tea, Mr Harris.'

She nodded toward the newspaper. 'Do they know anymore?'

'Alan's been talking to Sergeant Phillips.'

'Has he?' asked Mr Alphonsi. 'Phillips will always find someone to hang.'

'Someone deserves… eat your ice cream, boy.'

They talked and drank their tea and coffee. Mr Alphonsi lit a cigarette. 'Do you want one of these?' he asked over the flaring match.

'I mustn't,' answered his grandfather, 'it's bad enough without them, not that I wouldn't if I could.'

'Mmm,' said Mr Alphonsi, looking down his nose as he blew a stream of smoke toward the ceiling. 'One's not going to do you any harm.'

'Just one then.' His grandfather plucked a cigarette from the pack, lit it and leaned back.

After a moment of rare enjoyment he and Mr Alphonsi talked some more about things Jack didn't understand and people he hadn't heard of so he stopped being interested and watched Emma moving between the tables, smiling at him, as he slowly ate the ice cream that would not, could not, taste any better.

When they got home, his grandfather came with Jack into the house. He said to Jack's father, 'I told Mario you'd been talking to Sergeant Phillips. Any news?'

His father shook his head.

'I must be going. Look after them both, Alan,' his grandfather said, sternly, as if he was giving his son an instruction that must not be disobeyed. Then he pulled the front door to behind him.

After tea, Jack watched *Robinson Crusoe* on television in the front room.

His father said, 'Stay indoors, there's a good boy, you won't go out will you?'

Jack shook his head.

'Good. I've got to get the coal into the bunker before the rain gets to it. You know where I am and mum's upstairs giving Aled his bath.'

But, not long after, Jack heard a low rumbling, growing louder. He knew what it was so he forgot what his father had said and rushed out to the front garden and looked up. It was roaring and he waited for it to appear when, suddenly, a man's voice, next to his ear, said, 'You're coming with me,' and grabbed Jack's arm, pulled him down the drive and pushed him into the back of a smelly van.

A Vulcan bomber rose out of St Athan and slowly unzipped the sky.

Chapter Two

Basutoland, Bermuda, Bechuanaland Protectorate…

Huw and Jack began their lives from different places because Huw could not remember his father, killed underground before he was born. But they shared many first memories: running out when they heard the pop lorry; walking on the dunes with Jack's grandfather; the tower of stones and the people in the sand; Kenfig Pool; the dragon's fiery eyes over Port Talbot; the best ice cream he would ever taste in Alphonsi's; running on Rest Bay with the wind; but it was the first time he went to the pantomime that Huw began the story of himself.

From then, the theatre in Cardiff became enchanted, unreachable, but he dared to think of himself performing there. Never as the villain, glorious and detestable; Huw was Buttons, that's who he was going to be. That's who he was as one of the kings in the nativity play when he stole the show with his antics. '*Frankincense*,' he declaimed, holding up his tinsel-covered shoebox, 'a gift for the baby Jesus.' He strode to the front of a stage made of old boxes with planks on top and stood with his legs apart, just like Buttons had, but with his striped towel dangling in front of the seated Virgin Mary, bewildered at her eclipse, holding a doll with a painted cardboard halo. 'Lo, I come bearing gifts,' and he made a slow sweep of his arm over the heads of the startled audience and Mr Tanner sitting in the front row. 'And, now, we must give praise to the Son of God,' (obscured behind him, crushed in the crook of Mary's tightly folded arms, her face becoming a little girl's indignant frown) and waited for the applause – claimed it – before returning to his place alongside the other two kings, but unable to resist jiggling his eyebrows, just as Buttons had.

On that first Christmas of memory, his mother, Gwen, bought him *The Big Book of Theatre and Film,* full of colour photographs of plays, musicals, pantomimes and films on set, with explanations of what they were, where they had been performed and made – Hollywood, Pinewood, the West End, Broadway (not Cardiff) – and who the actors were, the most famous with pictures of their own, in character, grimacing in make-up.

Huw turned the pages slowly, wide-eyed, and touched the glossy paper reverently with his fingertips, breathing the heady smell of newness and ink. How could there be such a world? He didn't want to get to the last page and his heart sank as, page by page, its two halves became thicker and thinner until, lingering over the last page before it revealed the finality of the inside cover, he heaved it back to the beginning with a thump, let go his breath and dismissed from his mind that this magical book had an end. Over and over he did the same, beginning to end, beginning to end and never closed it shut. Each time, he noticed more details, each picture revealed something new and he began to memorise the names of the plays and films, the actors and directors, who were the biggest stars and how productions were different, the sets and stage scenery, the way the actors dressed, his favourites taking bow after bow as if the pages were curtain calls, the film premieres and the red carpets. He learnt the history of the theatre and film from the silent era, through talkies, to black and white to colour – there were chapters devoted to it – with old drawings and engravings and pictures of oil paintings, more lurid than pictures of the real thing, and still shots. He could only be happier than this when he was an actor in *The Big Book* itself.

It was a big book because he had to hold it in both hands to carry it up to his bedroom where he put it on his desk, open at the first photograph which he could see sideways when he was lying in bed, its sheen reflecting the dim light coming from outside.

Every night, before he fell asleep, he made himself imagine what it would be like to be an actor in one of the photographs: he designed his own make-up, he made up speeches and decided that he would read all the plays in *The Big Book*, '*All* of them,' he told himself. He couldn't wait to go down to the library in Bridgend to ask if they had copies. Then he began to be afraid they would not. What would he do then? Would school? They had lots of books but he had never seen anything like this. He began a list of all the films he had to watch. Would he ever be able to see them all? He fell asleep worrying. But, when he opened his eyes in the morning, *The Big Book* was the first thing he saw and wanted to see ('Still there,' the magic, he reassured himself), shining and waiting for him.

Huw was six years old and certain of what he wanted to be, as certain as if he was looking back over a long and brilliant career in *The Big Book*, at the highs and the lows and remembering the moment, *now*, when he knew and not regretting a single second of what followed.

He heard his mother in the kitchen and called down to her from the landing but she didn't answer so he went back into his bedroom to get dressed by himself (feeling grown up and wanting to surprise her). In *The Big Book*, as he fiddled with the buttons on his shirt, there was a picture of a boy in uniform standing in the middle of a stage surrounded by adults who were listening intently to what he was saying. Huw looked at himself in the mirror. Apart from his crookedly done up buttons, his school uniform was similar. He stood like the boy, with his hands held out trying to explain. Today, he was the Winslow Boy.

He ran downstairs to tell her, and to ask about the library (how many boys his age would want to read grown-up plays?) but she wasn't there. She always got him ready for school and he wasn't sure whether to feel a quite-so-grown-up reader of plays or to go and find her. She was either in Auntie Eve's next door or she had gone round to see Jack's mother. None of them were real aunties or uncles (not like Jack, who had lots of both): there was Auntie Eve and Uncle Roy, who lived in the house between Jack and his; Auntie Jean and Uncle Alan and Jack's grandfather, Mr Harris, who was never 'uncle'. They were all nearly parents, nearly, and they were always in and out of each other's houses, a pebble-dashed row, a road of them, semi-detached, with a bay window, three bedrooms and a box room; an alley running behind, then Gwyn the Milk's fields and cows grazing. He and Jack played in all three gardens without asking, taking shortcuts through the fences.

There was only his mother and him. So, he ate his cereal alone but waited for some time at the front door for her to come back – she did not – before shutting it.

When he got to school, the gates were locked and there was no one there. Was he early, was his mum looking for him now to get him ready? But no one came, not even Mr Tanner. There was nothing else for it, even though he dawdled, afraid he had done something wrong, so he went home and round the back where the door would be open.

He dropped his satchel on the kitchen floor. 'Mum,' he called, 'school was closed.' There was no answer. Then he heard someone crying. Through the door, he saw her in the front room, sitting on the settee, bent over with her head in her hands, tilted to one side toward the fading photograph of his father on the sideboard. He thought about taking it over to her but she was crying so loudly he started to become frightened and didn't know what to do. Her eyes were closed and red-rimmed. He had never seen her – or anyone – cry like this before. Was this what it was like for her, every day, when he was in school? 'Mummy?' he asked, through a gathering sob of his own, 'Mummy?' she didn't answer. He climbed up on the settee and put his arm around her. She stirred but didn't stop crying or lift her head. 'Mummy?' he whispered, but she buried her face deeper into her hands and cried through her fingers. He leant against her shoulder and, as her body convulsed, his little body did the same, as if he was unborn and still tiny inside her. He didn't know what to do or say except cling to her.

Suddenly, she lifted her head and said, 'Why did you? Why did it happen to you, why *you*? Now I have nothing left, *nothing*.'

'I'm here. Mummy, you've got me, don't forget about me?' She clutched her hands over her face again and, now, she was crying so hard, she was almost wailing. 'Please stop, Mummy, please stop.' She cried harder, as if she might break apart.

They sat for a long time, through the morning, he becoming an extension of her grief and thinking thoughts he could not understand. The sun slanted through the kitchen window into the front room as the afternoon began.

His mother stopped crying and fell asleep on her hands but, when she breathed, it sounded like paper tearing. He was afraid she would die and watched her face. Eventually, she tipped onto her side with her legs pulled up and was quieter. He wished he could go and play with Jack, but he wouldn't leave her. Gently, trying not to wake her and set off the awful crying again, he slipped off the settee and got into the armchair, small and curled in its depth, facing the picture of his father.

It wasn't a very good picture, black and white and already yellowing – so unlike *The Big Book* – but his father's smile gleamed from the middle of it like a white pebble, clean in the sand, and two smaller stones evenly spaced above it, darker, his eyes smiling too. Huw didn't know that he wanted what every son wants from his father; from a father who must love him as every good man loves his son. He must be a good man because all fathers are, *were* (present, past).

His father's face was slowly being erased by the sun coming through the kitchen door (even in Wales, it was bright and often enough) and, unless his mother moved it, there would be nothing left but pictures in the mind and these Huw did not have; his memories could not cling to a lost photograph. His father was a myth, a legend of deeds unknown and only in his mother's uncontained grief was there proof of what a great man he had been.

How would his father have loved him? With hugs, teasing and fun, being told off when he was naughty, and unending kindness even when he was cross? How would he have loved his father? 'Would you take me for walks on the sand dunes – we could take Jack, and Mr Harris can come too? Can we get a dog? Then he can play with Sam. A name? *Buttons*. Can we go to the café in Porthcawl, all of us, and have Alphonsi ice creams?' *Alphonsi.* He had to say it carefully, when he did, but he could say it. 'Mummy must come too; we can't leave mummy here, on her own.' He glanced at her, sleeping quietly now, before returning to the picture. 'We can take Buttons to play on the beach with us and down the fields,' like we used to? Not that, that he couldn't have. They were not words he would ever say: his father was dead. When asked about him (by those who did not know), he replied, 'My daddy is dead.' It was a fact he had always known; he couldn't remember when it happened and he didn't know of the terrible shock it caused. His father was an empty space. But, every day, he saw what it was like to have a father and a shop full of real aunties and uncles from the valleys who brought fish on Tuesdays. He silently observed Jack and Uncle Alan. It was there in everything they did together, but their cues were no use without a father of his own. So, he gave all his love to his mother, she gave all hers to him and it burned desperately hot in one and the same place. But, if Huw could do everything Jack did, he could be Jack? Wasn't that better than being Huw without a father?

In the sunlight, the picture seemed to move: either the shadow was progressing to the side of the frame or his father was quietly telling him, 'You're not Jack, you're Huw. What else could we do, Huw, what else could we do together?' guiding his young son toward the right answer.

'*I'm* Buttons.'

'I thought the dog was Buttons.'

'The dog has to have a different name now.'

'Alright, Huw, you be Buttons,' his father smiled.

He *was* Buttons and the curtain rose, the music struck up, the spotlight picked him in its brilliant circle. 'We can go to the theatre in Cardiff, you, me and mummy – and Jack,' he added, hurriedly. 'Sometimes.' Then, 'You can come and see me on stage, one day – look,' and the spotlight followed the little boy with the world applauding at his feet. 'One day, I will, I really *will*.'

'You will, Huw,' said his father, 'and I will come to see you with mummy.' The shadow slid to his shoulder and touched his face: time for one last smile. He smiled and hoped beyond hope that his son would never know of his pain.

Long after the sun had progressed beyond the kitchen window and his father's white, pebble smile had gone, Huw remained in the armchair watching his mother. He didn't even get up to go to the toilet. Finally, when his legs were stiff and his feet had pins and needles, she turned over and opened her eyes. 'Mummy?'

She pushed herself up. 'Huw?'

'I'm here, I've been here all the time.'

'What will I do without you?' She looked at the picture on the sideboard. 'What will I do?'

'*I'm* here,' Huw insisted.

'There's nothing left,' she sighed, slowly getting to her feet.

'But I am.' So small in the chair, like a pill of energy and comfort. She seemed to drift into the kitchen and he heard her taking down plates off the shelf to make tea. At last, he felt relief that she was doing something normal again. 'I'm just going up to my room,' he called as the water echoed in the kettle. He wasn't going to be the Winslow Boy again.

When Uncle Alan took Jack up to his aunties in Porth, Huw was lonely without his friend. He wanted to ask if he could go too, but his promise to his father not to leave his mother alone could not be broken. He watched Jack and Uncle Alan leave from the window as they disappeared at the end of the road. Jack had so many places he could go to find love and certainty.

A police car appeared, moving slowly, and stopped a few doors down. Two policemen got out carrying torches and began walking in opposite directions up and down the road, looking in front-room windows and up the drives. A second police car stopped behind the first and two more policemen got out and started doing the same on the other side of the road.

School was open the next day. All the teachers were waiting outside when Huw got there. A police car was parked not far away and a policewoman was standing next to it, trying to smile reassuringly at the mothers as they arrived with their children.

When Huw left the house, his mother had been sitting on the settee again, not crying, just slowly swaying back and fore with a screwed-up, tear-damp hankie pressed against her mouth in the ball of her fist. He had eaten his cereal in the kitchen and she hadn't moved. 'I have to go to school, Mummy,' he said but, when he said goodbye, she didn't look at him or answer. His father must have been a wonderful, wonderful man for her to miss him so much after such a long time.

Mr Tanner was stalking the corridors as they went into class. He was beaming at them all and bending down to ask how they were. He was never like this. Huw was less afraid of him.

Miss Williams was usually quite strict but she wasn't today. She took the register out and opened her mouth to start calling the names but stopped before she said, 'Adams.' 'No, I'll mark the register, you don't need to tell me you're here; I know you are.'

Huw watched as she ticked the boxes, her eyes moving from face to face, then she quickly put the register back in the drawer to shut it away.

Assembly. '*The Lord's Prayer*, children,' said Mr Tanner. They said it together, as always, in Welsh. 'Amen.' There were no hymns or announcements, so they filed back to class, line by line from the back.

Miss Williams told them to read their books quietly but the silence became so deep and unbearable that one of the girls started to cry. 'That's enough,' said Miss Williams, 'shall I read you a story?' the class brightened, 'then I shall.' She read them stories until breaktime and, afterwards, they recited the times table up to times ten, then more stories until the bell rang for going home time.

As they were leaving through the school gates, a fight suddenly started between two boys who were best friends. No one knew why. Everyone stood in silence. There were no choruses of '*Fight, fight*,' as usual as the boys flailed and kicked at each other in a tiny storm of fury. Mr Tanner came running over and pulled them apart. The boys hung like rags from each hand. Mr Tanner looked at Miss Williams with an expression of anguish then he let them go and they slumped onto their heels, sulkily, with their heads bowed.

Huw saw their mothers coming but Mr Tanner went to stand next to Miss Williams and said nothing about it.

The days passed and there was always a police car outside the school.

When Jack came home from Trebanog, Huw waited at the end of his garden path and watched as he got into his grandfather's car. He knew where they were going but he had made his promise to his mother and he didn't ask and they didn't ask him as they usually did.

He went back inside and up to his bedroom to his other world and sat with *The Big Book* for hours as the afternoon gave way to evening. There was a double-page spread of a play in a castle with the actors high on the battlements looking over an army threatening at the foot of the walls and waving swords and spears and banging their shields. He switched on the light in the middle of the ceiling and pulled his desk into the middle of the room where he could still see the picture and placed his bedside light next to it. Then he stood on the bed and raised an arm to defy the clamouring soldiers below. As he began his speech, he heard the growing roar and pretended it was the shouts from the besieging army, growing louder and louder. 'I will not surrender!' he shouted at them. 'You must obey me, I am your King!' not of Frankincense, a *Warrior*. 'Join me, obey me and we will have peace in the land.' The roar fell away as the Vulcan traced the Bristol Channel west toward the Irish Sea, dying until it was distant, dying more as Huw quelled the besieging army into silence. 'And now, my people, let me lead you,' words he had read (not of the same play, but just the words he wanted) and how he felt in that moment of victory, breathing heavily, sweating with the exertion of his indomitable will, with the lights above and below like the sun rising and reflecting in the waters of the moat. He clung to the moment as long as he could until, slowly, it became his bedroom again.

He was already in bed when his mum came in from Auntie Jean's. He heard the back door, but she didn't come up. He wanted to dream of the battlements, of being the Warrior King and what he would say to the barons now they had obeyed him. He began it in his mind as he fell asleep, but it turned to a dream of the lost boy, the stolen boy, buried beneath black, sticky mud that clogged his mouth so that he couldn't speak and filled his eyes and ears. He couldn't breathe or see. He tried to turn in his sleep but the weight was pressing down on him and he couldn't move. He heard the sound of waves above, washing away the mud, tide after tide, trying to set free the boy's kindling bones.

Chapter Three

Burma, Canada, Cayman Islands...

Outside Huw's bedroom, blue lights fluttered across the walls like a cloud of fleeing butterflies. He heard urgent voices and the sound of engines; police radios snarled and a siren grew louder. He threw off the blankets and ran out onto the landing to see.

It was early and the light was grey. The road was full of people, most of them in uniform, with police cars parked on both sides leaving only a narrow lane down the middle. Policemen were sitting in the cars with the doors open talking to the radios and then holding them up to listen; others were going from house to house, or disappearing down drives into back gardens without waiting to be invited. Everyone was walking quickly, as if they were trying not to run. A man in a tweed jacket and twisted woollen tie stood in the middle of the road holding a map, surrounded by more policemen who were trying to look over his shoulder.

A big, black car pulled up soundlessly and a tall man got out. He put on his peaked cap, yanked his tunic straight and ran the outside of his thumbs down his black moustache. Everyone looked at him.

'Sergeant Phillips,' Huw gasped, in fright and wonderment.

'Up to mischief are you? I know you are,' he asked small boys who were up to no good (even if they weren't, they were). But his clip around the ear knocked them off their feet and then he took them home and told their fathers how to punish them and made sure they did (he had ways to punish fathers too: a word here, a speeding ticket there, worse).

To be 'mischiefed' was almost a rite of passage and, when the boys grew up, they boasted about it but, beneath their bravado, was fear (no one had ever been mischiefed twice). He had terrified generations of miscreant boys with the vengeance of his particular interpretation of justice; he was omnipresent whenever they were bad (or were tempted to be).

Sergeant Phillips had ruled Bridgend for so long but no one knew where he came from except it was another part of Wales (the North?). He had no past, no loyalties, he was impervious to entreaty and he had no sympathy for what they were, their ties or their families. He did not drink with them or go to any of the pubs; he was never seen out of uniform and no one knew where he lived. If he had a wife she was never spoken of; if he had children they were never mentioned. They said he was a copper's copper, old school, but he was anthracite, hard as glass, without ash or dust.

Sergeant Phillips planted his heels heavily as he walked: time was his alone and must progress to the pace he determined. 'Jeffries,' he said, in a low rumble. The policemen crowding round took a step back. The man with the map turned it toward him and made a circle around the middle of it with his finger. Sergeant Phillips didn't look. 'Fold it,' he told him, as if he had no need for such things. He looked directly at Huw. 'There.'

Huw let go the curtain and ducked beneath the windowsill, cowering, waiting for the banging on the front door. It did not come. When Huw peered out again, Sergeant Phillips and his big, black car had gone and so had Jeffries. Gwyn the Milk was coming up the road from his farm, searching goggle-eyed through his dirty windscreen for somewhere to park and was waved on when he tried to stop outside.

Huw saw his mother hurrying down the pavement into Jack's house with the policewoman from school clutching her arm.

The policeman standing outside Jack's front door didn't take any notice of the little boy pattering past in his bare feet and pyjamas, but he was so tall in his helmet and Huw was so small and quick he might not have seen him.

In the kitchen, Huw saw his mother and Jean on the other side of the table holding each other's hands. Their knuckles were white. They stared at the tabletop and both their faces were like his mother's when he found her crying in the front room; they were not, but they had been and their cheeks were stained. Jean was shaking. The policewoman, who had introduced herself as Brenda, sat next to her, leaning forward, gently rubbing their gripped hands. No one spoke. Opposite her, Aled was in his high chair, reaching out over the wooden arm to his mother who didn't respond. He stretched half-out and strained to make her.

Huw stood at the door. 'Mum?' he asked, 'Mum?' She didn't answer. 'Mum, what's the matter? Auntie Jean, what's the matter?'

Aled squirmed and threw himself backwards and the chair rocked on its legs. Then he saw Huw and his face erupted with shock. He screamed and turned violently back to his mother. Brenda leapt up and grabbed at the high chair to stop it tipping over. Aled beat his hands about his cheeks and tried to push her away. They turned slapped-red with finger marks. He screamed louder and was not going to stop. Jean lifted her head and knotted her eyes, as if he had woken her from an exhausted sleep. She untangled her hands and lifted him out of his chair, wincing with the effort. Aled gaped at Huw and buried his head in Jean's shoulder, but with one eye still fearfully seeing.

Huw slid down against the radiator and pulled his knees up and wrapped his arms around them and rested his chin. His back was hot but his bare feet were cold.

What was happening to his world? Now, he didn't want to be in the kitchen where he had spent so much time with Jack. His mother hadn't asked him why he was still in his pyjamas – he expected to be told off: why hadn't she? He wanted to take her home where she could cry with the picture of his father. In here, like this, she was not his.

'Where's Jack?' he asked, needing the reassurance of his best friend. There was no answer. He pulled his knees tighter against him.

Aled had stopped screaming and was grizzling.

Brenda sat down.

Legs in a brown skirt came past Huw's face and made him jump. He looked up. It was Auntie Eve from next door.

Eve said, 'Let me take him,' and she took Aled from Jean's arms. Surprised, Aled started screaming again. 'He'll calm down in a bit, won't you, cariad?' But Aled didn't. He kept looking at Huw, gulping for breath between screeches. 'Oh, cariad, cariad? I'll take him next door,' said Eve, jiggling Aled up and down. She took him into the hall and he stopped crying.

Huw was grateful he had been taken away. Why didn't Aled like him anymore, he used to make him laugh?

Brenda stood up. 'Where's the tea?'

Jean's hands were entwined in Gwen's and she didn't try to move them, but a thin, dry crack split her lips as if she was about to answer. She didn't and it sealed shut.

Brenda said, 'I'll just have to look for myself, then,' but there was no response from these normally polite and friendly women. Brenda opened the cupboard above the sink and took down three mugs and the teapot, 'Here we are. Now, where's the tea?'

Huw pointed, 'It's over there, next to the bread.'

'I've found it,' said Brenda, 'by the bread bin.' She filled the kettle and lit the gas with a click, click. Then she sat back down to wait.

Another police siren, quickly going away.

The kettle began to whistle and Brenda stood up to fill the teapot and plopped a red and green striped tea cosy over it that she had found in the cutlery drawer.

'Where's Jack?' asked Huw, 'is he in his bedroom? We've got to go to school.' He went into the hall – the fraught air of the kitchen trailed behind him like a wake – and started up the stairs, looking through the bannister into Jack's room as he neared the top. 'Jack?' he called. The bedroom door was open. Within, it was still and empty; he could not feel the presence of his friend. The bed was neatly made (not by Jack). He looked into the back garden. There was no one, but in all the other gardens, policemen were prodding compost heaps with sticks and searching in sheds and greenhouses – he could see them through the mildewed glass, moving like ghosts between the tomato plants. More policemen were in the alley behind the house and a line of them was walking very slowly across Gwyn the Milk's field with their heads down, searching in the grass and the cowpats. Two alsatians pulled impatiently on their leads.

Huw went back to the kitchen and slid down the radiator. 'Where's Jack? He's not in his bedroom. Has he gone up to the shop again? Why are there lots of policemen?'

The front door was wide open and his feet were even colder. He decided, 'Mum, I'm going to get ready for school,' and he jumped up and ran out past the policeman with his helmet higher than the door frame and along the pavement, past the policemen milling at the kerb next to their cars, and into his house. He sprinted up to his room where *The Big Book* lay open at a double-page spread of a musical called *Porgy and Bess* he had been looking at when he should have been in bed the night before.

He read: *Porgy and Bess, Broadway, America,* 'America,' he repeated to himself, silently moving his lips, '*Porgy and Bess,* Broadway, America, 1935, a famous production,' he said, out loud, as if telling a group of young actors hanging on his every word because he was famous. He knew Broadway, he had acted there so many times he had an 'apartment' (he didn't know what that was, but actors lived in them). It was warmer than in Jack's house and he stopped worrying about his cold feet. Ten minutes went by until shouting outside made him jump and he started to get dressed. He forgot his satchel and went back for it. He ran all the way, expecting to catch up with Jack before he got there.

The school gates were chained and padlocked and children were waiting to get in. A policewoman ushered them into a group and, thinking he should, Huw joined them. He couldn't see Jack.

When Mr Tanner spoke to the mothers, they pulled their children's faces tight into their tummies with cries of '*Oh*', and hands leapt to cover their mouths. Miss Williams' eyes welled. There was a shocked silence filled by the sound of distant traffic, a few inarticulate words, repeated over with staring eyes. Then, as if they saw each other re-forming out of the morning light and became aware of where they were, a torrent of questions flew out for Mr Tanner, who shook his head dumbly, then to the policewoman, then to each other. Huw couldn't hear what they said. The children unfastened themselves, still clamped by their chins, and looked up between lapsed cleavages at their mothers' strained, white faces, and were told to '*Hush*'.

It started to rain but the mothers stayed and searched for more words to share, terrified of someone waiting, watching, drawn to the certainty of the school because, between there and home, were the empty streets of the town. As they babbled, they frightened each other more.

Mr Tanner held his arms wide to shepherd them away from the gates and the mothers began hurrying away in small groups, not to be alone until the last few steps up their garden paths and into their houses (where *he* could be waiting), still holding their children tight, making awkward creatures with four uneven legs.

The policewoman knelt in front of Huw and the others and said, 'We're going to take you home; there's nothing to worry about.'

Why was a policewoman telling them? Who was she? And now, the children knew there was something wrong that would not be explained because it was of adult enormity and not for their ears.

One girl from Huw's class asked, 'Is this about the boy who got lost?' but no answer came.

Miss Williams began guiding them toward waiting police cars that edged up in turn and drove away like an emptying taxi rank. For those who lived closer, including Huw, they were made to form a line with the policewoman at the back and Miss Williams leading, holding a piece of paper with all their addresses.

The crocodile started to move and Huw thought, 'Prisoners (or was it soldiers?) of the Revolution,' from *The Big Book* and he was determined to be brave like them. They were watched from bay windows as if they were a row of theatre boxes. He marched importantly.

Miss Williams held up her hand outside the addresses on the piece of paper. When she knocked, if there was someone in, she spoke to them and their mouths sprang open, black as rabbit holes. Miss Williams had to force herself away from their questions. The children were pushed inside. The doors clapped and shivered the windows. Miss Williams ticked her piece of paper. If there was no one in, the children came back and re-joined the shortening column.

Miss Williams asked, 'Would you like to wait in the police station until your mummy or daddy gets home?' She tried to make it sound exciting.

The children frowned, as if trying to weigh up what she was saying. 'I want my mummy.'

'So do I,' said another and a tremor of alarm rippled the tarmac beneath their feet.

'I'm sure there will be a big tin of sweets for special boys and girls, and biscuits and orange squash,' said Miss Williams, as they stared up at her like a nest of baby owls, 'and I'll be with you all the time.' But when they got to Jack's house, Huw ran inside before they could make him go down to the police station. He didn't look back to see if Miss Williams had ticked him off.

In the kitchen, no one had moved. The kettle was whistling. Brenda emptied the teapot of cold tea into the sink and made another. Then she emptied more cold tea from the mugs and refilled them and took the milk from the fridge. She put the teapot in the middle of the table next to the sugar bowl and covered it with the striped tea cosy and there it sat, slowly ebbing cheer from under its woolly vest. The tea in the mugs got colder faster and was untouched. With nothing else to do, Brenda sat back down and stroked the entwined hands. Gwen and Jean were as unmoving as flesh-covered dummies in a shop window, strangely arranged, and even their clothes looked dowdy and badly fitting. No mannequins would have faces like theirs.

The radiator was warm against Huw's back and he wriggled his toes in his shoes and took the satchel from around his neck. 'They've closed the school,' he announced, 'because of the boy who got lost. Where's Jack?'

BANG. The front door slammed against the wall.

Everyone jumped and Jean cried out.

Alan burst into the kitchen. He was panting.

Jean wrestled her hands free. Her eyes were white and sideways like Gwyn the Milk's cow that got caught in a fence during the summer and had to be cut free.

Behind Alan was Sergeant Phillips.

Huw pushed himself further into the corner between the radiator and the wall and tried to make himself as small and innocent as he could and craned his neck up the long, navy leg.

'A boy has been seen in Pencoed,' growled Sergeant Phillips, slowly and low, making the words pulsate.

Jean leapt up.

Brenda reached over to touch her arm. 'We don't know yet, Mrs Harris,' she told her, softly. 'Do we, Sir?'

Sergeant Phillips pouted his moustache and looked at each of their faces in turn with purposeful examination. 'I will,' he said, 'soon.'

'Sit down,' said Brenda. 'Sit back down, Jean.'

Jean sank back into her chair, 'When will you?'

'I will know, soon,' said Sergeant Phillips.

'But why have you told me if you don't know?'

A car started up outside. Its siren burst into the hall and detonated in the kitchen. Jean ran for the door, followed by Gwen, not to be stopped, and out into the street as if they could see what was happening in Pencoed from the end of the drive.

Brenda went after them, glancing at Sergeant Phillips who didn't move.

Alan leant against the edge of the table, then he slumped into a chair as if his legs wouldn't hold him any longer.

'When I know,' Sergeant Phillips said, 'but not before.'

'This will kill my father,' said Alan.

'Haven't you told him, Mr Harris?'

Alan looked up and shook his head, 'No, I haven't.'

'Why didn't you, Mr Harris?'

'He might already know, somebody will have told him.'

'But he's your father, Mr Harris, why didn't you tell him?'

'I couldn't. I wanted to see it all cleared up, so I never had to tell him the worst. He's not well. I would have told him something, but not this.'

'Is that the reason?'

'Yes. What else could it be?'

'What other reason, Mr Harris? He might have known where your son was?'

'But he didn't, he doesn't. He'd just brought him back.'

'Is that so?'

'Yes.'

'I must speak to him, Mr Harris.'

'Is that necessary?'

'Yes, it is, Mr Harris.'

Brenda came back leading the two women. 'Let's have some more tea.'

'I don't want any more tea,' said Jean and searched for Gwen's hand. They gripped. Their knuckles whitened.

Alan looked at his wife as if he was about to say something but didn't.

Sergeant Phillips looked at Alan. 'Your father, Mr Harris?' He left. The room became lighter.

'Why is Jack in Pencoed?' asked Huw.

The front door was still wide open to admit anyone with news. A blackbird panicked with a discordant cascade of notes across the lawn into the low hedge between the gardens and the siren faded into the frieze of sound coming from the main road. Nothing more.

Huw picked up his satchel and went into the front room. New voices were talking from the end of the garden path. Huw heard the word, '*Herald*,' and then, more clearly, 'Aw, come on Dewi?'

'No.'

'But the *Mail's* going to be here any second.'

'No. And if you start to take any photos I'll have the film off you and the camera.'

More quietly, as if trying not to be heard, the man said, 'He won't speak to the *Mail* before us, will he? Please Dew, we've always been straight with you, can't you warn them off so at least we can be at the front of the queue, that's all? We've got to have a better story than them.'

'I can't do that, Andrew. You know what'll happen if he even thinks I've been interfering.'

'What are we supposed to do, then, Dew? Not the *Mail*, please, not the *Mail*?'

'Well, for a start, you can go out onto the pavement and wait up there because you can't stay here like vultures right by their front door.'

'Dew?'

'Go.'

'Fair enough, Dew. We'll be waiting over there, then, like good boys.'

Huw looked round the door and saw the tall policeman who had been standing outside talking to two men, one with a camera hanging from his neck. A police car with no one in it was parked further up the road and the two men walked to stand next to it.

The one without the camera pointed at the pavement. 'Just here, Dew? Are we alright here? You be ready, Lloydy-boy,' he said to the man with the camera. 'I want a shot of anyone who moves in that house. We'll go round the back in a bit to have a look from there. I think they're all in the kitchen.'

'What are you talking about, now?' demanded Constable Dewi.

'Nothing, Dew, you won't hear a peep out of us, I promise.'

Huw went back into the kitchen. 'Mum, when can we go home?' She looked to the ceiling as if she was searching for the warmth of the sun in the single bulb hanging from its orange lampshade. Huw knew that expression and didn't ask again. He slid back down the radiator.

'*Speech, speech*,' they cried. He tapped the tip of his sword on the grey stone and let it rest there – *no*, his sword was a scroll – a proclamation – and they were not battlements, he was on the scaffold before the guillotine, a prisoner of the revolution who was about to die for his cause but he went willingly to his death because his cause was just and it was history that would never forget: not the death of one man, but a shining example for all who would come after him when the tyrants had all been swept away by the winds of time and forgotten. The executioner waited with his hand on the lever, but dared not hurry. This leader looked like Sergeant Phillips. His followers crowded at his feet. When he spoke, his voice thundered over them and filled the square. Huw shivered. 'For glory this day,' and held up the scroll. Huw loved that, so he said it again, 'For *glory* this day.' *The Big Book* said it was one of the great performances, coming so soon after the end of the war it had lifted men's hearts that were so weary of battle and death. *It reminded them of what they had been fighting for, that freedom from oppression is a universal right in any age.* He read that line again and again, *for glory this day*.

Sergeant Phillips was getting out of his big, black car. Huw jumped back inside the house. '*Ohhh*,' if Sergeant Phillips saw him now, he would want to know why he was hiding and

Huw didn't know why and he would be mischiefed for the first time. He quaked with the consequences of being there.

Alan passed him in the hall. 'What is it?' he asked, 'is it the boy in Pencoed?'

'Has Uncle Alan ever been mischiefed?' Huw wondered.

'I have someone in custody,' replied Sergeant Phillips.

'*Who*?'

'Who? I can't tell you, Mr Harris.'

'*What*? Why not? You've *got* to.'

'I haven't got to do anything, Mr Harris. But I will tell you that it's always someone you know.'

'Dear God,' said Alan, passing his hand across his eyes, 'tell me who it is, please?'

Sergeant Phillips ran his thumbs down his moustache and didn't reply.

Gwyn the Milk's van started to move from where it had been parked all day. As it got closer, through a gap in the hedge, Huw saw Constable Dewi driving.

'*No*,' exclaimed Alan, in disbelief. '*No*.'

'Have you told your father?'

'I can't tell him until we've found Jack.'

'*We*, Mr Harris?'

'*We, you*, find him, I don't care *who* does.'

'There is no *we*.'

'Oh dear God.'

'I must speak to your father, Mr Harris.'

Huw followed his mother home so close he almost tangled in her legs. Sergeant Phillips and his big, black car were nowhere to be seen but his late presence lingered like a spectre. Huw scampered up the stairs to the bright lights.

Chapter Four

Ceylon, Cook Islands, Cyprus...

Beyond the empty shore the fiery eyes burned, winking through the gloom in languorous Morse, a warning, too late the cows woke Huw from his sightless dream of mud, cold and salt. When he went to look, they were crowded against the gate at the top of the field making a noise.

Roy was in his garden, slowly and methodically digging over the vegetable patch. It didn't need digging again: the earth had been freshly turned and there was not a single weed but the policemen's boots had made a mess and it was waiting to be planted with winter vegetables. Roy didn't work from one side to the other. When he finished a row he went back to the side nearest the house and started on the next one so that he was always working in the same direction.

Huw watched him dig three rows until Eve came out with a mug of tea.

Roy leaned half a buttock against the spade handle and lit a cigarette and sipped at the tea. Steam lifted from the mug and vanished but the cigarette smoke hung around him and puffed out when he spoke: 'Who's going to milk those cows now, then?'

Eve shook her head.

'Somebody's got to – it's not going to be Sergeant Phillips is it? What's going to happen to the farm?' He looked into his tea. 'Have we got any more milk?'

'Not enough to last,' she replied.

'Then you better get some.'

'I'll go to the shops later.'

'Before I get home?'

'Yes.'

'A couple more rows and I've got to get off to work,' and he handed the mug back to his wife. 'I can't drink that,' he said, and carried on digging.

Constable Dewi was outside Jack's door, rocking on his heels with his hands clasped behind his back. Roy nodded to him as he got into his car; the two men from *The Herald* were walking to their allotted place on the pavement.

There was a crowd around the school gates: mothers and children, Mr Tanner, Miss Williams, Mr Hughes from Form Three and Mr Topliss, the caretaker, in his dusty overalls holding a broom.

The mothers were talking. 'They've got him, then, *Gwyn the Milk*,' disbelieving that the man they had known all their lives and his father before him, who came to their houses every day, who drank tea in their kitchens, could be this man. But, he had been caught and they let their children run free to their friends in the playground. Huw skipped after them.

The children talked and imagined what they had overheard. 'He's got a cloak and he lives in a cave and he only comes out at night. I saw him, he was in our garden.' This man was not Gwyn the Milk; they didn't know who it was, only that he had been 'mischiefed' by Sergeant Phillips.

At registration. 'Have they caught the man who did it, Miss?'

'Have they found him, Miss?'

'What did he do, Miss?'

Miss Williams still couldn't read out the names to omit the two missing boys or, worse, pronounce them 'Absent,' praying that she would hear them call 'Here' before she had to compile a new register without them in it (and always having to pause after 'Edwards' and 'Griffiths'). She ticked the register by sight, face by guileless face. She stood up and led them to assembly.

A hymn, *The Lord's Prayer*. Back to class.

She read them another story. Times tables. Lunchtime.

When they ran out onto the playground, Mr Tanner followed. 'Now then,' he said, 'how about a game of British Bulldog?'

The boys looked at each other in amazement. Mr Tanner had banned British Bulldog because it was too rough and they got hurt and their clothes got torn.

'You can today,' he said, 'just this once.'

The girls sat on the grass and watched as the two lines of boys ran at each other trying to break through to the other side of the playground without being caught. Quickly, the game became wild. Blood flew from their noses and mouths, it ran down their shins from scraped knees, from their elbows and over their knuckles. They refused to cry, it was a matter of honour not to. The tarmac scuffed their shoes; grass stains smeared their shorts; shirts and jumpers were ripped. All afternoon the game raged, resetting itself and beginning again. It was the hot breath of their lives and confused rage at the loss of their playmates. None of this was in their childish minds but it had expression in their savagery.

Mr Tanner, Miss Williams, Mr Hughes, with whistles hanging from their necks, watched from the edge of the playground near the school doors. Mr Tanner was as still as a beam of faint light against the blue door, as if trying to draw brightness from the children's vitality, briefly glowing then dimming like a failing bulb. Unmarried, lonely, upright, the school was his whole world. 'British Bulldog,' he said to Miss Williams, without turning to look at her. 'I wish I could join in.'

Miss Williams nodded and sniffed.

The afternoon roared on, all afternoon, but not with the piping voices of children at breaktimes or the flock of little birds chirruping excitedly that greeted their mothers when they came to collect them at home time. These were the nascent voices of the men they would become, as the boys before them became, their fathers' sons, because this was what they had been born to, belonged to, fiercely and unquestioningly, and would inherit: industrial and wild, visceral and pungent, ringed with mountains, littered with coal tips, each town with winding gear spearing its heart, deep green fields, rain and lazy or sharp sun, the sea close.

This was the country that Huw would bring to the stage in the sing-song accent he didn't yet know he had. The emotional little boy lost in British Bulldog, in the heat of it; how many of his performances would be of days like this when the time came?

The teachers let the game play on and didn't call them back in.

As Huw ran through the lines of yelling boys, he wished Jack was running with him.

When the mothers arrived and saw the ripped and bloodied state of their weary little soldiers as they trudged from the field, panting and sparky-eyed, they didn't say anything but draped their arms loosely over their shoulders, because there was no need to hold them tight, and kissed the tops of their glowing heads.

The streets were filled with children again and there were no waiting police cars.

As Huw walked home, he could not leave the game behind. He was still careering toward the waiting lines and his ears rang with thundering hooves as, all around him, his brothers-in-arms fell with their horses: *The Charge of the*

Light Brigade? *Yes*. He could almost smell the cordite (like at the tattoo in Cardiff Castle with Uncle Alan and Jack). His diminished army slowed to a trot, bent in their saddles, and waited for him on the hot Spanish plain. *El Cid*? *Yes*. The horses stamped, kicked up the dust, and tossed their heads. He felt the sweat on his neck; he was at the centre of a dervish of colours and sounds. The houses were bank upon bank of stands, the crowds of Rome. *Julius Caesar*? *Yes*. What would he say when he reached the steps of the Senate? A hush fell and, when all eyes were unable to look anywhere but to the small figure on the steps, he saw into every face, as if he was addressing each one of them alone and knew what was in their souls. Then came the director's instruction, '*Action,*' and he took a deep breath, and began the same speech he had rehearsed as a boy on his bedroom stage, rising to the Gods with the same resounding clarity.

Mr Elwiss, the cricket-loving vicar from Hampshire, was talking to a man in the porch of one of the houses at the top of his road. The whole school went to his church for Harvest Festival and Christmas and Huw had put his hand up to do a reading, but he didn't want to be a vicar because he had heard Uncle Roy say to Uncle Alan, 'That man knows all there is to know about God but nothing about sex or death, so what he's doing here is a new one on me.'

Huw asked, 'Mummy, why doesn't the vicar know anything about sex?' and knew straightaway he shouldn't have because she didn't answer.

Outside Jack's front door, Alan stood with his arm around Jean. Next to them, like a seam thrust vertically from the earth, was Sergeant Phillips. They were hemmed against the porch by reporters, many more now.

Flash. Cameras clicked. *Flash*.

Sergeant Phillips was at the centre of every photo, holding up the sky.

Jean spoke so quietly, Huw couldn't make out what she was saying. She kept stopping and Alan would put his head close to hers and, behind her, Brenda whispered, and she would carry on.

Constable Dewi stood in the drive.

The reporters asked questions and scribbled in their notebooks. After a few minutes, Sergeant Phillips interrupted. The air shimmered around his mouth as he spoke. His voice descended and his eyes did not move because he looked down on reporters: they were for his convenience and, from such a height, they knew he saw everything.

Huw could hear every word he said. 'You've got what you need and you know what to print so, from now on, stay away unless I tell you different.'

Herald Andrew asked, 'Sergeant Phillips, are you able to confirm you have someone in custody?'

'No.'

Herald Andrew ventured on bravely, 'Sergeant Phillips, does that mean you have no one in custody or you are unable to confirm it.'

Sergeant Phillips glared at *Herald* Andrew. 'No.'

Herald Andrew closed his notebook. The other reporters did the same. 'No, of course not. I'm sorry I have to ask, but it's my job.'

'Is it?' Sergeant Phillips tilted his head even further back and said, with a twitch of his moustache, 'There is no reason you have to ask anything because I will tell you what I want you to know and there is no question I have to answer until I decide to. You will do as you're told or I will tell you nothing.'

Constable Dewi began herding reporters toward the road. They kept looking back but dare not ask any more questions.

Brenda ushered Alan and Jean back inside.

'Dew?' whispered *Herald* Andrew.

'You heard Sergeant Phillips,' answered Constable Dewi, pretending he didn't know who *Herald* Andrew was.

Sergeant Phillips walked slowly toward his big, black car, taking great care to pull on his gloves, ignoring everyone. He got in and it glided away.

The noise of the battle on the scorched plain in the beating sun had not reached the kitchen where the air was icily still. It reminded Huw of the crypt in the church where Miss Williams had taken them and made ghostly noises from behind a tomb. The teapot was cold on the table with half-full mugs around it, just as it had been.

Alan said to Brenda, 'I'm going down the alley to avoid those reporters.'

Jean said, 'That was awful, just awful.'

'I know,' said Brenda, 'but it's over now.'

Jean closed her eyes, 'But it's not over, it's not.' She was colourless and her skin was translucent: the kitchen cupboards seemed to show through her, as if drawing her in. She started to shake. 'I think I'm going to… explode,' she said, forcing the words out one by one.

Gwen gripped her hand and started to shake too, as if it was an infectious malady.

Brenda slid her hand across the tabletop but drew it back.

Jean stared.

Another presence came into the small kitchen. 'Mum?' Huw asked.

Brenda leaned forward and touched their clasped hands. Gwen stopped shaking and opened her eyes but Jean did not. She was breathing too quickly. 'Jean?'

After some moments, Jean began to breathe more slowly. 'Where's Jack?' she murmured. 'Have those reporters gone?'

'Yes, they've all gone,' said Brenda.

There was no adoration here for the great actor, hoping for praise (and a cuddle). Huw dropped his satchel on the floor. 'When's Jack coming home?'

Aled saw him from his high chair, and let out a scream, struggling frantically to reach Jean. This time, the chair tipped too far and crashed to the floor. Aled hit his head on the sink as it fell. It shocked Jean to life. She slid from the chair to her knees. But even as he was screaming in her arms, Aled pointed at Huw.

Constable Dewi appeared at the door.

Jean held Aled tight and rocked him, trying to calm him and rubbing the bump on his head. 'That chair's not safe,' she said, angrily.

'Why did he wake up like that?' asked Gwen. 'Did he have a bad dream do you think?'

'I'll rub it better for you,' said Jean. 'Hush now, there's a good boy.'

Brenda filled the kettle and emptied the teapot.

Constable Dewi went back to stand at the front door.

Huw slid down the radiator and puffed out his cheeks. But the two women were preoccupied with Aled (Huw felt a surge of jealousy) and the kettle started to dance on the stove with a growing whistle. Brenda took it off and filled the teapot.

Huw thought, 'If I go and hide, they'll miss me and then what'll they do if I don't come back?' But the battle had made him tired and the heat of the radiator was making his head nod. Nearly asleep, he heard applause that sounded like waves. His head jerked back up but he was soon nodding again.

Constable Dewi's voice woke him up. 'This is Detective Jeffries.' With him was the man with the map. He was wearing the same tweed jacket with elbow patches and the twisted woollen tie that stopped halfway down his chest. 'He's looking for Mr Harris, do you know where he is?'

'He's at his father's,' said Gwen. 'Have you found something?'

'No,' replied Detective Jeffries, 'I need to ask him some questions.'

'I can answer any questions you've got,' said Jean.

'I need to speak to him directly, Mrs Harris.'

'I can ring his father,' said Gwen. 'Why don't you speak to him on the phone?'

'I'm going to speak to him in person. Mrs Harris, could I have his father's address?'

'I've got it,' said Brenda, 'I've got all the addresses.'

'Give it to me,' said Detective Jeffries.

'I don't understand,' said Jean. 'He will come straight back. His father is not well.'

'I know,' said Detective Jeffries.

'Is it about the boy in Pencoed?'

'No, it's not. I must go now, Mrs Harris.'

'Oh,' she slumped, and dread came back, 'then I'll ring him to tell him you're coming.'

Detective Jeffries looked at Brenda and beckoned her into the hall. 'Make sure she doesn't,' he told her. On his way out, he said to Constable Dewi, 'If Harris comes back here, I want to know.'

When Detective Jeffries had gone, Jean asked Brenda, 'What does he need to speak to Alan about?'

Brenda said, 'They're just getting their facts straight, that's all, it's only routine.'

'Is it?'

'Yes, they're trying to get every bit of information they can because, until they do, they won't know which bit is important and which isn't. They won't leave any stone unturned. Drink your tea, Jean, while it's hot.'

'I've had enough tea,' she answered, quietly.

'So have I,' said Gwen. 'Is this all we can do, drink tea?'

The stillness raged. The tea stewed and chilled. A frost came down even though the radiator was hot.

Huw thought, 'Is this how grown-ups spend their days?' He jumped up and grabbed his satchel, 'I'm going round to see Auntie Eve and Uncle Roy,' and ran out before they could tell him not to.

When he was outside, in the fresh air, the thrill of the battle returned – the burning plain, the pennants cracking in the wind, trumpets like sirens – and he couldn't help smiling. Huw went through the hole in the fence and went in without knocking because Jack and he never did.

Eve was ironing and looking out of the window. She folded a shirt and added it to the pile and started another. She asked, 'Do you want some tea?'

Huw was tempted but knew he shouldn't. 'Mum's going to make me some,' he said.

'Roy?'

'What?' said a familiar voice from the front room.

Huw looked round the door and saw the top of Roy's head with *The Herald* held up in front of his face and cigarette smoke rising above it.

'We ought to have some tea.'

Roy lowered his paper slowly and tapped his cigarette into the ashtray on the arm of the chair. 'I'm not hungry,' he said.

'I'm not either,' sighed Eve, 'but I'll make you something if you want? I've got the milk.'

'No. Later.' Roy raised his paper and disappeared.

'Let's have something later, then.' She went back to the ironing, 'I should have done these earlier and now it's teatime. Everything's going to pot.'

'What is?'

'Nothing.'

Behind the paper, Roy said, 'Tomorrow's edition, I expect it will be. There's not much they can say, is there? Not if they don't know and he's not telling.'

'They're making an appeal for information.'

'What for? They've got who did it.'

Eve gripped the ironing board. 'Gwyn the Milk, I can't bear to think of it.'

The paper dipped and Roy's eyes appeared over the top, 'You're going to have to; you never really know anyone do you?' Cigarette smoke gathered in the ceiling and came lower layer by layer. Only when Roy turned a page were they disturbed, momentarily agitated, before resuming their delicate strata.

Gwen came in.

Roy dropped his paper to his knees and the layers swirled and became a haze over everything.

Eve had her arms full of folded shirts. 'I'm finished now,' she said, 'shall I make us some tea? What about you, Gwen?'

Gwen shook her head tiredly, her eyes red. 'No thank you, Eve, I've got something in the house that's got to be eaten or it will spoil. And then I'm going to have a bath. I am aching.'

'Are you sure? It's no trouble.'

'Let her have her bath if that's what she wants,' said Roy.

'Honestly, Eve,' said Gwen.

Huw listened to the bath starting to run upstairs. Still hungry, trying to be as quiet as he could, he climbed up onto a chair for the bread, held the loaf to his chest like a rugby ball (as his mother did) and buttered it. Then he carved off a slice, drawing the knife toward him – looking up when he heard the water begin to slow – and tearing off the last bit before covering the lump with jam and getting it down his already stained, white school shirt. He took his shapeless sandwich into the living room to watch television.

When he woke up in the armchair, the plate was upside down on the floor and there were crumbs and lumps of jam all over the carpet. He didn't make a good job of getting them off no matter how hard he rubbed with the towel. He went to the other end of the room to see if they could still be seen. They could. He wet the towel and rubbed the carpet harder but that only spread the jam over a bigger area. He sat back on his haunches and rested against the chair. He rehearsed his excuses until it grew into a longer speech with included an entrance from the hall and an unconcerned pose leaning against the mantelpiece with an imaginary pipe between his teeth like the man in the war film with the dams. After a while, he had constructed a complete scene with camera angles and the light coming in through the bay window (or should it be a stage play?). He went upstairs to consult *The Big Book,* leaving the jam to dry out on its own (she would only send him up to his room when she found out anyway).

When he heard the cows beginning to moo, he looked up and went to the window. In the gloom, he saw Gwyn the Milk, arms outstretched, holding a long stick, walking behind his cows as they plodded up the slope to be milked.

Chapter Five

Dominica, Eritrea, Egypt…

There was a note pinned to the school gates. It said: *The School will be closed until further notice.* Mr Topliss came out of the brick toilets at the top of the playground holding a spanner.

The boys' toilets were Gonk, the school bully's kingdom. Huw had been summoned there more than once to see him on his tiny throne, door open, pants and trousers round his ankles, surrounded by his giggling cronies. 'Mr Tanner must be ill,' thought Huw.

The streets were almost deserted except for slowly cruising police cars. The police were back in the fields with their dogs searching amongst the relieved cows, grazing with stupid fixation and not a care.

Huw had a play (or a film?) in mind, one of his own. Adventurously, he was branching out already, and the idea had come to him that, as well as being a great actor, he could be a writer too. Practise was needed. By the time he reached his bedroom, another scene had already been added to the incident of the jam on the carpet. He paced up and down, sucking on his pipe. It could be a play which could be made into a film. He searched *The Big Book* for someone famous to be the star. Why not the man in the war film with the dams? Huw cradled his pipe. Was he a bit old? But all the actors in *The Big Book* were old to Huw. What was he going to call it? A good title was important: '*The Mystery of the Blood on the Carpet?* Mmm. *Blood on the Carpet? Blood*, just *Blood?*' He made a face as he said it. That was it. '*Blood.*' He leaned back and tapped his teeth with his pipe and stroked the silk scarf he didn't know was called a cravat and adjusted the dressing gown he didn't know was a smoking jacket. Slippers were slippers but he preferred not to notice they were purple and green and fluffy.

There was a knock at the front door.

Huw sat on the top step of the stairs. When his mother opened the door, he saw it was Reverend Elwiss.

'Vicar?' asked Gwen, surprised.

'Mrs Evans,' said the vicar, 'I'm sorry to disturb you. I hope to be able to offer my support to you, to the whole community, but particularly to you at such an *horrendous* time.'

'Come in,' said Gwen, and she stood aside to let the Reverend go through to the front room. Behind his back, she frowned and squeezed the bridge of her nose. 'Can I offer you some tea?'

'There's no need, only if you're making some, Mrs Evans.'

'Not for me, I've had enough tea, I don't think I'll ever drink another cup.'

'No? Will you not, Mrs Evans?'

'But, please, it's no trouble, I can easily make you one.'

'No, if you're not, I won't. Such a terrible time, *indescribable*. How are you bearing up, if that's not an absurd question to which the answer must be so painfully obvious? Sadly, I have no children of my own. Marriage is a blessing, but we are not blessed in that other way.'

Huw frowned to himself, 'Somebody ought to tell him about it, then.' But he wasn't sure he was on the right track.

'My concern is all for you, Mrs Evans.'

'I've been round at Jean Harris' most of the time.'

'That must be a great comfort to you both. I am going to call on her shortly. Would that be welcome, do you think?'

'It might be a distraction,' said Gwen, thoughtlessly, rudely, but couldn't care.

'And not a comfort? If distraction is possible in such overwhelming circumstances.'

'I'm sorry, Vicar. No, it isn't. At least she has Alan and I do not.'

'How long is it since Mr Evans was lost?' he lowered his voice and leaned towards her.

Too close and she leaned away. 'He's not lost, they know where he is, they just can't get to him – well, they could, but it would cost too much.'

'I'm sure they have made every effort to recover his remains.' He lifted his hands but she dropped hers to her sides where he could not reach them. He brought his hands together as if that was his intention.

'You don't know the Coal Board very well, do you, Vicar?'

'I have made visits underground.' He let his hands fall, redundant, and they bounced against his groin.

'With respect, that isn't the same.'

'No, I cannot imagine what it is like to toil in the bowels of the earth.'

'Why does he have to talk like that?' she thought, and said, 'It's even further from God.'

'We are never far from God, Mrs Evans. He is with you now, he is with Mrs Harris, with you all. If you call on him, he will answer, he will heed your pain. Please believe that.'

'I must take your word for it, Vicar.'

'I like to think of the colliery as a kind of church where men labour…'

'Vicar, it's more like a graveyard.'

'Where have you taken him? Where is he? Tell me.'

'Jean?' Gwen rushed out of the front room and through the front door followed by a flapping Reverend Elwiss.

Huw slid down the bannister.

'Mrs Evans?' the Reverend cheeped.

Jean was shouting at Constable Dewi. Her head was thrust forward and the veins in her neck were like vines strangling a tree. '*Where is he? What have you done with him? Tell me.*'

Her arms windmilled, bouncing off his chest as he tried to seize hold of her wrists. 'Mrs Harris, *please*, calm down, *Jean*.' His helmet tipped over his eyes. Brenda wrapped herself around Jean and held her tight. As she struggled, Eve and Roy came out. Gwen stepped over the low hedge and she and Brenda pulled Jean away from Constable Dewi. Roy wrapped the three of them together with Jean hidden in the middle.

Eve went in to Aled who was wailing.

Constable Dewi straightened his helmet and shook his head at Brenda.

Sergeant Phillips' big, black car pulled up with Detective Jeffries in the passenger seat. Alan got out of the back, pale and drawn, and came down the drive and into the house, looking straight ahead without saying a word.

Behind him, Sergeant Phillips rose like the night and watched him go, holding open the driver's door. 'Did she strike you, Constable Jones?'

Constable Dewi shook his head. 'No, Sir.'

'I'll ask you again. Did she strike you Constable Jones?'

'No, Sir, she did not.' Sergeant Phillips perused each of the shocked faces, then he got back into his car and left.

Alan sat with his forearms flat on the kitchen table and his fists clenched. 'They accused me of taking my own son,' he said, in a voice shaking with anger and disbelief, 'my *own* son… in front of dad… and they made me leave him there… with no one, *no one*… he's an old man, a sick old man.'

Brenda wouldn't look at him.

Gwen helped Jean sit down.

'I'm sorry, Alan,' Constable Dewi said, 'I'm sorry for that.'

The walls of the kitchen were being marked in scored days of laden time but, when new families came to live there, they would be covered with a fresh coat of paint.

Reverend Elwiss' head poked under Constable Dewi's arm like a sheep reaching for a clump of grass.

Huw looked up at the tilted moons clustered above him and asked, 'When is Jack coming home?'

Roy asked, 'Are you going to fetch your father now?'

'Yes, I want to talk to him in the car although I don't know what I'm going to say to him.'

'You won't need to say anything.'

'Won't I? Whatever I say,' Alan said, quietly, 'this will kill him.'

'Would you like me to stay with you for a while, Mrs Harris?' asked Reverend Elwiss.

Jean didn't reply. She rocked with her arms folded and her elbows bumping against the edge of the table.

'I'll be with her,' said Eve.

'I will too,' said Brenda.

'I need to escape for a while,' said Gwen. 'I need some air; I've got to breathe.'

'Would you like me to accompany you, Mrs Evans?' asked the Reverend.

'No, Vicar, I'm only going as far as the shops.'

'Are you sure, Mrs Evans?'

'Yes, Vicar.'

'I am here to give whatever help I can,' said Reverend Elwiss, raising his eyebrows, 'whatever help I can.' They made no response, of body or speech. 'You know where I am?'

'The church,' said Roy, 'where you should be.'

'Yes, of course,' Reverend Elwiss said, with a puzzled expression, 'the church or the vicarage.' He backed out of the kitchen, clasping his dignity in prayer, unwanted and excluded from their tragedy, his cloth wanting.

'Has he gone?' asked Roy, too soon, and quickly looked round the door, but not caring if the vicar had heard him. 'Yes, he has. Pity.'

'I must go,' said Alan, standing up.

Huw trotted along beside his mother as they walked to the shops. Faces at the windows watched them pass; a police car idled by but didn't stop. They saw no one until they reached the shops and then there were women coming in and out, many of them with children gripped tightly whom Huw recognised from school. The women went quiet as they approached and parted to let them through. Some of them made shy, fleeting smiles, others looked away. One woman touched Gwen's shoulder and pursed her lips; another briefly put her arm around her.

Mr Mason the butcher asked, almost inaudibly, as if he didn't want anyone to overhear, 'How are you, Mrs Evans?'

She nodded.

'And Mrs Harris? How is Mrs Harris? I can't tell you… I just can't say…'

'There is nothing to say.'

'The police are doing all they can, I'm sure.'

'*Are* they? They certainly *are*.'

'Of course, Mrs Evans, I'm sure, with something like this.'

'Yes, I'm sure.'

'Is there anything I can get for you, Mrs Evans?'

'I don't know. I only came out for some air.'

'How about some sausages? They're homemade this morning.'

Huw said, 'Yes, please.' Sausages were his favourite, especially with beans and chips.

'Ohhh,' breathed his mother, putting her hand to her eyes, 'no, not sausages.'

'Some liver, then?'

'I suppose so, Mr Mason.'

'Right you are.'

'Not liver,' muttered Huw, they had it at school in tar-like gravy.

'Is that about right?' asked Mr Mason, pointing to a piece next to the sausages behind the glass of the brightly lit display cabinet.

'Yes, that will do. Wait a minute, I haven't got any money with me. I've left my purse in the house.'

'Never mind that,' said Mr Mason, wrapping the liver in greaseproof paper, 'you can pay me next time you're in.' He placed the package on the counter top. 'Is there anything else, anything at all?'

'No thank you, Mr Mason, you've been very kind.'

'Not at all. All our thoughts...' he took a deep breath and was close to tears, 'are with those boys.'

When they were outside, Gwen said, 'Home, I can't breathe here either. There is no air left in the world.'

An old woman came up to her and grasped Gwen's hand in both of hers. 'God be with us all,' she said.

'He just was, a little while ago, but now he's gone back to the vicarage.'

When they reached Jack's house, passing again through the avenue of faces, Constable Dewi came to meet them. 'I've got some news,' he said.

Gwen stopped and stood perfectly still: a weather vane to be pushed in any direction by the impending wind. 'Yes?'

'They've taken in Bryn Hughes, one of the teachers at the school.'

'Mr Hughes?' thought Huw. He had seen Miss Williams kiss him behind the canteen. Was that sex?

Gwen shook her head. 'It's not him. Why have they picked on him?'

'It could be anyone,' said Constable Dewi.

'Alan? It wasn't him, was it? Yes, it couldn't be *anyone*, Dewi, but I'm telling you, it's not him.'

'Well, they've taken him in for questioning. Brenda's called Alan at his father's and he's on his way back.'

'Is no one safe?'
'Mrs Evans?'

'*Blood, Scene Three*.' Huw emptied his pipe and gazed thoughtfully into the darkening corner of the ceiling. A play – a film – either, he couldn't decide, even as he made it up, the script, the screenplay (a new word he had recently discovered), whatever it was to become. His desk lamp reflected off the glossy pages of a calm sea or a lake. It was a lake. Two swans sailed across it. Huw felt the cool air rising from the water to his face. There was a jetty and a rowing boat moored to it.

A man appeared at his shoulder and made him jump. He said, 'Hello Huw.' He had fair hair and a blue scar across his cheek.

The man climbed carefully into the boat and tossed the mooring rope onto the jetty. He took up the oars and began to row out across the lake. Ripples disturbed the pages' sheen and the oars gently splashed. The swans quickened. The reflected sun caressed Huw's eyes. The man stopped rowing and looked back at Huw. He smiled and folded away the oars. The small boat glided, turning at an angle until it stopped and the lake became mirror-still again. Suddenly, hands reached up from the water and began rocking the boat violently from side to side. The man hung on. The boat tipped over and the man fell headlong into the water. He came up with his blond hair clinging to his head. Then he sank. The last Huw saw of him was an uplifted arm like a retreating Excalibur. Huw had to catch his pipe before it fell into his lap in a shower of sparks. 'Oh,' he said, and scribbled over the scene and started again.

The swans sailed across the lake. The rowing boat was moored to the jetty. But, there was the man again, at his shoulder. He got into the boat. Huw couldn't stop him. He rowed out into the middle of the lake. The hands came up. His arm sank like the sword. Again, Huw tried. He wasn't writing the play, it was writing him. It had taken control of his characters and places, the lighting, the sound and, where he wanted words, he could not have them said.

Three times, *Scene Three*: then he recognised the dunes all around leading down to the flat yellow beach with waves heaving into breakers a long way out and the two flames in a smoke-heavy sky. He quickly turned the page.

Dorothy was holding Toto amidst a confection of colours. That was the end of *Blood.*

Stories to entertain, to make us laugh, to thrill, to frighten sometimes, to tell a moral tale and to warn and educate, but always to inspire, such are the many purposes of theatre and film. They contain the imaginative universe of our minds for there are no boundaries to what we are able to conjure up. Our minds take us to places we do not expect; our imaginations are free to roam and to discover and reveal, sometimes, what is within us. Huw read it again more slowly. He didn't fully understand but it was frightening to know that he couldn't control his own mind as if it had a separate life to him.

Now, he didn't have to look very hard to see a picture of himself on every page of *The Big Book* somewhere in the background, watching if not yet taking his part, as if it was inviting him in.

He went down to the front room, taking care not to wake his mother who had pronounced herself 'Exhausted' and gone for a nap. He pulled his feet up under him in the chair in the bay window and let his head rest.

He didn't recognise the bent old man he saw Alan helping into the house under the weak light over the door, gripping him by the elbow, shuffling the short distance down the drive to the porch step, with his stick almost bending under the strain, scraping and clacking its way over the concrete.

Jean came out and Jack's grandfather lifted his head but could not hold it up and it dropped level with his shoulders once more. Jean took his other side and he let the stick dangle. At the porch step, he couldn't raise his foot and tried again and would have fallen backwards onto the lawn if they weren't holding him. He had one foot up and the other down. He caught his breath and managed to raise the other. Side to side, they waddled him through the door.

Some minutes later, Alan came back out to fetch a bag from the car boot. He let the bag drop and stood in front of the porch. His shoulders heaved.

Huw had never seen a grown man cry and he wasn't sure that was what he was doing.

A dirty, grey van came slowly down the road and stopped. Alan bent to see through the back windows. He walked quickly to the end of his drive and bent down further with his head to one side. The van moved a few yards and stopped. Alan followed it. 'Gwyn?' he called. 'Is that you? Gwyn, stop.' Alan started running, caught the van and slapped his palms on the roof. And again. 'Stop, will you?' The van juddered and the fan belt squealed. Alan ran after it, slapping his hands on the roof over and over. It echoed and bottles clinked. As the van speeded up, the shadows between the orange street lights flickered over it like the frames from a cine camera. The van went faster, reached the end of the road and turned out of sight. Alan walked back with his head bowed and went inside. The door closed.

At the other end of the street, in shadow, was parked Sergeant Phillips' big, black car. It didn't move.

Chapter Six

Falkland Islands, Fiji, Gambia…

Mr Harris had cushions against his back to perch him upright in the chair in the front room. It helped him breathe. Between breaths, there was a pause as he gathered his strength for the next, as if every breath was the lap of a running track, round and round, slowing each time, stumbling over the line, before beginning the next because the track was all that was left. His skin was the colour of scallops and his eyelids fluttered, threatening to touch and stay closed. He took in the air that hurt his throat like emery paper and snapped the frayed veins in his lungs.

His labouring breaths could be heard in the garden where the women had taken Jean to warm her in the autumn sun – fresh air was always the answer – until Gwen quietly shut the back door and said, 'We shouldn't listen anymore.'

Jean did not move.

Alan saw the door close but didn't object. It was his father and he must listen and watch because there was nothing else to be done. The two ends of life, his son missing and his father dying, the first hastening the second, but a desperate cause for the laps to continue, the second praying he would hear his grandson's voice before the last and lift his hand to touch his head and whisper, 'Boy,' to share a memory of Kenfig Pool and the dunes. But he knew it was not to be: the dust was rising from his chest and into his mouth in a bitter upwelling. He could taste the mine and feel the grit between his teeth and every cough was black. 'Alan,' he said, trying to make the word wheeze out before it petered into wisps and, even then, he almost had to suck it back in before the sound emerged. He rapped his hand feebly on the chair arm in frustration.

'Dad?' Alan put his head close.

Mr Harris' pupils were finale bright, floating in yellowed whites like tiny, fetid ponds. 'Listen… now,' he said, with habit, wasting words, 'listen… now,' twice wasted.

'What is it, Dad?'

Mr Harris looked through the bay window onto the road, the way he was pointing, without having to move his head. Out there had been his life – or close enough – not long: he was fifty-seven and might have expected more. He knew what he should have done. But it would have caused too much pain to do it. What choice did he have? His life for theirs. He had warned Alan and Jack. He would not be able to tell Aled. Now he spoke because he had to. His thin lips were blue as they struggled to form the difficult words, not difficult words to say but difficult because of what they said. He pushed them out singly, crackling as they came. He did not have the strength or the time for proper explanations so he began where it mattered and meant to add what he could. He said, 'You have a brother, half-brother, Steven is his name, younger than you. It was the war, when I was in Eastbourne before we went over, his mother is Agnes, St Vincent's Terrace. I don't know now.' He had to stop, struggling for breath and his eyes rolled back. 'No one knew. The army, I wanted to stay, I could have escaped, but I came back to this. If Jack… God forbid… *forbid*…there is another. God *forgive* me.' His breath made a low whistle, an involuntary song, and his chest crumpled as the props gave way and the roof caved in. His head slumped to one side.

'Dad?' Alan shook his arm, but Mr Harris did not move. '*Jean, Jean*,' Alan shouted and the back door burst open. 'Call an ambulance.'

Jean did not move.

Brenda took charge. 'Get him on the floor. Lie him down.'

Jean got slowly to her feet and watched, transfixed, from the kitchen as Gwen called for the ambulance.

Huw asked, 'What's the matter with Mr Harris?' But everyone was too preoccupied with imminence to pay attention to a little boy who was so far from it and he was tiny amongst the legs so he slid down the radiator near Jean's feet and consoled Buttons. 'I'm sorry,' he told him, 'you're still my favourite.'

The ambulance arrived. There was no difference between its flashing blue lights smothering the walls and the police cars'. The ambulance men hurried in carrying a stretcher and busied themselves on the front room carpet with Mr Harris (where Jack and Huw had played with toy soldiers). The ambulance men carried Mr Harris out covered in a blanket with an oxygen mask over his face. Alan got into the back of the ambulance and the doors were slammed shut and it blared away through neighbours watching from the pavements on either side, disbelieving that so much could be brought on one family at the same time and that it could happen here, in their midst, where nothing ever happened.

Until it did.

Almost before the lint could settle, Constable Dewi came in. He waited until the three women looked at him. He said, 'Sergeant Phillips found Gwyn Roberts dead this morning in his milking shed. He hanged himself. Sergeant Phillips is coming here now.'

'Dewi?' asked Brenda.

Constable Dewi nodded slowly.

Jean lifted her white face to Constable Dewi's, rosily pink beneath the navy cupola, and shook her head. 'I don't understand,' she said, searching in him for what he meant. Then she did and her fingers flew up and made a cage over her nose and mouth. 'No, Dewi,' she said, between the trembling bars, and tears began to wash over them. 'What if he was the only one who knew? How will we ever find them?'

'We don't know if he was,' said Constable Dewi.

And there was Sergeant Phillips filling the doorway.

Constable Dewi stepped to one side.

Huw felt guilty and flinched small, thinking over his past few days for possible mischief.

Sergeant Phillips pouted his moustache and surveyed the misery. 'I went to ask Gwyn Roberts some questions this morning and I found him hanged among his cows in the milking shed.' His voice throbbed in their chests. 'They had not been milked,' as if this was a selfish omission, like his failure to make a will (had he not?).

'I have told them,' said Constable Dewi.

'Have you?' asked Sergeant Phillips. He didn't look at Constable Dewi. 'Did I tell you to do that?'

'No, Sir.'

Jean came half out of her chair across the table with her hands splayed. 'Did he do it? Did he take knowledge of it with him?'

'That is why I went to his farm.' Unexpectedly, inexplicably, Sergeant Phillips smiled with the slightest movement of his mouth, barely a twitch but, now, they thought to see a sympathetic man at heart, doing his job without fear or favour, but it would have been the same if he had pulled a wing off a fly – if he had ever been a boy, that boy – and he watched as the insect listed into blades of grass. 'And I must warn you that time is not on my side,' and he pulled the other wing off and the fly was condemned to crawl upon the ground, never to feel the air passing over its big, faceted eyes or scent decay, 'because he cannot tell us now.'

'*Ohhh*,' Jean moaned, and fell into her chair.

'Where is Mr Harris?' asked Sergeant Phillips.

'He's gone with his father to hospital,' said Brenda, too sharply and the points of her cheeks were white with anger.

It had no effect. 'Was that the ambulance?'

'Yes.'

'Yes?'

'Yes, Sir.'

'Bridgend Hospital?'

'I believe so, Sir.'

'You believe so?'

'Bridgend Hospital, Sir.'

'Then I know where to find him.' Sergeant Phillips left, taking faint hope with him.

For a while they sat, mute, even Brenda, not sure to despair and mourn or try to rally with possibilities. They emerged from themselves.

'Was it conscience? Couldn't he live with himself?' asked Gwen. 'But, if it was, why take it with him. If it was conscience, why not spare us?'

'Or the accusation,' said Brenda. 'It's a terrible thing to be accused of.'

'You mean he might not have done it?'

Brenda shook her head. 'I don't know.'

'But to hang yourself, to do that if it's not true? Did Sergeant Phillips threaten him?'

'Every question Sergeant Phillips asks is a threat,' said Brenda, 'but that is his job.'

'But what if he drove him to it,' insisted Gwen, 'what if he did?'

'Then he wouldn't know and he *has* to know.'

Jean raised her head. 'None of this will bring Jack back, either of the boys, both, if they are to be found. What if they are never found?'

'They will be found, Jean, they will be,' said Brenda.

'You can only say that. Only one man knows and he has died with it. How could he? When he was in our home every morning, when he saw Jack every day? Jack played in his fields, he helped him get the cows in. How could you know someone like that, a child, and be so cruel? Do you have an answer for that?'

'No, I don't,' said Brenda.

The storm continued to gather but not to break, growing more oppressive but not released.

At the door was Mr Hughes and Miss Williams. Constable Dewi was behind them.

Brenda said, 'They shouldn't be here.'

Mr Hughes looked at Jean. 'I had to come, I had to see you; I had to tell you to your face that I had nothing to do with it. I don't know why Sergeant Phillips or anyone could believe I did.' He stopped and waited for her. He was as small as a child next to Constable Dewi and it would not have been a surprise if he had reached up to grasp his hand.

Brenda said, 'Dewi, they shouldn't be here,' but her expression had softened.

'I had to let him say his piece,' Dewi replied. 'He asked me if he could and I said yes, and now he has.'

'Thank you,' said Mr Hughes. 'I will leave now.'

Gwen said, 'He didn't do it, I told Dewi that.'

'I didn't do it,' said Mr Hughes, again. 'He let me out but said he's not finished with me yet. What does that mean? What can I can tell him? Nothing. I keep telling him. It's as if telling him nothing makes it worse. I think he wants me to make something up. Laura was with me on the afternoon Jack was… *taken*,' he said, soundlessly, but they heard it said.

'Yes, he was,' said Miss Williams, even now, bashfully (their kiss behind the canteen for none to see and Huw by chance).

'I told him over and over,' said Mr Hughes, 'and all he said was that a woman like that – "*that*", he said "like *that*" – wouldn't have anything to do with the likes of me.'

'I told him too,' said Miss Williams, 'and he said he couldn't believe I was going to marry him. How could he say such a thing? We're going to get married.'

'Married?' thought Huw, 'with sex? But the vicar's married.'

Jean remembered another time, before the children were born, courting with Alan. 'Sit down,' she told them, quietly, 'and we'll have some tea. Tea, tea and more tea. Tea, tea and more tea, isn't it Gwen?'

Gwen said, 'I'll make it.'

Mr Hughes and Miss Williams sat, their legs touching, on the edge of the settee, like two waifs. 'Thank you,' they both said, grateful, when they had dreaded rage and would not have blamed the wronged for taking it out on them; grateful for being believed when they might not have been; and grateful for compassion when they might not have expected it.

Brenda said, 'Gwyn Roberts is dead.'

'Dead, what do you mean dead?'

'Dead, he hanged himself. Sergeant Phillips found him.'

Jean said, 'He did it and that's why.' She turned away, 'He did it and he's taken knowledge of it with him.'

Mr Hughes fell back into the settee as if pushed. '*No*.'

'We don't know that for certain,' said Brenda. 'Jean, we don't.'

'Yes, we do,' said Jean. 'What else? He's taken knowledge of it with him.'

'Is that why he let me out?' asked Mr Hughes, of no one who could give him an answer. He ran his hand through his hair and pinched his nostrils, 'So why didn't he tell me?'

'Oh God, Bryn,' said Miss Williams, in a way Huw did not think a teacher was capable, 'all that and he knew?'

'It's not like that,' said Brenda. 'Nothing can be settled until they are found. Do you see, Jean?'

'No, he has taken knowledge of it with him.'

'I didn't *do* it,' said Mr Hughes, angrily. 'He knew I didn't, so why put us through all that – and you too? Why did he do that?'

'Is Gwyn the Milk dead?' asked Huw.

'I'm sorry,' said Brenda, 'but you can't stay, finish your tea. If he catches you here? Dewi shouldn't have let you in – even if he was right to.'

'But thank you from the bottom of my heart,' said Mr Hughes.

'Thank you,' said Miss Williams.

Detective Jeffries appeared as if he'd been waiting and listening from the porch. He greeted no one and didn't ask if he could come in: he wasn't his own man but seas must part for the man who was. 'Get up,' he told Mr Hughes. 'You too, Miss.'

'I've got nothing else I can tell you,' said Mr Hughes.

'You're coming with me,' said Detective Jeffries. 'Do you want me to get these two to make you?' He looked at Brenda and Constable Dewi as if hoping to order them to.

'Where are you taking us?' asked Mr Hughes.

'Back where you came from.' Detective Jeffries beckoned Constable Dewi to follow. When they were outside on the path, he told Mr Hughes, 'You're interfering in a police investigation.' He looked at Miss Williams, 'and we'll see about you when we get down to the station. Get in the car.'

Sergeant Phillips was sitting in the driver's seat, slowly drum-rolling his fingers over the top of the steering wheel. He did not turn around or say anything as they slid onto the back seat.

Detective Jeffries hung back. 'Go and get Colcannon,' he ordered Constable Dewi.

Constable Dewi went in and came back out with Brenda.

'What are you two playing at?' demanded Detective Jeffries. He didn't seem to care who heard him. 'Letting them in? He will have you for it.'

'How did you know they were coming here?' asked Constable Dewi.

Detective Jeffries said, 'We might have suggested it to flush out the guilty.'

'How?'

'Guilt. Facing the mother and now we're going to question him again.'

'You might have suggested it, and now you're arresting him again?'

'I said might.'

'She's lost her son; the two boys could be dead.'

Suddenly bashful, Detective Jeffries snapped, '*Keep* your voice down.'

'And you want to use *her* to flush out the guilty?'

'Don't speak to me like that and don't try to tell me how to do my job. Do you want to tell him that? No, I didn't think so.'

'Isn't Gwyn Roberts enough?'

'What about him? He didn't leave a confession, did he? I did it, it was me, look no further? What does it change? Nothing. Now you stand out here and, you, Colcannon, go back in there and do as you're told.'

Constable Dewi could think of nothing more to say. He stood in the porch. His eyes were round.

Jean said, 'I think I'm going to fly apart,' and she wrapped her arms about herself, as if it was about to happen, and rocked.

When Alan came home, they had resumed their places in the kitchen because, at such times, the front room was for best and ceremony: they would go there when all was lost. Alan glanced through the kitchen door and went into the front room and sat in the dusk without turning on the light.

Gwen asked, 'How is he, Alan?'

It was a moment before he answered, but no one expected good news. 'He's not going to wake up, whatever they say. He's done. They told me to go home, they said they'd call me if there was any change.'

A car pulled up outside. They heard urgent voices. Constable Dewi came in, looking flushed, holding his helmet in both hands. He said, breathlessly, 'They've *found* him, they've *found* him.'

'Who have they found?' asked Huw, but everyone had gone.

Huw could see his name in the programme and the titles; he had a speaking part; he was close to the leading players and his acclaim grew with every page. On stage, when he came out to take his bow, there was cheering, not as loud as the hero, but growing louder with each performance. He wanted to live in *The Big Book,* where every picture and description was of a triumph, the landmarks of theatre and film; where there were no struggling actors or hard times – he didn't know they existed – fame awaited him and it was granted, full of light and warmth, glorious words and everything a little boy with such precocious dreams could ask for. It grew dark outside but his face was bathed with rippling colours. Buttons doffed his cap at him.

Chapter Seven

Gibraltar, Gilbert and Ellice Islands...

The furnace opened and the western sky was lit red from its blistering core, strong enough to silhouette the searchers in a brilliant glare. It died away and the fiery eyes reappeared, imperturbable and steadily burning. In the dark, they stumbled through half-full ditches, through wet sand and marram grass, wading through brine pools, torch beams criss-crossing like veering lances, their breath snorting through the light, dogs yelping, men shouting, then, suddenly, '*Here*.' But nothing disturbed Huw from his black dream beneath a sodden blanket.

Morning came. 'Mrs Brown?' asked Detective Jeffries, when she opened the door.

'Is there any news? Is Jack coming home?'

'Could I come in?'

Eve had Aled on her hip. He sleepily opened his eyes

and regarded Detective Jeffries grumpily at being woken up. 'Roy's out with Alan,' she said.

'I know.'

She frowned. 'Oh.'

'It's you I want to talk to. Can I come in?'

'I'm looking after Aled.'

'I can see that. Can I come in?'

She shook her head. 'What do you want to talk to me for?'

He didn't answer and stepped through the door, almost forcing her against the wall. She pushed open the front room door with her free hand and he went in and sat without being invited.

'Sit down, Mrs Brown,' he told her.

She pulled Aled into her lap and he stuck his thumb in his mouth, watching Detective Jeffries, 'I don't know what help I can be,' she said, uncomprehending his rudeness – a policeman – and in her own home.

'How long have you been married to Mr Brown?' he asked, abruptly, dismissing her right to an explanation.

'Pardon? I don't understand? Why do you need to know?'

He ignored her and crossed his legs and folded his hands in his lap. 'How long, Mrs Brown?'

'Why,' she bristled, 'why do you need to know?'

'How long, Mrs Brown?'

She tightened her lips and glared at him.

'How *long*, Mrs Brown?'

'Why do you need to know that? Ten years in November.'

He took his notebook out of the pocket of his tweed jacket and wrote in it. 'And how long did you know him before that?'

'Since school.'

'All your life then?'

'Yes, nearly. Will you please tell me why you need to know?'

'Have you ever had any time apart other than a day or so, a prolonged or reasonably prolonged period of time?'

'If you don't tell me why you're asking, I'm not going to say another word.'

He looked up to the ceiling, then he levelled his eyes at her. 'I am looking for two missing children. I don't have to tell you anything, *Mrs* Brown, except to say I wouldn't be asking if it wasn't important.'

His insolence was baffling. 'He is my husband.'

'Which is why I'm asking you,' he said, feeling her resistance breaking. 'Have you spent any prolonged periods of time apart in the ten years since you were married?'

'But they've found him. They've found Jack.'

'Have they? That may or may not solve anything.'

'I don't understand. They said they've found Jack.'

'Tell me, Mrs Brown, have you and your husband spent any significant time apart since you were married? Or is there any reason why you think you shouldn't tell me?'

'No.'

'Then?'

'When he was working on the railways he had to spend some time away, on occasion.'

'How long for?'

'It varied, a few days, a week sometimes.'

'Where?'

'Lots of places.'

'Such as?'

'Doncaster, York, Crewe, Scotland sometimes.'

'But he works in the same factory on the trading estate as Mr Harris now?'

'Yes.'

'How long ago did he leave the railways?'

'Five years, something like that.'

'You never had any children of your own, Mrs Brown?'

'No, we didn't.'

'So you enjoy looking after this boy?'

'Yes, of course I do, it's the least I could do.'

'Do you look after him often?'

'Yes, quite often.'

'And Jack Harris? Did you look after him too?'

'He's in and out of here all the time, and Huw, it's a second home for them both.'

'So you have a close relationship with Alan and Jean Harris and Gwen Evans?'

'Roy and I were in school with Alan and Jean.'

'And Gwen Evans?'

'She moved here from Carmarthen when she married Geraint – he was in school with us too.'

'Was he? And when you're looking after Aled and with Jack and Huw in and out of here all the time. Does Mr Brown help you do that?'

'Why shouldn't he? Why are you asking me this? They've found Jack.'

Detective Jeffries tapped his chin with his pencil. 'Does he look after them when you're not here?'

Her eyes were slits. Policeman… detective, this was inexcusable. She told him, 'You can leave now.'

Detective Jeffries made a show of studying her. 'Yes, Mrs Brown,' he replied, slowly. He was not finished and wanted her to know it. He would not tell her why. 'I have a job to do, Mrs Brown – which is why I'm here.' It wasn't up to her when he left but he stood up. 'Thank you, Mrs Brown,' he said, and pointedly turned away as he went into the hall to let himself out.

Eve watched from the bay window, holding Aled, until Detective Jeffries reached the pavement, then she faded into the shadow of the room and went into the kitchen. 'Why are they asking questions about you, Roy?' she asked herself. 'Surely it's nothing to do with any of this?' She rested her chin on the top of Aled's head. 'No, it can't have, they're just doing their job. I'm sure they're asking everyone lots of questions.'

Outside, Detective Jeffries asked Constable Dewi, 'Did Brown go with Harris?'

'Yes, he did.'

'How long ago?'

'The same time as Alan Harris. They went together.'

'And who told Brown that Jack Harris had been found?'

'Alan Harris did.'

'Then what?'

'They came running out and left in Alan Harris' car.'

'And you're sure Alan Harris told him?'

'His son had just been found. I know Alan Harris.'

'Do you?'

'Yes, I do.'

Detective Jeffries came closer. 'And how well do you know Roy Brown and his wife?'

'About the same.'

'Do you?'

'Yes, they went to the same school as me, not at the same time, I was after.'

'And how well is that?'

'I have a beer with them when I see them in town sometimes, that's all.'

'That's very cosy, Constable Jones? Is Roy Brown a keen gardener?'

'A keen gardener? I don't know. It's a neat looking garden, they all are.'

Detective Jeffries looked up and down the road at the gardens, each with identical, low hedges separating them. 'Yes, they are,' he said, 'and what about his back garden?'

'I haven't looked, or I haven't noticed to look, that is.'

'Then I shall.' Detective Jeffries stepped over the hedge back into Roy and Eve's garden and went up the side of the house to the top of the drive next to the garage. He saw the vegetable patch had recently been dug over where the earth was still dark. He stayed only a few seconds, as if he knew what he would see.

Constable Dewi watched as Detective Jeffries made his way up to the end of the row of houses, looking in each of the front gardens as if comparing their neatness with Roy Brown's.

Huw played in Jack's front garden with his mother inside with Jean and Brenda. The stage was grass, below the wall was the orchestra and, in the road, was the audience. When cars came past, they sounded like applause. It was a new game of his but very few cars went by so he looked up and down the road and timed his best lines for when he saw one coming.

The same police car cruised up and down every few minutes, taking in all the roads on the estate. Constable Dewi and the policeman in the car no longer acknowledged each other when it came past, if they noticed each other at all, but its circuit took almost exactly the same amount of time, which became the length of Huw's scenes and, because the police car was going slowly, the applause was longer.

Mr Tanner, the headmaster, appeared. He hesitated at the top of Jack's drive and smiled. 'Dewi Jones,' he said.

'Hello, Mr Tanner.'

'Is it true there's news?'

'We've had some information and they're out looking now. They've been out all night.'

'Is Jean Harris inside?'

'Yes, but she's not on her own.'

'I used to teach her, she loved to read, but that seems like a long time ago.'

'Not since you taught me, Mr Tanner.'

'That's true, Dewi.'

'I wouldn't go in at the moment, Mr Tanner.'

'I wasn't going to, it would be very wrong of me to intrude at a time like this.'

'No, I think they'd be very grateful you came, but I don't think Jean would cope with a visitor very well, just now.'

'Yes, of course, but, if you have the opportunity, would you tell them I came and let them know they are in my thoughts?'

'Of course I will.'

Mr Tanner tugged at his earlobe. 'I never thought you'd become a policeman and that's a fact.'

'Neither did I.'

'Has it improved your spelling?'

Constable Dewi smiled. 'There's not much call for good spelling in this job but, no, I'm afraid not. I never could spell, could I?'

'There's never an excuse for bad spelling, Dewi.'

'Well, I can only try when it's needed.'

Mr Tanner frowned. He had been waiting to say what he wanted to say and now he did. 'I must say, if no one else does, I knew Gwyn Roberts well. We grew up together. I knew his father too. He was never very academic – a bit like you, Dewi,' Mr Tanner shook his head, sadly, 'but he had a good heart. He was nothing if not kind and I, for one, do not believe he was capable of this or anything like it. And Mr Hughes, for goodness' sake, for goodness' *sake*.'

Constable Dewi listened but said nothing.

'I know you can't have an opinion, Dewi, or express one if you do. You're still not much older than some of my boys now but I know how badly this must affect you behind that uniform, believe me, I do. Come and talk to me, will you, if you want to? Even policemen need to talk sometimes and, with something like this, all the more so. You know where I am.'

Constable Dewi shuffled his feet in the way he always had when waiting outside Mr Tanner's office to be called in.

Mr Tanner ground his fist into his palm. 'I want those boys back where they belong. How is it our children cannot walk these streets in safety anymore? There are bad people in the world, I know, but schools are places of learning, they should *not* be closed.' He looked at the ground, almost embarrassed at his anger but unapologetic. He sighed. 'Well, tell Jean and Alan I was here, won't you? Tell them they're in my thoughts?'

'I will, Mr Tanner.'

Mr Tanner walked away in the direction of his empty school with his hands behind his back and head down.

'Mr Tanner must be feeling better,' thought Huw.

Constable Dewi remembered being caned by Mr Tanner, more than once, every time deserved. He owed the headmaster a lot. Next was *Herald* Andrew, cigarette bobbing in his mouth, with Lloyd at his side, camera round his neck. 'Not them,' said Constable Dewi, under his breath. 'What do you want?'

'We heard one of them's been found alive?'

Mr Tanner's courtesy, his compassion and sense of duty, a good man and, now, this pair, hunching along the pavement, weaselling and sneaking. 'Not now, Andrew, right, not *now*.'

'Alright, Dewi, alright, we've got a job to do the same as you.'

Constable Dewi gritted his teeth, 'If you don't get away from here, I will find something to arrest you for and then you can spend the next few hours down the station and what'll happen to your story then?'

'Calm down, Dewi.'

'Go away from here, Andrew, do you hear me?'

'I'm not sure you can stop us,' said *Herald* Andrew, defiantly. 'This is a public footpath and we're going about our lawful business.'

'It's also a crime scene.'

'*Was* a crime scene.'

'Don't play games with me, Andrew.'

Herald Andrew looked at Lloyd. 'Come on,' he told him. Then to Constable Dewi, 'We'll go round the corner, then, where you can't see us.'

'You do that, Andrew.'

The kitchen door flew open and Alan stormed in. Between both hands, he was holding a skull. He smashed it down on the table and chips pinged off and the teacups bounced. He struggled to get his breath. 'It was a *fucking* sheep.' He pounded the top of the skull until it cracked. 'A *sheep*, a *sheep*.'

Huw had never heard such language. He didn't know what the word meant but he knew it should never be said. He looked into the skull's nostrils and into the sockets of its eyes to the space where its brains would have been, and its soul, now both gone. He touched the side of his head. Beneath his hair and skin was his brain and soul and, when it was empty, he would be dead and then someone could look into those tunnels and see where he once was.

Constable Dewi said, 'Somebody must have put him up to it, Alan, he wouldn't have thought this up on his own. He's been in and out of the Parc Hospital for years. He's twp. We've got a new man on the desk and he didn't know who he was. If he had, we wouldn't have told you until we'd seen for ourselves, but it wasn't his fault.'

Alan turned to Constable Dewi. 'What do you mean, *somebody* put him up to it? Who?'

'I don't know. Someone must have.'

'But he said he was alive, *alive*, not a dead fucking *sheep*.'

'Yes, he did say that. He might have been told to say it, he might even have believed it.'

Jean stared at the skull. It stared back. It mocked her. It said, 'I am your son.' She shuddered and it turned her flesh; she quivered to a rising falsetto note that could not distinguish between pleasure or pain and, waiting for her, high above, was grace or madness.

'Jean?' Brenda asked, 'Jean? Can you hear me? *Jean*?' Brenda shook her but Jean's eyes were glazed and she did not respond. Brenda turned to Alan. 'Do you have any brandy?'

He pointed at the sideboard in the front room. 'I don't know if we've got any. If we do, it'll be in there. I know we've got whisky.'

'That'll do.'

'*Jean? Jean?*' Alan rubbed her cheek, but her head fell to one side.

'Hold her.' Brenda got up and pulled open the sideboard. She moved bottles around until she found the whisky. She didn't bother with a glass but swilled out Jean's teacup and half-filled it. 'Drink this,' she said and tilted it against Jean's lips.

Jean did not move: she could see angels, her troubles forgotten, and did not want to leave. Brenda pressed the cup closer, demanding she return to the living, unaware of what she was asking. The fumes went up Jean's nose as if they were smoke creeping under the bedroom door in the dead of night. The whisky stung her lips and drops rolled over her tongue. The angels moved away and waved to her. She would not see them again, not while she breathed. Her parting thought, as the whisky brought back her senses was, 'If that's where you are, Jack, you don't need to come back, just so long as I know.' The whisky reassembled the kitchen around her. She tasted it and felt the tabletop under her fingers and saw Alan and Brenda's faces, with Gwen behind. She murmured, 'I knew it. He has taken knowledge of it with him.'

A camera clicked, *Flash.*

The crowded room blazed with light.

'*Right*,' Constable Dewi rushed out. After a few minutes, he came back. He waited and swallowed. He took off his helmet. 'Another boy has gone missing in Llantwit.'

Jean gasped, 'Oh thank *God*.'

The phone rang. Gwen picked it up and listened, then she held out the receiver to Alan. 'It's the hospital.'

On every page of *The Big Book*, Huw was the hero, the leading man, the first name on the titles and in the programme. He wanted to step inside and pull the cover closed above him and live there forever. *The Big Book* was Huw's Heaven.

CHAPTER EIGHT

Gold Coast, Granada, Honduras...

There were men in Gwyn the Milk's fields. They herded the cows toward the top of the big field near the milking shed, beating their backs with sticks if they didn't move quickly enough – thwacks that could be heard in Huw's bedroom. It wasn't time for milking and the cows were reluctant and confused. But these men didn't care that Gwyn had always been gentle, walking behind them at the slow plod they had become used to. Two cattle trucks were waiting with their doors open and slatted, wooden ramps down. The men shouted and hit them harder to get them to go inside and the cows scrabbled on the muck-strewn ramps. They had never been in a lorry before; for them there was only one journey, their last, with Gwyn to pat and encourage lest they suspect its purpose. This was their last and they went to it with terror. When the cattle truck doors were closed and the ramps were lifted up like drawbridges, their mooing was dulled but pitiful. The trucks drove away down the farm track, rolling and splashing in the ruts, leaving the fields empty for the first time in three generations of Roberts.

Huw watched his mother put on her grey dress and wrap a black shawl around her shoulders. She was trying to hold back tears behind her make-up, dabbing her eyes with a lace hankie to keep them at bay. Her lips and jaw were tight but she could not stop the flurries of anguish sweeping over her cheeks and dipping the corners of her mouth. She took deep breaths through her nose and stiffened her shoulders. It was a losing battle as she prepared to face the world.

In the front room, she touched her husband's photograph. It was fading more quickly as if he was trying to escape its silver frame. She caressed his face with the backs of her fingers.

His gentle expression, but he was not looking at her. 'You cannot stay,' he said, and smiled, 'but do not be frightened, I will explain.'

'Six years, my love,' she said. 'I must have a life now. I'm sorry, but I cannot help myself, even if it must be hidden and borrowed. It is because of the loss of you, not instead of you.' She tilted the photograph toward the light.

He raised his eyes to hers to say, 'How can I stop you? What right do I have? But, if I could, I would, not to be selfish but for your own sake. I would never ask you to be alone, but in this way? All I have are memories and that is all I can be to you too.'

'Huw has your eyes and hair. He looks so much like you.'

'Yes, he does. I see me in him, what there is left to see.'

'You liked Mr Harris, didn't you? He could talk about the colliery with you, he couldn't with Alan. It was too late to stop you going underground. I wish he had, but would you have listened?'

'It is too late for both of us – but he has more stories than me.'

Roy was smoking in his back garden in his shirt sleeves. Eve came out with his suit jacket. He flicked the cigarette butt away and put it on.

Cars were arriving and parking up and down the road where police cars had been, now moved temporarily. The hearse appeared, quiet as a draught, followed by another funeral car, huge and heavy, and came to an imperceptible stop outside the Harris' house as if fate had materialised. The coffin was pale oak with shining brass handles and it was not to be believed there was anything as vulgar as a body inside. The driver was sepulchral still. The undertaker got out, stiff and straight, and put on his top hat. He stood by the car with a solemn expression and clasped his hands across the front of his dark striped trousers with his coat-tails hanging to the backs of his knees like the crisply folded wings of a bat. He made a single bow of the head to Gwen as they walked past, perhaps rueing the funeral that never was. 'How are you, Mrs Evans?' he asked. 'Our thoughts are with you all at this terribly difficult time.'

Gwen remembered that he was known as Bowen the Box, and prone to getting worse for wear at wakes when the formalities were over. 'Scotch, just the one mind,' and his decorum was instantly tarnished – thankfully, because it made her less tearful.

The mourners gathered like stooping crows at the door to the Harris' house and, one by one, they filed inside to the hush of pressed bodies sitting or standing around the walls of the front room. Others were squeezed out into the kitchen and more still were bunched in the garden and up the drive.

At the centre of the room, on the small, remaining patch of paisley carpet, Reverend Elwiss, black and sudden white, clasped the good book with one finger jammed into it to mark his reading.

From between the legs, Huw thought he looked like a penguin.

Reverend Elwiss asked, 'Are we all here?' but, whether they were or not, there was no space left. He had been dreading this moment (as he always did in the intimacy of their homes). They gave him the friendliness of acquaintance and the deference his office deserved but he was separated by blood and belonging. He was a kindly man but their sensual muscularity repelled him; they were elemental and his delicacy of breeding would not allow him to join in – or so he believed, but he was afraid of what he did not understand and refused to admit it. On his evening walks, humming tunelessly for company –

hymn-like, as befits (who would question should they hear?) – sometimes down to the playing fields by the river where there was a cricket square, he hoped to come upon a good deed waiting to be done by a Good Samaritan. It would have given him authority and standing amongst these people. There never was and South Wales remained a mystery to his Saxon soul (Norman – Elwiss? Worse? Not a Celt) and a penance.

But, to his surprise, feeling their physical warmth so close, smelling the old-fashioned scents of valleys aunties and hearing the melancholy wheezing of the old miners, his finger slipped from his carefully marked page, and strange words came from him that they could understand. Briefly, as he spoke, he was admitted to the dark lands. 'It is here, in the family home, that love finds its greatest resonance. It was not John's home, a fiercely independent man, but where those closest to him live, a place where he was at home. The formal service at the crematorium is a full stop to a life but most certainly not to existence itself, which continues in another place, its mysteries one day to be divulged to us all. Until then, by faith we continue.

'John was a man of coal and, apart from a brief sojourn in the army when he fought for his country and for us all, he spent his life underground and, for that, his body carried the burden of its trials into retirement and, sadly, it hastened his end. But, during that life, he made a considerable mark. He will be remembered well. How many of us can say of our lives that it will be so?

'He left us at a time of great trouble and pain and he would have given everything, his life itself, to be with his family, to be their support and guidance, but he was called by a greater power and, perhaps, we should look upon this as an act of mercy for we can be certain that all was revealed to him at his passing and, finally, his own pain could be put aside. It is for us, the living, to endure. We are mortal and must be accepting of its limitations, but always in the knowledge that God's eternal love is with us even if, at times, it is sorely tested and seemingly impossible to understand.' Restrained sobbing came from the walls. Reverend Elwiss looked at Alan and gestured toward the door. One by one, the room emptied into the fresh air.

Alan was last. He looked at the chair where his father had died to tell him at the end. Why? To what purpose? He wondered whether to leave be. What good would come of it?

Constable Dewi touched him on the wrist and took him to the side and glanced around to make sure no one could overhear. 'Gwyn Roberts did not die by his own hand, he was already dead when he was hanged. I thought you should know before the service. I know your father was friends with him for many years. Gwyn would have been here today. You should remember him well, Alan. He deserves that and the truth will out in the end.'

The cortege moved sedately away and a line of cars fell in behind. As it reached the end of the road, Sergeant Phillips' big, black car came round the corner and stopped where the hearse had been. It was followed by a police van, a tipper truck and two more police cars, full with policemen in overalls.

The mourners gathered outside the crematorium, their feathered weeds ruffling in the wind, waiting for the previous service to finish and leave out the back entrance.

The crematorium overlooked the railway line and the edge of the trading estate. The view lifted over Ewenny Priory, ancient as a rock formation, toward the open hands of the Vale of Glamorgan, lit by the western sun when it came, cherished and sweet with no coal in its guts.

It was time. Alan and Roy felt the weight of the coffin as it slid from the hearse, more wood than man, and it dug into their shoulders as they lifted it up. The mourners followed them inside.

Reverend Elwiss began by reading the text. Light came through the window above his head and gave his bald patch a hue.

A hymn. Another reading. Another hymn and the Reverend stood to one side and Alan climbed up the steps to the pulpit and looked over the heads of the mourners and they all looked at him. 'One Christmas, when I was not more than Jack's age, my father gave me a very old book about a place he loved. He took me there often and he loved to take Jack too. I would like to read from it. Nothing reminds me more of him.' He paused and began, faltering at first, but his voice gathered strength: *'There is a wild and lonely solitude of sand where the sad cry of the seabird and the unceasing lap of the tireless tide are almost the only sounds that meets the ear of the wanderer who tracks along Glamorgan beach over the site of the buried town – Kenfig – formerly the pride of its possessors, content and happy in its castle. This once active centre lies deep below the all devouring sand which has engulfed everything but one solitary fragment of wall, yet left, in cruel irony, to mark the actual spot where clash of sword and buckler, clatter of hoofs and clang of arms was heard half a thousand years ago.'*

He closed the book and the mourners dipped their beaks in sadness, heavy-eyed in envy of their friend his passing. Alan continued. 'I was asked if I wanted to wait for Jack before we held my father's funeral so that he could say goodbye to the grandpa he loved. But, Dad is gone and Jack is a boy. He will be left with memories of his grandpa – not enough, I grant you – but, with Dad's health I do not believe there would have been many more, whatever the circumstances. Let him have those memories, he does not need the memory of a funeral to go with them. It will be down to me, now, to take him for walks over the lost city and I look forward to it as, one day, he will take his children and I will be the grandpa.' Alan stepped down from the dais and returned to his seat.

Reverend Elwiss read the last of it. There was music and the coffin sank and disappeared.

Everyone left through the back entrance and shook hands or kissed Alan and Jean. Barely had they left than the next funeral came in and the sound of someone else's special music could be heard playing inside.

There were plaques with names and dates all down the wall behind the crematorium and alcoves with pots of flowers, some of them dried out and dead. A garden of roses stretched down the hill toward the road. Each rose had a peg with a name in front of it. The grass between was clipped short. There was not a weed, not even a buttercup or a dandelion. Gwen said, 'That was so moving, Alan.'

He sighed, 'Thank you. Dad's time was done – it should have been longer, but it was done. Why has this happened to us? Out there, look, *look*, someone knows. All those houses and I ask is it that one or that one? I want to go into every one of them. If we go into every one of them, we will find them, won't we? So why don't they? I don't know if I can stay here after this. I suspect them all and I'll never stop.'

'Is it going to be over, Alan?'

'No and yes, it must be, but I'd sooner it never was if they aren't returned to us as innocent as the last time we saw them. It will be beyond me to heal the harm done. It's unbearable but I'll bear it until the day I die if I can bear it for them and, if that is not to be, I ask only one thing and, if I can have it, I'd gladly join Dad in the furnace.' He didn't tell her about Gwyn and he would tell Constable Dewi not to tell his wife. They would find out soon enough, but not today. It was an evil tarring but this was not the place.

'You couldn't have chosen a better reading, Alan.'

'Couldn't I?'

'No, it was just enough. Our thoughts weren't with your father today. That's not fair, but I know he wouldn't have minded.'

'No, he wouldn't have. Not fair is it? You fight your whole life, one way or another, and this is the finish of it? There's not much justice is there?' He kissed her gently on the cheek.

Roy came walking towards them. 'Are you going to plant him a bush, Alan?' he asked.

Alan looked at the garden, 'What do you think? He wasn't a fan of all that prissy stuff. I know a place he'd much prefer.'

Roy nodded. 'I can guess.'

'I'm going to wait for Jack, though, to do that. Dad's not going anywhere is he?'

They walked together to the car park where the funeral car waited to take them home. The hearse had already gone. Alan got into the back next to Jean and Gwen. 'I feel like a king in here but I bet it doesn't do much to the gallon.' Before he closed the door, he said to Roy, 'I'll see you back at the house, perhaps there will be news.'

But the funeral car couldn't get near the house because the police vehicles were in the way. It had to wait halfway up the road with the queue of following cars trailing around the corner. Policemen in overalls pushed wheelbarrows filled with soil and rubble up Roy and Eve's drive and up a bouncing plank to empty them into the tipper truck. They left a trail that was being trodden into the concrete. A pulsing hose from a compressor snaked into the back garden to where a jackhammer pounded deafening obscenities, drilling insults, a frenzied, demonic liturgy to shatter the reverent calm of the crematorium. Dust rose over the houses in a jarring, brown cloud. Where the undertaker had waited patiently beside the hearse, now stood Sergeant Phillips beside his big, black car, as if he had been manifested by the monstrous invocation of the jackhammer's cacophony.

Alan got out and shook his head in disbelief. He walked down the middle of the road followed by Jean and Gwen with Roy and Eve, carrying Aled, close behind, almost staggering in the pummelling air. Eve's mouth fell open with shock when she saw the devastation.

Sergeant Phillips pouted his moustache with his upper lip and looked down at her.

Alan shouted, trying to make himself heard. The jackhammer took no notice and hammered on.

Sergeant Phillips flexed his brown gloves tight over his knuckles and raised a finger at Roy and Detective Jeffries and another policeman, not in overalls, pulled Roy's hands behind his back and put him in handcuffs. They were saying something, perhaps a reason, but he couldn't hear and they didn't care. They bundled him into Sergeant Phillips' big, black car and got in on either side of him. Sergeant Phillips ran his thumbs down the sides of his moustache and yanked his uniform straight.

As if it was a signal, a pack of reporters, led by *Herald* Andrew and Lloyd and many more, surged from behind a house a few doors up. Cigarette smoke wreathed behind them and their eyes were thrilling.

Sergeant Phillips adopted a pose with one hand on the roof of his car as the reporters took photographs of him from every angle.

Eve pressed her face to the window of the big, black car with her palms flat against it. She tried to mouth words. Roy's frightened eyes peered from within. One of the policemen raised his hand to block her view.

Sergeant Phillips leaned very close to Alan and said, 'Roberts was seen off before he was strung up. But you knew that didn't you, Harris?' Then he pushed him to one side and adjusted his pose and there was more blazing. *Flash… Flash.*

The wheelbarrows kept trundling past to empty their muck and the jackhammer kept up its numbing racket.

Sergeant Phillips swung himself into his big, black car and it drove away taking Roy. The funeral car edged down the road and took its place. The driver took a pocket watch out of his waistcoat pocket and looked at it, then he shrugged his shoulders and drove away too.

Alan shouted into Constable Dewi's ear, '*Why?*'

Constable Dewi shook his head, 'Can't say.'

'Can't, won't?'

'Can't.'

'Where have they taken him?'

‘Bridgend.’

‘I’ll take Eve then.’

‘They won’t let her see him. Don’t try, it will make it worse.’

The mourners parked their cars where they could and made their way to the Harris’ house with strained expressions and their feathers twitched. The black throng gathered in the front room and the kitchen and nibbled at sandwiches with plates held close to their chests and sipped at beer and sherry that now tasted sour or sharp. They only had sign language, but they tried to pay their respects in the din even if it was making some of them ill.

Alan went out and waved his arms over the garden fence to try to make them stop. The man with the jackhammer bouncing over the foundation of Roy’s greenhouse ignored him. The patio that Roy had taken so much time to lay was already a pile of broken paving. Alan went round and tried to find the *Off* switch on the compressor but he was ushered away. ‘*Make them stop, Dewi?*’ But Constable Dewi held up his hands and shook his head. Alan returned to his vibrating guests. He mouthed, ‘Red Lion?’ at them and pointed.

They left plates of half-eaten sandwiches wherever there was a space, lifted catatonic aunties out of armchairs and off the settee and led them through the front door.

Eve was left, small and staring in the corner next to a standard lamp. Gwen gently touched her elbow but she refused to follow. Instead, she stepped over the low hedge between the houses and went in to her own house where she drew the curtains and became one with the shattering noise that made no sense of her fears.

Even in the lounge bar of The Red Lion, the *drrr drrr drrrrrr* could still be heard. For the rest of the town who could hear it, it was only roadworks. But, for the mourners, they were too shocked to talk about what it meant; too shocked to speculate why Roy had been arrested and afraid of what he might have done. If they thought it, they did not say so in front of Alan and Jean. They were relieved that Eve had not come. For the moment, on a sad but not unexpected day that had become more awful than could be imagined, their anger searched elsewhere. 'Why did Sergeant Phillips have to do it like that? Surely there was no need?'

'Where's the vicar?'

'Another funeral, I imagine.'

'You're probably right, but he might have been able – you know?'

It was not long before only Alan, Jean, Gwen and Jack's uncles and aunties were left. The crows had gone their ways, some to other pubs where they could talk more freely to try to make sense of it. *Drrr*.

A lighting set was put up in Roy and Eve's garden. It was wound up to its full height with the lights on top and its diesel engine came to life in acrid, blue smoke. The raucous search went on into the night.

Alan said, 'We can't stay here, let's go home.'

'We shouldn't have left Eve,' said Gwen.

They straggled home with the aunties and uncles in the rear, surrounding Jean, who was pale and transparent, shuffling and frail.

When the jackhammer finally stopped and the lighting set was turned off, they could only bring themselves to whisper in the silence, grateful for the sudden calm, because they did not want to provoke another outburst. It had defeated them as surely as if they had lived under a cruel tyranny and could not believe it would not return.

Sam the labrador regarded them mournfully with his head between his paws.

Alan said, 'If we can't find anyone to take him, it's going to have to be the vet's.'

When Huw looked from his bedroom window, the moonlight reflected in the panes of Uncle Roy's dismantled greenhouse leaning against the fence, some of them cracked, some with all their glass splintered on the lawn and in the mud. The concrete foundation had been split apart and pulled up and the footings beneath had been dug out to reveal the bare earth. Nothing had been found. Boot marks were everywhere, the grass was mashed and smeared and the neatly turned vegetable patch was flattened. The jackhammer with its umbilical hose was plunged upright like a striking snake into a rodent's burrow and the lighting set waited, spiky and tall as a stork, to spear the snake.

Chapter Nine

Hong Kong, India, Jamaica...

The tide revealed small fingers poking out like white asparagus. Green silkweed caught around them and they began to make a tiny bank of mud on the leeward side. Crabs fussed, knitting with their mouths. Not yet his face, still deep in the gelatinous silt, because his hands were reaching up.

The tom cat's screech woke him with a start. He went to the window expecting to see it parading down the fence and lording it over the other cats in the alley below. It had been some time, not since he and Jack had laughed at its antics. But the cat wasn't there. Instead, a man with blond hair was staring up at his mother's window.

The sound wasn't coming from outside, it was coming from her room across the landing: whining, truncated cries, punctured moans and an insistent creaking that was getting faster and ended abruptly with a single cry. Breathless voices whispered. Steps: one, two. Floorboards.

A pause. More footsteps at the top of the stairs then slowly descending.

The man in the alley stepped into the shadows.

The back door opened and Alan Harris came out. He shut it quietly and skirted the fence until he reached the gate at the end of the garden and went into the alley, past the wreck of Roy and Eve where the front room light was still on, slanting through a gap in the curtains, and into his own garden and into the house.

The man in the alley stepped forward again. One side of his face was lit by the street lamp in the road, the other by the moon. He was familiar. But Huw could not pick him from what memories he had. When their eyes met, Huw waved and the man smiled. Huw knew that smile. Then the man slipped away toward the end of the alley and Huw did not see him reappear under the street lamp or see which way he went. He watched for a while, hoping he would come back. He didn't. There were no more sounds from his mother's room. Huw went back to bed.

The Big Book, open on his desk, glowed with stories of fantastical moons. Half asleep, he heard the cows going in for milking in the musket light and Gwyn's gentle voice. It was as if nothing had happened, nothing had changed and the world had been stopped for the little boy tucked up in bed, kept safe, for now, by the soft Welsh night that was probing uncertainly at the verges of another day. A screech of tyres brought him fully awake and the world resumed.

The moon had gone and rain had taken its place. It drifted in lazy sheets from an unremitting, grey sky on a day that would never fully be so. It was bad tempered.

The blue police lights streamed over the windscreen of Alan's car and all the wipers could do was push the water from one side to the other. He bent over the steering wheel, trying to see the road he knew well in the spray. They sped up the dual carriageway to the top of Stormy Down, which was, and up came the fiery eyes over Port Talbot making steam of the rain. They turned off the dual carriageway and onto the quarry road. Huge dump trucks hauled through the traffic lights that would not, could not stop, even for a police car. They shook the ground. Alan sped on, following the police car, until they reached the outskirts of Porthcawl and off into the lanes with high hedges and blind bends. The police car switched on its siren. The lanes opened out onto golf links, deserted and hemmed in by the dunes with Sker beach behind. The siren was turned off. Up a rough track and the police car slid sideways and almost hit a fence post. Alan had to slow down. He followed, fighting the car as it slewed down the track. Dirty puddles heaved over the bonnet and muddy streaks ran down the windscreen and were gathered up by the wipers into filthy borders. In the distance, there was a cluster of more blue lights, closely bunched: transfixed by a spectacle; it was their duty to be there – prurient, all the same. The police car reached a half-open gate and stopped, blocking Alan's way. Beyond, the police cars were circled around an old box-car with no wheels. Its doors were closed. All the headlights were pointing at it. Torch beams, effete, danced between them skittishly. It was silent except for the rain lashing in the wind but every droplet hoped to see as they crowded in from the sea. The waiting was over: the performance was about to begin.

And… *now*…

A tall figure in a long black mac approached the box-car. He stopped to look over his shoulder. All the torch beams leapt to his face: Sergeant Phillips, with his skin glistening like bronze and his moustache dripping. He grasped the door handles, tilted back his head and threw his arms wide to slide the doors apart. They flew open. The torch beams snapped into a single spotlight and there the demon was, crouching, with yellow eyes, its mouth open, bloodied over torn flesh. Disturbed, it snarled and drew back and cowered beneath its bone-thin knees like tent poles holding up rags. Sergeant Phillips towered: righteousness come to avenge and banish it from the realm of the living...

The torches frantically searched the box-car's depths.

It was empty.

Sergeant Phillips let his arms slowly fall. His shoulders lifted as he took a deep breath. He stepped inside and reached down. The torches followed his hands. Sergeant Phillips picked something up. It was too small to be a child. He looked at it and bent down again and picked up what looked like a piece of cloth. He turned, holding in each hand what he had found. He walked through the phalanx of police cars with the torch beams shortening. He kicked open the farm gate and stood in the middle of Alan's headlights.

His *eyes*.

Sergeant Phillips stretched out his arms: in his left hand there was a dead black and white cat, rigid and flattened, its fur matted and its neck bent back and broken. In his right hand was a small, red jumper, getting heavy in the rain. He came round to stand next to the car window. His hands were level with the bottom of the frame.

Alan wound the window down and smelt putrefaction.

'Is this your son's?'

Alan looked at it and didn't want to know, but he did. 'Yes,' he said, 'it is.'

'I know so,' said Sergeant Phillips, 'we are too late, he is not here. He has killed the cat and left the jumper for us to find. I know his mind.' Sergeant Phillips put his face almost through the car window. 'I know you saw off Roberts,' he hissed, so no one else could hear. 'I know you did, Harris, and I will have you for it.' He strode away and thrust the jumper and the dead cat into Brenda's hands without saying a word.

She did not drop the cat. She glared at Sergeant Phillips' back, with the mac flapping about him like a cape. She turned to Alan, his face melting through the rain-soaked windscreen and then she looked at the cat, rigid and stinking, with her thumb beginning to leave an indentation in its board-like skin. She saw where Sergeant Phillips' fingers had grasped it, wrung it as if it had still been alive, killed it again, and at the unnatural angle of its snapped neck with vertebrae poking out, twisted with such rage it would have been killed many times over. A child's stem-like neck, a sapling fresh and lithe?

She would have to return to her kitchen vigil with Jean and Gwen, Constable Dewi outside. There was no end to it yet. She opened the passenger door of Alan's car and got in with the jumper on her lap and dropped the cat into the footwell. 'I'm sorry,' she said, 'but if I throw it away he will ask what I've done with it.'

Alan didn't answer. He stared straight ahead into the rain and his teeth were bared.

'Can I come back with you?' she asked. 'I have to go back to the house now.'

'I have to stay here to help them search.'

'You have to tell Jean about this, Alan,' and she held up the jumper, 'she's waiting. They'll tell you if they find something.'

He turned to her. 'Someone is playing a terrible game.'

'Yes, they are.'

The torches yawed and criss-crossed, tarrying with the insides of the box-car but there was still nothing there.

Some of the police cars reversed to get out of the way as van loads of police began to arrive to search an ever-widening area around the voided epicentre of rage.

The box-car's doors were left open and the insides brightly lit, a tardy study of febrile emptiness because that's where Jack had been and was not now (and the other boys?).

Sergeant Phillips' big, black car steamed away like an ocean liner in too much of an important hurry to stop for an abandoned life raft adrift on an empty sea. Somewhere the sun was shining, but not here.

When Aled saw Huw he started crying and reached for his mother.

'Not now, Aled,' said Jean, weakly, 'not now, *please?*'

Gwen picked him out of the dangerous high chair (there was no one else and Eve was closeted away).

'What's the matter with him,' thought Huw, as he curled up in a ball in what had become his place. 'Is he always going to be like that?' He had begun to dislike Aled, but couldn't help feeling guilty about it because Aled was such a little boy. 'Where's Brenda?' he asked.

'Is Dewi outside?' asked Jean,

'Yes, he's still there,' answered Gwen, rocking Aled who was grumbling to himself.

'Did he say anything?'

'No.'

'Why is it taking so long?'

'It hasn't been long, Jean.'

'It's been forever.'

'He hasn't heard anything or he'd tell us.'

'At least Brenda's gone with them, all those men.'

'Gone where?' asked Huw.

'All those men,' asked Gwen, quietly, almost to herself, 'does it matter who finds them?'

'No, as long as they find him.'

'Find *them*.'

'Find them, find them, find *them*.'

'I can't stay living here after this. I should have gone after Geraint was killed. I could have gone back to Carmarthen. Huw was still a baby, it wouldn't have made any difference to him. But I didn't.' Aled had gone to sleep. Gwen pushed the high chair against the wall with her foot and placed him carefully back in it.

'We can never move from here,' Jean said.

'Can't you? I think Alan could,' said Gwen, before she thought.

'No, he wouldn't, he *never* would.'

'That's not what he told me.' It was a pointless dispute to have with her listless, weakened friend and she had no right.

'When did he say that? He wouldn't say that.'

Gwen tried to retreat from her trespass, before she was seen and known. 'It doesn't matter.'

'But, it does. When did he say that?'

'At the funeral.'

'Why would he say that?' On another day, at another time, Jean might have caught Gwen and confronted Alan, but this was not that day and she was not that Jean.

'It was just something he said, that's all, when he was looking at all the houses and thinking about Jack.'

Aled smacked his lips in his sleep.

'He's never said anything like that to me. Why would he say that to you?'

'I don't think he meant it.'

'Jack's got to have somewhere he knows to come home to, where he feels safe. This is his home.'

'They all need to be safe,' said Gwen.

'Of course he didn't mean it.'

'No, he didn't, of course not. Let's have some tea after all,' said Gwen, and she got up to wash the cups in the sink.

'Where is Eve?' asked Jean.

'Next door with the curtains drawn.'

She frowned. 'With the curtains drawn? Why? Oh.' She closed her eyes and kneaded her forehead. 'Oh. What did he do, Gwen? It can't have anything to do with this can it?'

'Perhaps she doesn't know.'

'Doesn't she? But if she does, why doesn't she tell us?'

'I don't know. Perhaps she's too upset?'

'Too upset to tell us?'

Gwen stroked Aled's head that was bent over the plastic tray of his high chair and her breath lifted strands of hair.

He reached up in his sleep to scratch.

'Ashamed?' Gwen poured the tea they wouldn't drink into the now clean mugs.

'Ashamed?' asked Jean, 'ashamed of what? I don't want any more tea,' and she pushed the mug away.

Mr Hughes, the teacher, was let out of the cell for the second time without an explanation. He was given back what possessions he had had with him (watch, belt, tie, not much money) and was shown to the entrance of the police station and sent out into the rain. He stood under the awning and pulled his jacket collar up and stuck his hands in his pockets. He wanted to get away as quickly as he could before anyone saw him. He had been asked the same questions over and over again; he had been told what his answers should be over and over again. 'Where are they? Say you did it because we know you did.'

Not once had they asked why he would; not once did they tell him why they thought he had. Every time, he shook his head and said, 'No, I didn't,' until he was in tears of fear and frustration.

They kept on. 'Where are they?'

'I don't know.'

'Say you did it because we know you did.'

'I didn't, I didn't.'

Sergeant Phillips let Detective Jeffries ask the questions. Then he leaned across the wooden table and said, in his voice of tumbling boulders, 'You can't resist me, no one can.' The clipped ends of his dyed, black moustache trembled like a seismometer and he folded his arms and let silence do the rest. The muffled sounds of the police station outside the interview room did not disturb the stillness of the long moment that followed.

It began again. Detective Jeffries: 'Where are they?'

'I don't know.'

'Say you did it because we know you did.'

'I didn't, I didn't, I *didn't.*' After hours of the same, they put him into a windowless cell with a toilet and a bed and left him there. He didn't know if it was day or night; he didn't know if anyone had tried to come to see him. He thought about Laura.

Then Detective Jeffries came and took him back to the interview room. 'Where are they?'

'I don't know.'

'Say you did it because we know you did.'

'I didn't, I didn't, I *didn't.*'

'What are you crying for? Where are they?'

'I don't know.'

'Say you did it because we know you did.'

'I didn't, I didn't, I didn't,' he whimpered. They let him out and, here he was, utterly perplexed but grateful for his freedom under the cloud-filled skies and wanting to be home and wanting to be a simple primary school teacher again and wanting Laura.

Flash.

Herald Andrew appeared from the corner of the building with Lloyd.

Startled, Bryn Hughes spun round.

Herald Andrew took out his notebook. 'Mr Bryn Hughes?' He didn't give him time to answer, 'What have you got to say about the disappearance of the three boys? Why have the police released you? Are they going to ask you any more questions, Mr Hughes? Are you still under suspicion?'

Flash.

Before he could stop himself, Mr Hughes started to run. Another flash lit his fleeing shadow. He ran down the hill toward Cardigan Street.

Lloyd took one more picture for luck and the shop fronts flashed back through the rain and stilled Mr Hughes like a cartoon in lightning. Later, when they saw the developed photograph, *Herald* Andrew told Lloyd, 'You'll get an award for that one, matey – nothing without my words, mind, and knowing where to be and when. Secrets of the trade, Lloydy-boy. You just stick with me and I'll tell you where to point it, right?' *Herald* Andrew looked up to a first-floor window where Detective Jeffries was tapping his chin with his pencil. He nodded at *Herald* Andrew and the three of them watched as Mr Hughes disappeared up Cardigan Street with accusations hard on his heels and all over the next day's front page.

When they pulled into the drive, Alan told Brenda, 'Don't leave the cat, it'll stink. Kick it under the car and I'll get rid of it later. I'll tell you where I've put it so at least you can dig it up if he asks.'

She wrinkled her nose.

They sat, reluctant to get out, even though the rain was stopping.

Constable Dewi came out from where he had been sheltering in the porch, glad to be able to stand up straight.

'Come on,' said Alan, 'we've got to go in to tell Jean.'

Brenda gingerly picked up the cat and held it away from her as she opened the door. She let it drop onto the drive and eased it under the car with her toe.

'What's that?' asked Constable Dewi.

Brenda shook her head, 'A dead cat, he found it.'

Constable Dewi looked mystified.

'Don't ask, Dewi,' she told him, 'I'll tell you later – don't tell them inside, will you?'

Alan carried the red jumper into the house.

Dewi gripped the back of his neck when he saw it. 'Jack's?'

'Yes.'

Jean and Gwen looked up when Alan came in.

Aled opened his eyes and closed them again.

Jean took the jumper. 'It's wet,' she said, matter-of-factly, and laid it out on the radiator with its arms spread out and the rest of it hanging down next to Huw. Against the white enamel, it was the colour of arterial blood, as if life was still in it or had only very recently gone from it. They sat in silence. As it began to dry, the kitchen filled with the musty smell of stale straw and dirt from the floor of the box-car, redolent of where Jack had been, even if only Alan and Brenda had seen it, and the rancid breath of the perpetrator.

Sam was lying on the carpet in the front room next to the chair where Alan's father had collapsed. He had barely moved, only to visit the back garden. He hadn't barked or made any sound. His eyes swivelled up when he saw Alan through the kitchen door.

Alan said, 'We'll keep the dog. I just don't have the heart. It won't be fair on Jack to lose his Grandpa and Sam at the same time.'

At his name, Sam's ears twitched.

'There we are, Sam, you have a reprieve. What do you think of that, then, boy?'

Sam's ears made a bigger twitch; Alan had his father's voice.

Alan realised what he'd said. 'Boy,' he said again, 'boy,' hearing his father and the wind in the marram grass and remembering picking tiny, wild strawberries.

Brenda sat down next to Jean and clutched her hand. She drew Gwen's hand into their clasp. 'Almost,' she said, 'we came so close. We will next time.' She made no mention of the cat.

'I ought to wash it, really,' said Jean, looking at the jumper, 'if Jack's going to wear it.'

Chapter Ten

Kenya, Leeward Islands…

Eve sat alone in the empty house. Her small voice was loud now. It asked, 'But how could you not have known?'

And Eve replied, 'I didn't, I still don't.'

An apparition of guilt bent down and whispered in her ear, 'I don't believe you. You are his *wife*.'

Still, Eve insisted, 'But I don't know what it is.' Who had she married; why had she married him? What had she known – not then, but as the years went by? Could she forgive him? 'But I don't know what I'm forgiving him for.' Others would have to forgive him too, as she would have to be forgiven by them for the part she had played. 'What did I do?' But, when she realised she was capable of suspecting him, she leapt up with a cry of shock.

The small voice became quietly cruel, 'So, you could have stopped him.'

The police came back in their overalls to take the jackhammer and compressor away and lower the lighting set and tow if off.

Eve peered around the curtains and watched them.

They left the garden as they had desecrated it: the patio a pile of rubble; the greenhouse foundation broken, panes of glass with shards still attached to their frames leaning against the fence or shattered completely in the grass; the vegetable patch (winter beans unplanted) full of holes like looted graves; the flower borders stamped down and plants unearthed; the lawn flattened and besmirched by muddy boots. No one came to the door to tell her whether they were going to come back to put it right. He was guilty. She must share in it. Why should they care? So they left.

She went back to sitting alone in the silent house with her thoughts a frenzy until she was beaten numb and her mind was full of noise.

A knock at the front door made her jump. Detective Jeffries had come back. What could she tell him? But she was resigned. She put her head to the edge of the bay window and saw that it was Jean. Jean and Gwen didn't knock, they came in through the back door and announced themselves with 'Yoo-hoo'. Today, a stranger was knocking. Eve didn't want to see her: she was sullied and afraid the dirt would show.

Jean knocked again. 'Eve?'

Eve didn't reply.

'Eve? I know you're in there. Let me in?' Jean's voice was reedy.

Eve went into the hall and knelt on the other side of the closed door where her shadow could not be seen through the frosted glass at the top.

'Eve?'

Eve closed her eyes tight and answered. 'What?'

'I want to come in and talk to you.'

Eve couldn't remember if she had locked the back door. 'I'm sorry, Jean, I don't want to talk to anyone. I'm sorry.'

Jean said, 'It's only me. Let me in.' She was not 'only me'.

'I'm sorry.'

'Have you spoken to Roy?'

Eve breathed through her nose and let her head rest against the door. 'No.'

'Why not?'

'It's a private matter, Jean.'

'Tell me, I'm your friend.'

'I know.'

'*Tell* me.' There was a scratching sound.

'I rang the police station but they wouldn't let me speak to him.' The letterbox clattered open. 'I'll huff and I'll puff and blow your house down,' Eve whispered to herself.

'Why do they want to speak to him?' Jean's voice was louder through the letterbox.

Eve could see her mouth moving, fleshy like a blenny's, as if she was trying to worm her way in, lips first.

'Tell me, Eve, I'm your friend, I can help, I'm your *friend,* tell me, please. Tell me, I must know.'

'I told you, I'm sorry, they won't tell me anything.'

'But you're his *wife.*'

You're his *wife*. 'That doesn't make any difference, they still won't tell me anything.'

'Have you tried calling them again?'

'No.'

'Why don't you go down there and demand to see him? I would.'

'But then I would *know,*' Eve groaned to herself. 'They told me not to.'

'Why did they dig up your garden, Eve?'

'They didn't find anything – whatever it was they were looking for.'

'Have they finished? Are they going to come back?'

'There's nothing to come back for. They didn't find anything.'

'So why hasn't Roy come home?'

'I don't know.'

'Tell me, Eve?'

'Roy had nothing to do with it, Jean. *Nothing.*'

'How do you know?'

'He had nothing to do with it, Jean. It was something else.'

'But why did they dig up your garden, Eve, if he had nothing to do with it?'

'He didn't, he *doesn't.*' How could she admit to being married to a man who could have, might have… and not have known?

'Then why don't you open the door and tell me that to my face?'

'He hasn't been arrested, they're just talking to him.'

'In handcuffs? About what? How do you know if they won't tell you?'

'I'm sorry, Jean, I can't talk to you anymore.'

'He's my child, Eve, my *child*.'

Eve heard Brenda's voice. 'Come away, Jean.'

'No, not until *she* tells me.' Eve was *she*. 'Do you know, do you?'

'No, Jean, I don't,' said Brenda. There was a single bang at the door that jarred Eve's head resting against it, then fingernails clawed slowly down the wood. '*Jean*,' said Brenda, 'come away. Please, Jean.'

'I'm so sorry.' Eve put her hands over her ears and pressed herself into the corner between the wall and the door. If Jean said anything more, Eve didn't hear it. She didn't know how long Jean stayed demanding an answer or if Brenda pulled her away. It was lost and irrecoverable: her marriage, her friendships, the boys she loved as her own, her life as it had been.

Huw went through the hole in the fence into Roy and Eve's garden. It was no longer a garden. He was bemused as he stepped over the piles of broken concrete. What was this? Grown-ups brought order not chaos: his world was defined by what he saw around him and the people he saw every day; limits were defined, geography was defined and Uncle

Roy and Auntie Eve were part of his world. *The Big Book* had wars and arguments, there was shouting, anger and happiness and that was where all that happened. He knew it was all made up. They were actors – which was what he was going to be. But, as he looked around him, he couldn't understand: there was no sucking of pencils here or striding of stages or 'Action' on film sets. Why were the curtains closed? He went up to the window to try to see inside. There was no one in the front room. He couldn't hear Eve and Jean at the front door and the back door was locked: why? It never was, except at night and then he was in bed. He sat on the step and puzzled. After a while, he came up with an answer and brightened: Uncle Roy was going to build a new greenhouse. They've gone out to buy it – and he's going to let me help him put it up – but he was disappointed they hadn't taken him with them. 'I'll wait until they get back then, if they're not too long,' and he settled down.

'Hello, Huw,' said a man's voice, after no time at all. The blond man was watching him over the fence from the alley.

'How do you know my name?'

'I know all about you,' the man smiled his nearly familiar smile. 'I know your mum and Uncle Roy and Auntie Eve and Uncle Alan and Auntie Jean and Mr Harris.'

'Do you?'

'Yes, I've known them all for a long time.' He looked around the upturned garden, 'It's a bit of a mess, isn't it?'

'It's always like this when you're building something. Uncle Roy's building a new greenhouse.'

'Ah, is that it?' The man had a blue scar on his cheek.

'They've gone out to buy all the stuff to build it with. Uncle Roy's going to let me help him. I'm waiting for them to come back. Are you a coal miner?'

'Yes, I am,' the man smiled again and touched the blue scar. 'That's very clever of you, Huw.'

'I knew you were,' said Huw. 'I've seen them before.'

'How's your mum today?'

'Well, she's been crying a bit lately because she misses my daddy – he's dead, he was a miner too – but I think she's better now. She's in with Auntie Jean and Brenda in Auntie Jean's kitchen. They've been spending a lot of time in there,' he sighed, 'and I have as well because school's closed because Mr Tanner's ill but I think he's getting better.'

'Mr Tanner used to teach me when I was your age.'

'Mr Tanner is the headmaster,' replied Huw.

'I know. He is now, but he used to teach when I was in school. Doesn't he still teach, Huw?'

'Sometimes he does, I think, but not me. Did you go to my school?'

'Yes, I did.'

'How long ago? Do you know Miss Williams? She's my teacher.' He lowered his voice, 'She kissed Mr Hughes. Are teachers supposed to do that? The vicar knows nothing about sex.'

The blond man laughed. 'Doesn't he? Don't tell him will you? No, I don't know Miss Williams. I think I was probably in school before she was born.'

Huw absorbed the fact and struggled with the thought of Miss Williams being little and not always a teacher as if she had been made that way (if she had ever been made. Sex? Of course not). But Mr Tanner couldn't be any other than a headmaster. 'Before she was *born*?' asked Huw, amazed.

'Yes,' the blond man laughed again. 'Do you like school, Huw?'

'I think I do, especially if we can play British Bulldog but Mr Tanner doesn't usually let us, except once, because we were good.'

'I watched you,' said the blond man. 'Mr Tanner never used to let us play British Bulldog, you must have been especially good.'

'Uncle Roy and Auntie Eve are a long time. I'd better go and see mummy or she'll be wondering because I told her I was going to play in Uncle Alan and Auntie Jean's back garden – she won't have minded me coming through the fence, though, but perhaps I should have told her. Mummy's always *wondering*. Goodbye,' and he jumped up. Before he went back through the hole in the fence, he looked back but the man had gone. He squeezed between the boards.

The cat was still under Alan's car. A reddish liquor had run from it in the rain and dried to a stain on the drive after it stopped. It led back to where the animal lay twisted by the hands that had killed it, a cruelty made permanent in death. The sun was trying its best and it was warmer. A stench was beginning to rise around the tyres and up inside the car like the heat from its engine. Constable Dewi caught whiffs of it in the porch. He went inside to wave at Alan and point.

Alan came out and smelt it straightaway. 'Alright,' he said to Constable Dewi, 'I'll bury it.' He fetched a spade from the shed and tried to slide it under the cat that had attached itself to the drive with its thickening fluids. It took two jerks, the metal scraping along the concrete, before he could get it safely on the spade to lift it up. He held it as far from him as he could and turned away, trying to squeeze his nostrils together, but the cadaverous perfume had been liberated and, with the spade held out in front of him, he walked in its cloud. He turned around and walked backwards. Better, but not odour free.

He went into Gwyn's field, dropped the cat on the ground and started digging. The soil was wet and it didn't take long. He pushed the cat into the hole. It fell in sideways with a paw sticking out, waving, as if it didn't want to go. He prodded it, sliced and bent it with the spade until it lay flat at the bottom, less cat than its butchered parts. Then he buried it and the stench grew less as it was consumed by the smell of fresh earth. He patted it down and breathed again. The cat didn't deserve its cruel entombment.

Alan stretched his back and looked toward the farm buildings at the top of the field, as desolate and angular as standing stones. There was a *For Sale* sign on the side of the road next to the farm entrance. That, at least, was new and shiny. Alan didn't know if Gwyn had any relatives – he was surprised by not knowing – or who was selling the farm or who the proceeds would go to. It was the sale not of a farm, but a man's lineage. He worried that they might get permission to build houses on the land, a farm no longer, and the view of the fields would be gone from behind his house. It would be another reason to leave.

The weathered old man in his greasy, flat cap, parking in his drive and drinking tea with him every morning, Gwyn gossiped as only a milkman could. He knew all the gossip, but never in a nasty way: do they say, 'He never had a bad word about anyone' of all the dead? It was true of Gwyn the Milk. Alan's father had told him always to take a man on his merits and Alan had tried to. Gwyn had been noble. 'How could I have doubted you? Here I am burying a dead cat in your field and I don't even know when your funeral is – not already, surely?'

The door to the milking shed had been left open and it was as black as a vault inside. He thought of Gwyn hanging among his cows as they shuffled and chewed the cud, bumping into him and making him swing like a side of beef, waiting to be milked and wanting his voice.

Alan turned to look at Roy's garden behind him: at his feet, to left and right, the sacrilege of lives. He marked the cat's grave with a stick both as a token memorial and also in case Sergeant Phillips wanted it dug up. Alan could not believe he would – except to make someone do it, like Brenda, or Dewi, but not me, Alan told himself, not me. He wiped the spade clean on the grass but he still thought he could smell decay clinging to its blade. He held it by the handle as he went back onto the road, to his house, and washed it under the garden tap.

Jean came into the kitchen. She kept turning to Brenda who was following her, 'Go and make her come out.'

'Sit down, now, Jean,' said Brenda.

But Jean wouldn't. She paced up and down the kitchen on her tiptoes as if the floor was burning hot. Her eyes fretted. 'Eve won't come out, Gwen, Eve won't come out of her house. She talked to me through the door, but she wouldn't open it. You *must* know why, Brenda?'

'Sit down, Jean.'

'No. Does Dewi know why?'

'He won't know, Jean.'

'Why doesn't he?'

Brenda stood in Jean's way to stop her pacing. 'It's all part of a wider investigation; they have to investigate every possibility, no matter how unlikely.'

Gwen reached up and tried to pull Jean into the chair and Brenda pressed her down with both hands on her shoulders.

'Eve must know,' said Jean. 'She's his wife, so why wouldn't she tell me?'

'Sometimes that's the way investigations are conducted,' Brenda told her. 'Until they know all the facts, no one is told.'

'Oh,' said Jean, 'oh. But why have they dug up his garden if Roy hasn't done anything?'

'It might have something to do with when he was on the railways,' said Alan, hearing Roy's name, as if thinking out loud, distracted, as he closed the back door. Then he saw Brenda shaking her head vigorously and mouthing, 'No'. He frowned and stopped.

But Jean was already rising to her feet. 'What do you mean?'

'Nothing.'

'Yes, it is, or you wouldn't have said it.'

'No, really,' he said, turning to wash his hands in the sink and making the tap run loud, 'it's nothing.'

'Tell me.'

'Really, it's nothing.'

'*Tell* me.'

Alan's shoulders slumped and he reached for the towel. 'He left the railways quite suddenly. I wondered why at the time, that's all. It's nothing, I shouldn't have said. He only came to work in the factory after.'

'Eve said it was because he didn't want to be away so much.'

'Well, that's right, he didn't. That seemed fair enough to me.'

'What else is there, Alan?'

'Nothing. We grew up with him.'

'I don't care if we grew up with him.'

'Jean, it's Roy we're talking about.'

'You knew all this time and they dug up his garden looking for what?'

Huw slid down the radiator next to Jack's still unwashed jumper, now dried almost as stiff as the cat. 'When are they going to open the school again? I'm bored.'

Alan looked out over the holes in Roy's garden through the kitchen window. 'They didn't find anything.'

'Where *is* Jack?' asked Huw. 'Uncle Roy is building a new greenhouse and he's going to let me help him.'

'But they still dug it up,' said Jean

'That's enough now, come on now,' Alan told her, quietly, but he looked again at the ravaged garden, pitted as if it had been shelled, and he was tempted to fetch the spade and look where the police had not.

'Sit back down, Jean,' said Brenda. 'They have to follow up every possibility, even if there's the smallest chance. As Alan said, nothing's been found. Come on, sit back down.'

'I'm going to fly apart, fly apart.' Jean clutched herself and rocked. 'Eve knew and didn't tell me. She didn't *tell* me.'

Chapter Eleven

Malta, Mesopotamia, Montserrat …

On hearing the news of Mr Hughes' release, Mr Tanner hurried over to see him. When he arrived, Mr Hughes was ashen and thin – he was normally thin, but the experience had drawn what fat there was out of him and he was gaunt. Mr Tanner went in.

Laura Williams was sitting in the front room, the little girl Huw could not imagine. She stood up without hesitation.

Mr Tanner was shocked at their appearance but he pretended to be cheerful. 'How are you both?'

They shook their heads and lowered their eyes in apology: Sergeant Phillips had built a wall to seal them off from the town that had nurtured them. Miss Williams remained standing with Mr Hughes now at her side.

'Sit down the pair of you, it's your house, Bryn.'

They sat. Bryn stared at the floor with his hands clenched; Laura stared at Bryn, dejected, because he would not speak of it to her.

Mr Tanner sat next to them. He gave up his lame cheerfulness. 'It's over, Bryn,' he told him, 'all over and done with. It was wrong, I know, very wrong.' He had never questioned the three pillars of natural order: police, school, church and, by implication, his own authority to maintain it, his whole life's dictum and, if it collapsed, what would replace it? It must be restored.

'A man from *The Herald* was there,' said Bryn, reliving it, still seeing the nicotine walls and feeling the freshness on his face beyond the doors.

'Who was?'

'Bryn?' said Laura, 'you didn't tell me.'

'I don't know his name, but I know he works for *The Herald* and there was another one with a camera.'

'What of it, Bryn?' asked Mr Tanner, frowning. He held the freedom of the press dear, too (if they behaved responsibly).

'They took photos of me.'

'Did they? I suppose it is their job,' said Mr Tanner, uncertainly, but willing to stretch a point, 'but, well, what of it, what's a few photos, they'll be chip papers tomorrow. You and Laura can eat your chips out of them together.'

'I was running away.'

'I'm sorry, Bryn? Running away from what? What were you running away from?'

'I don't know – nothing. They surprised me when I came out of the police station and the man from *The Herald* started asking me questions – more questions,' he took a deep breath, 'and then the other one started taking pictures and I started running. I don't know why.'

'But you didn't have anything to run from, Bryn. Honestly, I don't know what the police are up to. I am at a loss.'

'How could they think I had anything to do with it? How could they?'

'Did they tell you why, Bryn?'

'No.'

'They didn't say at all?'

'No. They just asked me the same questions over and over – it was worse than the first time… the *first* time? I can't believe this. And then they let me out and *The Herald* was waiting and they started taking photos and I ran away.'

'They were waiting? Are you sure, Bryn?'

'I think so. They were there when I came out.'

'The press must spend a lot of time at the police station,' said Mr Tanner, 'it's where they gather a lot of news, I imagine – a squalid business, but where else can they glean it if not from the horse's mouth? Unfortunate, but perhaps we shouldn't read too much into it?'

'Perhaps so,' said Bryn, with a despairing shrug. 'How lucky for them.'

'But the police, they trouble me more,' said Mr Tanner. 'The press will follow whatever stories they are given, but the police? Leaving no stone unturned, you expect that, that's their job, moving heaven and earth to bring about justice, but this sort of thing, hauling in anyone they feel like and interrogating them without an explanation? We have to go on living together and that includes the police or, without our cooperation, where would they be?' He filled his lungs through his nose, puffing up and growing angry as he thought of it more. 'Doesn't this business test our trust in each other enough without the police wilfully trampling all over it? They need our trust if they are to find those poor boys, they *need* our cooperation more than at any time.' They had not heard him talk this way before: he was a righter of wrongs, justice personified, the explanation and the wound's salve. 'They must have proper cause before accusations are made. You can't suspend the rule of law, no matter *what* the circumstances.' He stopped, red in the cheeks. Then he said, 'I'm going to speak to *The Herald*, Bryn, Laura, to tell them we're going to open the school. Yes, we are, we will reopen the school. That should keep the pair of you busy. These events will not defeat us. We will go on, come what may. Now, you and Laura have a rest and you, Bryn, try to put it out of your mind and then, next week, we'll be back in harness. There we *are*.' He slapped his knees and stood up. 'There we *are*. Right, I'm off to *The Herald's* offices in town.'

They went with him to the door. He was reminded of two five-year-olds dreading their first day and he pitied them (all of them, every September). But, as he left, the weight of his self-imposed expectation grew heavier with each step. 'This is beyond me, it's beyond the reason of any man.' He didn't know if he could make it right, if anyone would listen. 'If reasonable arguments fail… if reasonable arguments fail, what then? The disappearance of the three boys cannot be an excuse. A crime, no matter how heinous, how tragic its consequences… oh, my word, the consequences…' he stopped himself, the ending was not known, 'but it must not, cannot be an excuse.'

He went into the newsagent and waited next to a man he used to teach, once a sullen boy and sly, who had a habit of speaking through his fingers when he was lying (often), now a father, whose son was in Mr Hughes' class and happily following his father's example. 'How are you, Ellis?' he asked. There was no reply. Mr Tanner saw what he was looking at.

'I know what I'd do to him.' He turned to Mr Tanner, 'And you.' His adult voice was menacing. A feral child, he had grown into an odious man. 'How can you have somebody like that as one of your teachers?'

Mr Tanner rounded on his former pupil. 'Now, you listen to me, Ellis, that's enough of that, he hasn't done anything wrong.'

Ellis waved *The Herald* in Mr Tanner's face and slapped at it with the backs of his fingers so that it crumpled and the inside pages fell out onto the floor and he was left holding tomorrow's chip papers. '*No*? What's he doing then? What's he running away from?'

'He was surprised.'

'Surprised? What by? Being caught? I don't know why they let him out but there are other kinds of justice if they're not up to the job.' He screwed the front page into a ball and threw it on the floor. 'You're not fit to be headmaster of that school. Don't think I'm sending my boy anywhere near *it* or *him*, or *you*. To think I went there, too?' and he stamped out.

Mr Tanner bent down and picked up the ball of paper and picked at a corner. The words *teacher at* appeared. He looked at the shopkeeper. 'You don't believe any of this, do you?'

The shopkeeper pursed his lips but said nothing, which could have meant, 'No, I don't' or 'No smoke without fire' or 'I don't know what to think.' He wasn't going to say one way or the other until he found out what a lot of other people thought and then he would agree with them.

Mr Tanner felt betrayed, for Bryn Hughes, for himself. It shook his faith to the core.

It wasn't her friend at the door again, it was Detective Jeffries. 'You can see Mr Brown,' he said. How could she refuse?

Early in the morning – the police were not concerned with civilised hours and it helped to add to the strain – Eve was allowed into the same interview room where Bryn Hughes had endured his ordeals. As she waited, Eve noticed details that might escape someone being questioned: the abused table, never polished, and how deep its scratches, an empty ashtray as big as a dog bowl, the overlaid rings of tea mugs (like tree rings of crimes petty and bad); the two rickety chairs on either side, the two nearest the door the worst because that was where the policemen sat and pushed them back on two legs with their hands behind their heads to wait; the undecided green of the walls and the yellowed ceiling that was once fresh white; the smell of stale alcohol and old cigarettes that had permeated everything; and the light-blue lino that was covered with black marks from the chair legs and the table where policemen (usually) had banged it.

They made Eve wait (or was it Roy) and offered her nothing while she did. But, eventually, the door opened and the policeman held it as Roy came in and sat down without acknowledging her. The policeman made sure, watching them as the door closed.

Roy wasn't shackled; he wasn't wearing a suit covered in arrows. By all appearances, he was her husband; it would have been easier if he had been decked out as a criminal. He was as he had been taken away but without his jacket and tie. Sweat had stained his shirt under the arms (the colour of the ceiling, she thought) and it was very creased because he had slept – or not – in it. His eyelids were held open by the crease between his eyes that had lines radiating from it up to the top corners of his forehead. Eve couldn't tell if it was the expression of a man wrongly accused or guilty (and ashamed?). He was unshaven, but his beard had always been fertile, and his hair was madly uncombed, whether by neglect or for want of a razor and comb, but he had always been quite dapper (one of the things that had first attracted him to her and later became irritating fastidiousness).

He took a half-empty pack of cigarettes from his shirt pocket and rattled one out. It trembled between his fingers and between his dry lips and the match blackened the pristine cylinder halfway up before he got it properly lit. The smell of fresh tobacco smoke was welcome and she was reminded of the smell of him, mixed with aftershave which, now, it was not.

She waited. He slumped to one side of the chair (nearest the door, to which he was not lately accustomed, but that was the singular change) with his head barely held up. Was he so consumed that even she no longer mattered or was he afraid of what she knew (nothing, of course – that was the policeman's game)?

'Why must I speak first?' she asked herself, but she did. 'Why are we here, Roy?'

He stiffened his shoulder and turned his head further away. The smoke quivered as it left the end of the cigarette, steadied itself into a perfect column and went straight up. He disturbed it, suddenly, as he put the cigarette to his lips, pulled on it and let his hand drop. Ash fell on his thigh; smoke streamed from his nose and mushroomed into his lap. He steamed as it diffused.

'Roy,' she leaned forward and lowered her head to get under his eyes, 'why are we here, tell me?' She poked his arm with her finger. 'Tell me.'

He took another drag to fend her off. He didn't move his head, only his arm levered up and down. The rest of him was frozen into a wince.

She poked him again. His forearm was braced and hard. It hurt the tip of her finger. 'I'm here because of you, Roy, so you're going to have to tell me... *aren't* you?'

His cigarette burned down. He stubbed it out with a glance at the ashtray to see what he was doing – the little heaps of ash dotting his thigh stirred into the movement – and lit another.

'Do you want me to find out from the police? Roy?'

He pulled his other arm tighter against his stomach and held the burning cigarette near his mouth, almost close enough to pull on it without moving his hand. The smoke wreathed over his eyes and through his hair. He pushed the nail of his thumb between his teeth and the cigarette lifted to the bridge of his nose, and planted itself there like a tiny, flag-less pole. Away from his breath, the column of smoke neatly divided him, with a missing downward line slicing through his ash-littered groin to the scuffed lino: good from bad and so swayed the smoke.

'Do you want the police to tell me, is that it? Do you want me to have to ask them? Is that it? Are you afraid to tell me yourself? Is that it? Roy? Answer *me*.'

He took another drag and bit his thumbnail. There was a tiny *crack* as a flake broke off. He didn't spit it out and it hung on his lip like a tiny chip of marble from a crumbling bust. His eyes stayed turned away.

'I am here because of you, Roy. Do you think that's fair? Do you think I deserve this? In a police station? In a prison cell? Roy? Answer me. If you don't answer me, I will leave. Do you hear me? I will wash my hands of you. Are you listening to me?'

He stubbed the cigarette out and lit another.

'I'll go, Roy, I'm warning you.'

'It was nothing to do with me.' He still didn't look at her, not even a bob of his eyes.

'What wasn't?'

'This.'

'What is this?'

'All this.'

'Then why have the police dug up our garden?'

He shivered pre-emptively (only his wife would notice why) and, knowing she was about to ask, he said, 'I didn't do it.'

'Do what, Roy?'

'All this with the boys. I didn't do it.'

'Are the police saying you did?'

'They're trying to say anything. But it wasn't me. I didn't do it.'

'Then why would they suspect you?'

He shrugged one shoulder and pressed his legs together.

'Look at me, Roy, look at me and tell me.' He shook his head imperceptibly except to her (how well she knew him – and her excuses would be… what? 'I'm sorry Jean,

I'm sorry?'). Eve leaned forward again. 'Tell me, Roy, what I have given my life to? Tell me that I haven't wasted my life?'

He took another drag and exhaled (but not to that), 'When I was away – but not this, nothing like this. On my *life*.'

Her voice fell to barely a murmur, as if the truth would be rude. 'On whose life, Roy?'

'I am not a monster.'

'A monster?' Were the police listening; was that why she was here? 'Who said you're a monster? The police? What did you *do*, Roy?' She looked down at her hands and braced herself for the blow (he had never done that; not that sort of man – not to her).

'No,' he said.

She looked up. 'Do I have to find out from the police, is that it?'

'It was nothing like that – like this, Eve.'

Yes, that was her name (not *she*). 'Are you going to tell me, are you?'

He stubbed out his third cigarette and lit a fourth. Another flake of nail cracked between his teeth, another chip clung to his lip next to the first.

'Are you so ashamed? Roy, what did you *do*? Am I going to have to read about it in *The Herald*? Am I going to have to give them an interview and have my picture taken? Is that how I find out because you won't tell me? I can't do this, Roy. I won't. I don't know who you are, I don't know you.' But she did, she did know. 'Here I sit and I wish I had never met you and I have myself to blame – and I do, for believing you all these years, fooling myself. I just didn't know what.'

He gathered himself tighter but did not move. The door opened on cue. He had told her nothing. That was their life together. The policeman's ruse had failed, if that's what it had been.

The policeman said, 'They've come to take you to Doncaster, Mr Brown. They're waiting.'

Roy got up. Even now, for forever, he didn't look at her. He left. The door closed.

Eve sat alone in the pinched little room, filled with cigarette smoke that was already being drawn into the furniture and the walls (could they but speak, they wouldn't tell).

The policeman came back. 'I'll show you out, Mrs Brown.'

Her maiden name had been Guthrie, Eve Guthrie. She followed him to the front door of the police station and stepped out into the cold.

Flash.

Herald Andrew came round the corner of the building with Lloyd. He looked up toward the first floor and jiggled his eyebrows. He had his pad ready.

Flash.

'Mrs Brown?'

'No,' she said, and put up her umbrella, although it wasn't raining, and slung it over her shoulder defiantly.

Herald Andrew quickstepped around it as she turned it into his face and tried to pester her with questions that went unanswered behind its black dome. Lloyd ran ahead, turning to take photographs that framed her face against it like a huge bonnet, as if she was in grand, conspicuous mourning. She walked down the hill and turned into Cardigan Street. *Herald* Andrew puffed out his cheeks. 'Come on, Lloydy-boy, we'll have to make do with what we've got, we've got plenty.'

The Herald's offices were in a short dead-end alley off the High Street that backed onto the river. *The Herald* sign was faded green with the '*r*' missing. There was no reception, only an office with broken-down venetian blinds over the windows. It was untidy and dusty. It was where *Herald* Andrew and Lloyd worked. They were out. Mr Tanner called, 'Hello?'

A voice upstairs answered, 'Yes, come on up.' There was no carpet on the stairs. A man was working at a desk on the landing which was covered in papers. He asked, 'Can I help you?'

'Are you the editor – if it's the editor I need to see?'

'No,' the man replied and pointed with his thumb over his shoulder toward a half-open door, 'he's in there, go straight in.'

Mr Tanner pushed the door fully open. There was a big desk in front of a sash window that hadn't been cleaned in a long time. Thick grime had gathered in its corners. Outside, the river flowed by.

The man behind the desk was Mr Tanner's age or older (indeterminably aged by the affectations of his profession – but less proud now the years were real). He was crumpled with grey, bushy eyebrows. He didn't stand up when Mr Tanner entered. Why should he care? 'What can I do for you?'

Mr Tanner held out his hand. 'Raymond Tanner,' he announced himself. 'Headmaster of the Primary School.'

'Are you indeed? Still closed, I take it?'

'That's what I came to talk to you about – one of the things.'

'Is it? And what have you got for me?'

'I'm sorry, I don't think you told me your name.'

'Doug Protheroe,' sighed Doug Protheroe, with the weary effort of pleasantries to those who bothered to visit his hole. They didn't have to; did he ask them to?

'The school will reopen next week and I was hoping you could put that in the next edition of your newspaper?'

'We could? With your picture?'

'Is that necessary?'

'It was a question. Do you want your picture with it?'

'If it helps but, otherwise, no.'

'Well, that's modest. It might help. A picture of you vouching for the safety of all the children in your care might be compelling. Will you vouch for them, Headmaster?'

'I'm not sure that…'

'No?'

'I didn't say that.'

'But you're going to reopen the school?'

'I came in,' said Mr Tanner, carefully, 'to ask if you would put an announcement or a short article, whichever is most appropriate, in your newspaper to inform parents that the school will reopen next week.'

'You generally have to pay for an announcement in the *Classifieds*.'

'An article, then.'

'Headmaster to reopen school?'

'Yes.'

'Headmaster says school to reopen with children still missing?'

Mr Tanner frowned. 'That is not how I would put it, no.'

'Mmm, wouldn't you? But they haven't been found.'

'No, they have not been found. But I most certainly do not want to create any further alarm. The school must reopen at some point. It cannot remain closed forever.'

'Forever?'

'That is not what I meant.'

'I think a pic of you looking reassuring might be a good idea. Standing outside the school gates, perhaps? How about that?'

'Yes,' said Mr Tanner, not sure, 'perhaps.'

'Alongside all your other teachers? All of you looking reassuring?'

'Well.'

'All of them, Mr Tanner, including the one who was taken in for questioning by the police? We couldn't leave him out, could we?'

'Now, Mr Protheroe, you can *stop* right there. Mr Hughes is an exemplary form teacher. I am at a complete loss to understand why the police questioned him at all. He is a fine young man.'

Doug Protheroe regarded Mr Tanner from under his bushy eyebrows with the mien of one who believes honourable men are charlatans. 'But he ran away, Mr Tanner.'

'Wouldn't you, if you'd just been falsely accused of an appalling act and a journalist and a cameraman accosted you by asking questions and taking photographs?'

'No, I wouldn't run away. Headmaster defends accused teacher?'

They heard a familiar roar. The building shook. It quickly became too loud to speak without shouting. Mr Tanner looked away and waited but Doug Protheroe continued to study him with curious disdain as if he were a pornographic image that had ceased to titillate. The roar fell away.

'I will always give whatever support I can to any member of my staff whenever they need it.'

Protheroe's eyes had not moved. 'Mmmph,' he grunted, finally, and shifted in his ancient leather chair, yawned and arched his back. 'Would you, Mr Tanner, at any price?'

'Of course, and Mr Hughes is an outstanding teacher and a credit to the school. I believe you were wrong to print that picture, entirely so.'

'Do you? I was wrong to print the picture of an accused man running away from a police station?'

'Yes, if he was coerced into doing so.'

'Coerced? Ah. And what picture should I have printed instead?'

'I am saying, Mr Protheroe, that perhaps you should take more care.'

'Should I? And, I might say, perhaps I was doing my job?'

'Mr Protheroe, will you include an article in your next edition to announce that the school will reopen next week?'

'I never had any intention of doing otherwise. It would be my civic duty to do so, *Mr* Tanner.'

'Thank you.' Protheroe did not get up as Mr Tanner left. His head was bowed as he walked past the indoor market, with its metal grille already pulled down across the entrance. He passed the chip shop near the bus station and went inside for a bag of chips (indulging himself with a rare treat after a difficult day, because he didn't approve of eating them in the street). It was only when he was carefully unwrapping them that he realised what he had done, even if it wasn't the offending front page. 'Just to cap it all,' he sighed, and dropped the bag of chips into the bin.

Huw saw Eve come home and heard her front door slam. He ran upstairs and knelt on the chair to look out of his bedroom window. He hoped to see Uncle Roy starting work on his new greenhouse, but the garden was still untouched with some weeds beginning to appear on the disturbed mounds of earth. Disappointed, he got down and went to *The Big Book* for consolation but carried on listening for any sounds outside that might tell him Uncle Roy had begun and was ready to keep his promise.

Chapter Twelve

Morocco Agencies, Newfoundland…

'Stable doors,' said the policeman as he padlocked the box-car. West toward Port Talbot's blazing scrutiny, east towards Porthcawl, inland towards Pyle: the eye of the storm widened, creeping as slow as a watched clock but relentless in its progress. The ground was searched so thoroughly every insect, slug and snail hiding in the wet grass was turned over and inspected. On into darkness, the next day…

Jean tried to fold Jack's jumper but it was too stiff with dirt to lie flat on the kitchen table so she pressed her hands down on it.

'Shall I give it a wash for you?' asked Brenda. 'It won't take a moment.'

'No,' replied Jean, stroking it, 'I want it as Jack last wore it.'

Jack had not, it had been a woolly shroud, and its smell was reminiscent of the dead cat, but Brenda could not tell her.

Gwen leaned across and placed her hand gently on top of Jean's. 'It won't wash Jack away, only the dirt and the rain, then we can air it properly and he can wear it straightaway when he comes home.'

Jean jerked the jumper away from her and clutched it against her stomach. 'He will want to wear it like this, just like when he took it off.'

'It's dirty, Jean,' said Gwen, softly, 'it smells. Jack wouldn't want to wear it like that.'

'It smells of Jack,' Jean snapped, 'that's what it smells like and it's *not* going to be washed before he wears it again.'

'Something smells,' said Huw, from his corner. 'I'm going out into the garden,' and he ran out to look through the hole in the fence.

Gwen and Brenda exchanged glances. 'But you said you wanted to wash it when Alan brought it in, Jean?'

'No, I didn't, I didn't say that. Why would I say that? It doesn't need washing. It was only wet from the rain, God's rain, and the rain won't do it any harm. If anything, it will have helped to keep it clean – and it will have helped to keep Jack dry. Did you think of that, *did* you?'

'No, I'm sorry,' said Gwen, 'of course, washing it would be the wrong thing to do.'

'Yes, it would. I don't know what it is with you.' Jean's hands tightened around the jumper. 'Were you going to take it to your house to wash it, is that it?'

'No,' said Gwen, 'we were going to wash it in the bowl here, very carefully, weren't we, Brenda?'

'It doesn't belong in your house. What else have you got in there that's mine, Gwen?'

'Nothing at all,' Gwen drew back into her chair.

'Haven't you?' Jean thrust her head forward, 'haven't you, *indeed*?'

Gwen swallowed. 'No, Jean, I haven't, why would I?'

'*No*? I know what you want, don't think I don't.'

'I don't want anything, Jean?'

'Something you haven't got and something you're never going to get, not now,' she cuddled the jumper to her face. 'Not now, not ever.'

'I don't understand?'

'Don't act the innocent with me, Gwen.'

'Gwen's only trying to help, Jean,' said Brenda.

Jean whirled round. 'What's it got to do with *you*? You don't live here. What do you *know*?'

'I don't know what she means,' Gwen said to Brenda.

'I don't think she knows herself.'

'Know what?' asked Jean, almost panting now, her eyes fixed on the tabletop, the jumper at her neck. Unaware, she was dragging her nails through it and threads were starting to run.

Brenda stood up and put her head round the front room door. Sam was sitting at Alan's feet. His ears pricked and he looked up. 'Alan, will you come and talk to Jean?'

'What's the matter?' he asked, disturbed from his thoughts.

'She's not herself, I think it might be an idea to call the doctor. Perhaps he can give her something?'

'Oh.' He pushed himself up out of the armchair. Sam lifted his head as Alan went into the kitchen. He squatted next to his wife. 'Jean?'

'*What*?' she snapped.

'They're doing all they can, we'll have some news soon, I'm sure.'

'That's what she's for,' Jean nodded angrily at Brenda, 'and we haven't had any.'

'I'll do whatever you want me to,' said Brenda.

'You're not washing Jack's jumper, and that's an end to it.' She rocked with her arms wrapped tight around the stinking jumper, still breathing so heavily her cheeks fluttered like bloodless diaphragms and her nostrils flared.

After an afternoon of silence, Bryn Hughes said, 'I need to get out, we can't stay locked in here. Let's go for a walk?'

When they reached the playing fields by the river, away from the watching streets and his tiny house in the oldest part of town (his first home – to be theirs – and rather proud of it), he felt able to talk.

It was growing dark and the sun had almost gone but it still glowed enough to see where they were walking, although the river was black in its channel between high banks and stars were coming out in an almost clear sky. The air had been flushed clean by the rain earlier in the day and it had the freshness of renewal. They walked hand in hand. They had nowhere to go and nowhere they needed to be but he had to go on living and she with him, for love.

'At least the school will be open,' he said, searching, in his bewilderment, for reassurance, a constant, to convince himself of the possibilities of resumption: school, Mr Tanner, her. 'At least we can get on with that again.'

'Yes, back to school,' she pulled him close and nuzzled his shoulder.

But he stopped on the path. 'How will I get over this? I wanted to be a teacher and now they've accused me of wanting to be a teacher for other... reasons.' He looked into the sky above her head.

'No, they haven't, Bryn.'

'Yes, they have, that's exactly what they've done. How can I ever go into a classroom again?'

'When they find the boys, Bryn, and catch who did it.'

'When and if?'

'No, *when*.'

They carried on walking. 'Do you really think Mr Tanner is right to reopen the school now?'

'I don't know, when is the right time?'

He stopped again. 'While I'm still a suspect?'

'No, you're not.'

'And who is to say I'm not? Sergeant Phillips, the papers, the whole town – what else are they supposed to think until they know different?'

'Bryn, as Mr Tanner said, it's over, that's the end of it. They were wrong, just wrong.'

'I don't think even Mr Tanner can put this right. How can I go into school on Monday? As things are, as we speak, how am I going to be able to do that?'

'I'll be with you, we'll go in together.'

'I don't know.' The last of the sun faded. It was dark. Behind them were the lights of the town. 'We'd better go back,' and they turned to retrace their steps.

The first blow caught Bryn on his temple and he staggered. The second hit him in the small of his back.

Laura screamed. Hands grabbed her arms, swung her round and threw her to the ground. She banged her head. In a daze, she heard the punches and kicks.

Two men bent over him, raising their fists high against the stars. They were as methodical as oil derricks. They did not speak. They stopped as suddenly as they had begun. Then they were gone, disappearing into the darkness.

Bryn did not move: he was draped over the ground as wearily as a fallen soldier, as shapelessly as a small, worn-away tumulus.

It was very quiet when Laura raised herself on her hands and crawled over to him. His skin was wet. She couldn't tell if he was breathing. 'Help,' she croaked. Her head would not clear. 'Help,' a little louder, 'help... *help*.' No one came to the aid of a little girl crying in the fields by the river. She might have been a lost gull, calling on the wing, unseen in the night. No one answered.

The three pillars: police, school, church?

She got unsteadily to her feet and held out her arms to find her balance. She tried to run toward the house lights and almost fell over the bank into the river. She kicked off her shoes. The mud was slippery so she went onto the grass. The lights came closer until they stretched out over the field and met her. She ran up the path of the first house and banged on the door. When it opened she couldn't get any words out. The man leaned out to look at her. She pointed. 'My...' she gasped, 'my... call an ambulance, he's been attacked. *Please*.'

The man said, 'I know you. You're Miss Williams from the school. Who has? Oh, is *it*?' He shut the door. Inside the light went out.

She tottered back up the path to the road, sobbing, and dropped to one knee and it was only the garden wall that stopped her from sprawling across the pavement. She hit her chin on the gate.

Distantly, from another world, she heard humming, more sombre than jaunty, a hesitant dirge that was uncertain of its purpose but was coming closer. Her head was heavy and she couldn't turn it enough to see his face but saw he was dressed in black and walking slowly. She stuck her arm out beyond the wall and waved. The humming stopped. There was a pause as if the man wasn't sure what he was seeing, and then the sound of running feet. She felt him touch her and she shied away, suddenly realising, with alarm, that he might be one of their attackers. But he was gentle and helped her lean against the gatepost.

'Oh my *Lord*,' he exclaimed, with a sharp intake of breath when he saw her face and the purpling bruise on her forehead. 'Oh my *Lord*, Miss *Williams*.'

Easter, Harvest Festivals, Christmas: 'Reverend Elwiss?'

The lonely vicar, out for his evening walk, half-finished crossword awaiting his return on the small round table by the fire. He looked down her body, at her torn stockings and scraped knees, at her muddy, shoeless feet. 'Did you fall?'

'No, we were attacked.'

'Attacked? Oh my *Lord*. Who attacked you? We? Who was with you?'

'Bryn Hughes.'

'Oh no.'

She said, in words that could not be hers, but she said them: 'He's down by the river. He's dead.'

'Dead?' The Reverend heard, but he had to repeat it before he understood. 'Dead?' He shook his head and tried to gather his wits. '*Dead?* I must get help. I must leave you for a moment.' He squeezed her shoulders.

Her head lolled against the bricks. 'Yes,' she said, sightlessly, into the night.

'I will be straight back, I promise.' He hurried up the path to the refused door. No one answered and it remained dark inside. He rushed past her to the next house and rang the bell. When the door opened, a rectangle of light unfolded onto the road. 'Do excuse me, but there is an emergency. May I use your telephone?'

'Vicar?' asked the woman, standing aside.

'Help her, would you, please?'

The woman saw Laura, slumped, and went to her.

After a few minutes Reverend Elwiss returned with the woman's husband, wearing a white, string vest with a mass of grey chest hairs poking through it. 'Where is he, Miss... Laura – may I call you Laura?' asked Reverend Elwiss. 'We cannot delay. If we help you, can you show us where he is?' Reverend Elwiss and the man lifted Laura to her feet. He asked the woman, 'Would you wait for the ambulance and tell them where we are?' and they stumbled out of the comforting rectangle of light toward the blackness of the fields with Laura supported between them.

'You'll catch your death like that,' the woman told her husband, who glanced over his shoulder at her, witheringly, and didn't reply.

She stood in the middle of the road to watch for the ambulance. When it arrived, she told them and it bumped over the kerb and went careening over the grass, following the line of the river, searching.

A big, black car arrived and made a void against the distant lights of the ambulance stopped on a bend of the river. Sergeant Phillips got out. He considered the woman. She gathered her cardigan tighter round her neck and shrank away. Sergeant Phillips said nothing. A police car came speeding up the road and onto the fields. Sergeant Phillips got back into his big, black car and, soundlessly, left.

Constable Dewi came in. He saw Jean and looked at Alan. 'Eve is outside,' he said.

The mention of Eve's name electrified Jean. She sprang up and charged out of the kitchen. A vase went flying and smashed over the hall floor. Jean's eyes were wide. Her lips drew back over her teeth. There were bubbles at the corners of her mouth. She growled as she reached for Eve's throat with strands of red wool under her nails.

Eve didn't move.

Constable Dewi threw himself around Jean. Her fingers brushed Eve's shoulder as Constable Dewi pulled her away, taken aback, again, at the strength of this slight woman writhing in his arms.

Jean strained to reach Eve.

Alan kicked the front door closed with his foot. It slammed shut in Eve's face. Jean went limp. They helped her back into the kitchen and into the chair.

'Jesus *Christ*,' Constable Dewi breathed, taking off his helmet. 'Bloody *hell*.'

Jean picked up Jack's jumper and held it against her. Her eyes were milky. A tendril of saliva descended from her mouth as if it was lowering a money spider onto the table.

Gwen said, 'She needs a doctor, Alan.'

'Yes,' he said, out of breath, 'she does.'

The doctor came, a kindly practitioner in the town for many years, a man of tweeds and autumn, with reading glasses hanging from his neck on a cord and balancing on the yellow waistcoat of his tummy. He rubbed his chin as he perused Jean, and wouldn't be hurried. She stared, but not at him. 'Alas,' he said, after some moments, 'I cannot alleviate the cause, wish that I could, but we can treat the symptoms – at least, to mask them and make them seem as if they do not exist, for her – but I cannot make them go away. Mr Harris, there is no medicine that will return your wife to you as she was, but that cannot be a surprise in these most dire circumstances.' He sighed. 'The price of alleviation is for Morpheus, or a twilight close to him. But temporary, one must hope. It is your decision but, I fear, to continue in this way would be to risk permanent damage to her mind and well-being and your son will want his mother as you will want your wife. Do you understand?'

'Yes.'

'What I will prescribe must not be taken lightly, the dosage must be strictly adhered to. They are powerful drugs.'

Alan nodded.

'If she worsens, we will have to take her in. Do you understand?'

'Yes.'

'You wait here. I will get the prescription for you and, if you think of any questions in the meantime, we can talk about them when I come back. Do you understand?'

'Yes, thank you, Doctor.'

'There's no need for thanks, Mr Harris.' He looked at Jean, as if to be certain of his decision, not afraid to be seen to change his mind. He wasn't going to. He snapped his bag shut. 'I won't be long.'

Huw came in from the garden, looking crestfallen and grumpy. 'It's getting dark,' he said. 'When's Uncle Roy going to start building his new greenhouse?' He slid down the radiator. 'Can we have tea soon, Mum?'

Reverend Elwiss sank down to kneel in the mud next to Bryn Hughes and did not know what to do. 'If not now, when?' he whispered to himself. 'What use am I? Where are you, Lord? Guide me now, through my hands let me help this man? Lord?' Reverend Elwiss waited, fearing to be found out because no answer came. 'Please, Lord, does this man deserve to die?' Laura's face was a blanched ovoid even though he was close enough to feel her breath. He waited, stranded under the rustling trees, his bearings lost, waiting for her to ask and he would have to tell her that he could not save him, neither body nor soul, as her breath quickened on his cheek. 'Lord? I beseech you, come to my aid. I do not know what to do.' A needle, barely supported by the meniscus, slowly revolved and stopped, pointing, and it came, flowing into him, a gift or inner fortitude he never questioned – in adversity, at *last* – and through him into the body of the sufferer. 'He's not dead, Laura, thank the Lord, he is alive.' He lifted his eyes and gave silent, tearful thanks to the firmament. 'We are not too late – I am not too late – it is not too late. I am your instrument, Lord, thanks be, guide me now.' He felt Laura's tremulous sigh of relief. 'We should not try to move him. We must wait for the ambulance to arrive. It will be here soon. Come and hold his hand and talk to him. Let him know he's not alone.'

Laura reached through the grass for Bryn's hand and found it, upturned and limp, with half-closed fingers, and gripped it. 'Bryn, I'm here with Reverend Elwiss.'

'That's it,' he whispered, and slid his arm around her.

She knew he smiled.

'Keep talking to him. Say the first thing that comes to mind. It doesn't matter what it is. I am praying for him. God is with us, he is listening.' The wind suddenly rose in the trees. 'You see?'

'My mum wants me to wear her old wedding dress, but I don't want to.'

'That's it, Laura, happy times to come, the future, your lives together.'

'It would be a very nice dress if we were getting married in about 1920. I don't know how to tell her. It would save some money though. Perhaps you can tell her, Bryn? What do you think? But, you're not allowed to see it, are you? That's awkward.' She stopped.

'Keep talking to him, Laura,' the Reverend urged.

'He never met my mum.'

'Would you wait up there and tell us when you see the ambulance?' Reverend Elwiss asked the man, ghostly in his white vest.

When it came, when she saw what had been done to Bryn, Laura fainted.

The hospital was bright and hot. They took Bryn away, rattling down the corridor on a trolley and through swing doors to a serious place.

'Do you know how I can contact Bryn's family?' Reverend Elwiss asked Laura, 'and your family, too? Your mother and father will want to be with you.'

'Mum died,' said Laura.

'Oh, I'm terribly sorry.'

She shook her head. 'I'll telephone dad.'

'No, I'll do it,' said Reverend Elwiss. 'You wait here and get that head seen to and then I'll see if I can get us something hot to drink. I won't be long.' He left.

Detective Jeffries appeared. He sat down next to her without asking. He took out his notebook. He made no greeting or asked after her obvious injury which she was dabbing with an antiseptic pad. 'Did you see who attacked you?'

'No,' she answered, afraid of him, wishing the Reverend hadn't left.

'Of course you did. It would have been impossible not to see them.'

'It was dark and they knocked me over.'

'I see.' He didn't write anything down. 'And what were you doing by the river in the dark?' It was irrelevant whether what he meant was true.

She couldn't understand why he needed to insult her.

'Do you often go down by the river in the dark, Miss Williams – with Mr Hughes?'

'No, we were on our way back.'

'And what happened?'

'We were attacked.'

'Were there any words exchanged to provoke this attack?'

'No, they came on us from behind.'

'I see. Really?' His pencil still had not touched his notebook. 'So, it was a spontaneous attack in the dark next to the river and neither you nor Mr Hughes did anything to provoke it and you didn't see who did it? Is that what you're telling me, Miss Williams?'

'No.'

'No, it wasn't spontaneous or no you didn't see who did it?'

'Yes and no.'

'I see.' He tapped his chin with his pencil. 'Which way round would that be?'

'Excuse me, who are you, might I ask?'

Detective Jeffries looked up. But Reverend Elwiss was haloed against the ceiling light. It hid his dog collar and all Detective Jeffries saw was a shape. 'Police. And who are you?'

The Reverend hovered in the light, shocked at Detective Jeffries' rudeness, unaware that his office was obscured but firm in his belief that they were supposed to be on the same side. It was as a man of God that he admonished him, attributing it, charitably, to the difficult circumstances (even for a policeman). 'This young lady has been assaulted and her fiancé critically hurt and this is the way you address her?'

'This is a police matter and none of your business.'

But a servant, the Reverend was insulted for his Church and he bent out of the light to put down the two cups of tea. 'Show some respect, young man, if not for me then for my office.'

'Oh,' said Detective Jeffries, with his pencil poised over his blank notebook. 'Vicar?'

'Indeed, *oh*. Might I have your name?'

'Detective Jeffries.'

'I am not a policeman, but do you not think it would be appropriate for you to enquire about my involvement in this matter or why I am here – other than pastoral care, perhaps? Might it not be appropriate for you to ask if I have any information that might prove useful? You haven't made a single entry in your notebook. Is that what you normally do, Detective Jeffries?'

'I wanted to hear what she had to say first before I made my notes.'

'Is that so? Miss Williams is the victim of a dreadful crime, she deserves your support and sympathy.'

'I am trying to ascertain the facts.'

'You have an unusual way of going about it, Detective Jeffries? If you want to interview Miss Williams, shouldn't you begin by asking if she feels able to answer your questions?'

'Let's get it out of the way,' said Laura. 'I want to see Bryn.'

'Are you sure, Laura?' Reverend Elwiss asked. 'I am sure Detective Jeffries can come back. Can't you, Detective Jeffries?'

'Yes.'

'Very well, I will stay with you. Your father is on his way, and Bryn's parents.' He looked at Detective Jeffries, 'Please proceed.'

Detective Jeffries had a sullen expression as he wrote the date, time and place in his notebook. 'Can you confirm your full name?' he asked Laura.

'I told you that in the police station,' she told him, with quiet defiance.

'Once more, if you would, Miss Williams?'

'Take your time, Laura,' said Reverend Elwiss. He tilted his head slightly back and half closed his eyes to listen. The ceiling light was like the sun on his face.

Chapter Thirteen

New Zealand, Nigeria, Niue...

They searched the old manor house, long derelict, like an old man supported on sticks of fallen rafters, struggling to stay upright and surveying the desolation from empty windows, too proud to die because he had seen the lost city swallowed and was futilely holding back the inevitable. They searched its roofless rooms and lifted aside rotting timbers, moving carefully and testing the boards with timorous feet, afraid the whole structure would concertina with a crash and a cloud of dust. They found nothing and came back out into the light with relief and drew a ring around it on the map with an *S* in the middle which meant *Searched.*

East, along the pebble foreshore of Sker Rocks to Pink Bay where the rocks turned pink; west, daring the fiery eyes closer, the smell of sulphur growing stronger on the wind, to where the River Kenfig met the sea; inland beyond the dunes onto the golf courses and found nothing. But, one of the boys – now they knew which one – had been there, for certain.

On top of the tallest dune, as stark as a war memorial, Sergeant Phillips shaded his eyes to see the now distant box-car, with police cars still circled around it. He told Detective Jeffries, who was sinking in the sand on the steepest side of the dune, 'Tell that reporter that Roberts was murdered and let's see what it stirs up. Start with Harris' wife.'

'What about Hughes?'

'What about him?'

'I don't know.'

'Then don't ask. Do as you're told,' said Sergeant Phillips. He pulled on his gloves and tightened them over his knuckles. He looked down at Detective Jeffries and pouted his moustache. 'Go,' he said, and dismissed him with a flick of his leathered fingers.

Detective Jeffries waded, knee-deep, down the dune and filled his shoes with sand.

Huw left *The Big Book* open on a favourite page and went downstairs to wait for his mother who was getting ready in her bedroom for the next vigil in Jean's kitchen.

Huw's father was almost gone from his photograph. There was still the outline of a man and a place for his face with the vestiges of eyes and a mouth but they had become smudges. The photograph was sepia as if it remembered old sunlight even as fresh sunlight burnt it away. Huw did not understand: if its loss made his mother so sad, why didn't she move it to the shady end of the sideboard where the remainder of him might linger?

But, for Gwen, trying to make out Geraint's features was like a creeping glaucoma slowly smothering her pupils – age no excuse – but almost a relief because, if she could not see him, crisp and plain, she would sooner not see him at all. She had memories of their life together; she did not want this fading image to remind her of what she had lost – but neither could he watch her, pressing his judgement between her shoulder blades to make her ache with the shame of disappointing him. He had been the love of her life; all else, anyone else, was a distraction. Guilt at a life after.

Huw did not even have that. He had nothing.

She never talked about Geraint now, holding up the photograph and telling stories about him that began, 'There was a time when…' as if Huw was a grown man. How could Huw imagine what times they might have had, the three of them together, if his mother would not tell him? In her grief, she was not being fair: he could not understand even to forgive her, so she bore the burden twice.

The early sun was full on the photograph, doing its relentless work, making a wraith of him. The silver frame shone like a precious casket.

Huw went outside and sat on the doorstep, hoping that, today, finally, Uncle Roy would start on his new greenhouse.

'Hello, Huw.' The blond-haired man had come through the alley gate and was standing in front of the bush – much grown – where his father's picture had been taken.

'Hello,' said Huw.

The man smiled. 'Hasn't school reopened yet?'

Huw shook his head and sighed. 'No. I hope Mr Tanner gets better soon.'

'So, what are you going to do today?'

'Uncle Roy might start building his greenhouse.'

'He might.'

'But if he doesn't we'll have to go round to Auntie Jean's kitchen *again*.'

'Will you?'

'Yes, and Brenda will be there and the policeman called Dewi outside the front door. I wish Jack would come home and then we could play and it wouldn't be so boring all the time. When's he coming home from the shop?'

'You can play with me, if you like, Huw.'

Huw's face lit up. 'Could we? *Really*? *Now*?'

'Perhaps not today, but very soon. It will give you something to look forward to.'

'Tomorrow, then?'

'Maybe. What would you like to do?'

'Could we go to the beach,' and then he dared, 'or to the fair at Trecco Bay?'

'Yes, anywhere you like.'

'*Really*?'

'Yes and for as long as you like. But I can see your mum in the front room. I think she's ready to go now.'

'*Ohhh*, Auntie Jean's.'

'I'll see you soon, Huw. Don't keep your mum waiting,' he said, as Huw reached for the door handle. 'I won't forget, I promise.'

When they entered the kitchen, Aled became rigid in his chair and stopped breathing, then he screamed. Alan picked him up, but it wasn't his father he wanted.

'Let me try,' said Brenda, and took him. He didn't want her either. She passed him to Gwen. That didn't work.

Jean had been consigned to the armchair in the front room where there were no sharp edges. Her head rested to one side as if she was asleep but her eyes were open. She didn't respond to Aled's cries.

Alan took him back. Aled saw his mother and reached for her.

Alan shook his head in exasperation. 'Have you seen Sam?' he almost shouted to Brenda.

'I think he went into the garden.'

Alan went outside taking Aled with him. After a few minutes, Aled quietened. Alan came back in. 'Sam's not there,' he said. Aled began screaming again. 'What's the matter with this boy?'

Gwen bent down to look into Jean's eyes. 'What on earth has the doctor given her?'

Aled's face was red and, between screams, he gulped for air with dry, tearless sobs.

'Has something frightened him?' asked Gwen.

'I don't know,' Alan replied, 'but we can't carry on like this. He seems to be having a lot of these bouts recently.' He took Aled into the front room. Aled bucked in his arms trying to reach his mother. Gently, Alan put him into Jean's lap and put her arms around him.

Aled nestled against her chest. He could feel her slow heartbeat and smell her familiar smell. He stuck his thumb in his mouth and his eyes began to close. He clung to her as if she was his favourite teddy but much bigger than the one in his cot.

Jean blinked every few seconds because her body told her to and her breathing was shallow. Further than that, there were no other signs of life.

Gwen pulled up a kitchen chair and sat close to them. If Aled moved and Jean's arms slipped, she put them back.

Aled made contented sucking noises and Huw slowly took his hands off his ears.

Mr Tanner opened his front door and was surprised, but pleased, to see Reverend Elwiss. That changed when the vicar told him why he had come.

When they got to the hospital, Laura had been taken away by her father. She hadn't wanted to go, but he made her, and Bryn's parents were huddled together in a waiting room next to a low table with old magazines in an untidy pile. A consultant was busy with their son and had banished them. Bryn's father became alarmed when he saw the priest.

'No,' Reverend Elwiss reassured him, 'I found your son. I spoke to you on the telephone.'

After brief introductions, Bryn's father said, 'He's not very good.' His mother couldn't say anything. Both her hands were fastened to his.

Mr Tanner and Reverend Elwiss didn't stay long. They were intruding on a privacy that crossed a boundary that prohibited both a headmaster and a Good Samaritan. The aftermath and its consequences which, however much they cared, they would not have to endure and they knew nothing of the years that his parents had made of him before he walked into Mr Tanner's school as a young teacher. But they promised to come back.

'Thank you, you're very kind,' said Bryn's father.

'I have to see someone,' said Mr Tanner to Reverend Elwiss as they left.

Herald Andrew and Lloyd stopped talking when Mr Tanner entered their scruffy office.

Mr Tanner climbed the stairs, past the man at the top who had no obvious purpose except to move the mass of paper around his desk, and into Doug Protheroe's office. He didn't sit down and was not invited to.

'Again? Yes?' asked Protheroe.

'Do you know what's happened?'

'I do, if I'm correct in understanding what you're referring to and the reason why you're here. Police stations and hospitals are a constant source of information for any newspaper. They are usually the start and the end and quite often the middle.'

'If you hadn't printed what you did, this wouldn't have happened.'

'Don't shoot the messenger, Mr Tanner. We have had this conversation. Are you suggesting we should not have printed it? Wouldn't that have required a judgement on my part – and who am I? Newspapers don't make the news, we report it.'

'But you decide when and how it's reported?'

'We do, but less when and more how, usually – old news is not news – but who will choose the words for us? *The Herald* didn't arrest Mr Hughes.'

'He wasn't arrested, Mr Protheroe.'

'There you have me, the wrong word again, I promise to be more careful in future. *Questioned*, then, and only the police have the power to take suspects to police stations, not a newspaper. Tell me, Mr Tanner, should I refrain from printing news of Mr Hughes' assault? No. Of course not.'

'Mr Protheroe, I object to the idea that one news story, an unnecessary news story, can lead to consequences that become the source of another news story. It is self-perpetuating.'

'As I said, Mr Tanner, that isn't for me to decide. Journalists are frequently portrayed as a grubby lot, but the news is the news and it is misleading to confuse our methods with what we print.'

'I believe I am wasting my time here.'

'No, you're not, but I cannot help you. I must ask, however, if you will be reopening the school on Monday?'

Mr Tanner glared at Protheroe. 'How is that going to be possible?'

'I don't know, Mr Tanner, I don't run schools, but you did ask me to print something to that effect and, now, I take it, you don't want me to?'

'No, I do not.'

'Then I will do as you ask. What would the town be – any town – without its local newspaper? All we are is a communicator of events, good and bad, deaths, marriages, fetes and everything else that goes on. That's what *we're* for.'

'Has Sam come back in?'

'I haven't seen him,' said Brenda.

'He wasn't in the road when you came round?' he asked Gwen.

She shook her head.

Alan went through the back garden and into the alley and looked over the fence into Gwyn's fields. There was no sign of Sam. He stuck his head round the back door. 'I'm going up to the farm to look for him,' he told them. 'My father used to take him up there with Jack.' He closed the door quickly before they heard the catch in his voice. But he was secretly glad to be out of the house and away from the vacant shell that was – had been – his wife.

The farm out-buildings were empty. Everything that could be moved had gone for scrap or sale. To a stranger, there was not a trace of what it had been like. The passing of an era could not be felt in its dirty, once carefully whitewashed stones.

The milking shed was still and gloomy. Here, Gwyn had died but he had left no presence. Parts of the bolted down skeletons of milking machines remained and the spar from which he had been hanged, already dead, was still there.

Under the window, at the far end, with just enough light coming in, Sam lay on his side. Next to him was a spade. The sharp edge of its blade was bloody. Sam's fur around his neck was bloodied too. His tongue flopped from the side of his mouth. There was a trail of blood droplets, still wet, leading to his body. He had been killed elsewhere and brought here.

Alan squatted next to him and laid his palm on Sam's flank. He was warm but Alan could feel the cold creeping into him. Alan slid his arms under the dog. Sam was heavy and his head hung from the crook of his elbow. Alan slipped his hand through the spade handle and it hung from his bent wrist, banging against his leg as he carried Sam out of the milking shed, dripping more blood onto the floor and down his trousers. Smears of blood covered his shirt.

At the bottom of the farm track, under the *For Sale* sign, a big, black car was parked and, leaning against the bonnet with his arms folded, waiting for him, was Sergeant Phillips.

Alan stopped, holding Sam, spade dangling, as if he was offering a sacrifice to a potentate.

Sergeant Phillips pushed himself upright. He walked toward Alan, slowly, with his head held back, examining him down his Roman, navigator-straight bridge, imperiously sovereign; lidded; and tightened his gloves over his knuckles, first one, then the other. He jerked his tunic straight, half smiled as if he had cocked a pistol and ran the outsides of his thumbs down his moustache – slowly – deliberately – again – and pinched the ends. 'Mmm,' he breathed, but neither to inhale or exhale, 'mmm.' He stopped a short distance from Alan, whose arms were beginning to ache and the spade pulled on his wrist. 'I've been watching you, Harris,' he said, like distant thunder from beyond the Styx. 'I see everything. There is nothing you do that I do not see.' He looked over Alan's shoulder to the farm building, 'You have blood on your hands. Is that where you go to kill? But I'm not interested in animals.'

Alan answered him with brittle calm, straining to hold back his desperate, but impotent, anger, 'Animals are all you have been able to give us: a sheep, a cat and, now, my father's dog.'

'Is that how you began, Harris, with animals?' He leaned closer to Alan, 'I know your mind,' he whispered, as if he could conjure retribution from the wind. 'I know your mind. Oh, but I do, *Harris*.'

'I don't know how the sheep died, but we found it dead, we were led to it. I didn't kill the cat, I didn't know anything about the cat, and I did *not* kill my father's dog.'

'Is that your spade, Harris?'

'Yes, it is, and the last time I saw it, it was in my garden shed.'

'Was it?'

'Yes, it was.'

'You can kill as many animals as you like, amuse yourself, but I *will* get you, Harris. I know your mind.'

'Until then, Sergeant Phillips, I have to bury Sam.'

Sergeant Phillips made Alan walk around him. As Alan passed him, he said, 'Remember where you bury it.'

Alan went into the field and found the freshly dug cat's grave marked by the stick. He began digging next to it. Sam's blood came off into the earth and the steel of the blade was soon shiny and clean. He dug a much bigger hole and gently laid the still supple dog in it. The earth thumped onto Sam's body, but he had to look away as it covered his lifeless eyes. 'I would never have sent you to the vet's. Goodbye, boy.'

'Do you know who did it, Ellis?' Mr Tanner remembered the shifty boy who had stood before him many times when he was a teacher and was standing before him now.

Ellis' house had peeling paint and a rusting, metal headboard in its overgrown garden. He had stains down his tee-shirt and the insides of two fingers of his right hand, resting against the doorpost, were dark yellow. He had missing front teeth and the rest were rotten. He hadn't shaved for days and he smelt of sweat and last night's beer. He was no advert for the school or Mr Tanner who, if he had felt no responsibility for how Ellis had turned out, wouldn't have been there.

'What do you want? You're not my teacher now.'

'No,' sighed Mr Tanner, 'but I was. Ellis, before I go to the police, I wanted to ask you myself, do you know who did it?'

'Did what?' His ugly fingers went to his mouth.

But Mr Tanner was well practised at interviewing small boys, his technique was as sharp as any policeman's. Ellis was no match: all the petty, juvenile crimes he had committed, that came within the ambit of a bad child, for breaking things, for stealing, for bullying. Schools have boys like that and Mr Tanner knew, from bitter experience, no matter how hard he tried, they rarely changed course. Constable Dewi was an exception, but he had been misguided and biddable, not nasty. Ellis Maynard had been steeped in vitriol since birth. 'Mr Hughes was assaulted and seriously hurt last night.'

'What's that got to do with me?' asked Ellis, hiding his words behind his fingers.

'Because I'm asking you, Ellis.'

'What's it got to do with you?'

'Mr Hughes is a teacher at my school and, after what you said at the newsagent, I have a duty to report it to the police because, and I say this with a heavy heart, I believe you to be capable of it.'

'*Do* you?'

'Unfortunately, yes, I do. But I used to teach you, Ellis, so I'm giving you the opportunity to convince me that you had nothing to do with it. Did you?'

Ellis took a step forward.

The stench of beer was repellent and Mr Tanner had to fight the urge to turn his head away, but he stood his ground.

'Who are you to come round here and start making accusations, Tanner?'

'I'm asking you, Ellis, before I go to the police.'

Ellis' fingers went back up to his mouth. 'Go to the police, then, it's got nothing to do with me.'

'Hasn't it?'

'I don't see why I have to tell you anything. I wasn't anywhere near the river. I never go down there.'

His guilt certain, Mr Tanner turned away for the police station but Detective Jeffries made only vague promises to, 'Look into it.' He didn't thank him for coming forward and he left Mr Tanner speechless with anger.

Chapter Fourteen

North Borneo, Northern Rhodesia...

They reached the foot of the dune where the last stones of the castle flew in the clouds, and put their hands on their hips for a breather, sweating. After a few minutes, one of them said, 'Come on,' and they surrounded the dune and began hacking away the brambles. Under the tangle, there were bare, sandy hollows to hide in or be hidden. The thorns snagged and had to be ripped apart, uncoiling like barbed wire. It took hours to strip them away and they piled up in wiry heaps. When they reached the top, the dune was as shorn to its tufts as the head of a collaborator and the stones were naked. There was nowhere left to hide or be hidden – except deep beneath in the lost city. 'We're like locusts,' said a tired policeman, but the dunes stretched away down the coast, both east and west, like dun-coloured Alps. They had found nothing.

The headline said ***Farmer Murdered.*** The other front page story, between the adverts for an exhaust fitter and a local jeweller, was ***Local Man Arrested.*** It was not ***Farmer Murdered, Local Man Arrested***, but it might have been: … *neighbours… school friends… missing boys… overlooking Blackbrook Farm… recently searched garden… in connection with… awaiting trial.* Two stories, one front page: wily, old editor Doug Protheroe nudged them together.

Herald Andrew and Lloyd were despatched to take more photographs of the deserted farm. Their hearts leapt when they saw the pool of dried blood under the window.

Flash.

Then they worked their way up the road, house by house. 'Did you know Gwyn Roberts? Did you know Roy Brown?' Two stories became one and almost everyone had something to say to add to it or were prodded into imagining they did. 'There was something odd about him, now you mention it.' If Gwyn Roberts hadn't done it, they wanted someone else locked up and it became more certain who it was with every door *Herald* Andrew and Lloyd knocked on. Guilty: Roy Brown. The next day's story was writing itself. Finally, saved until last, they arrived at Eve's house armed with all the information they had gathered, primed to confront her, as all good journalists – and policemen – should be.

'Aw, come on, Dew, you can't stop us asking her, can you?' they cajoled over the hedge between the houses. 'Come on, it's in the public interest.'

Constable Dewi didn't reply.

Eve didn't answer the door.

Herald Andrew knocked again. 'Mrs Brown, we only want to ask some questions. Will you answer some questions?'

Roy had brought this on her, cleaved her from her friend, brought reporters to her threshold, banished her from the town and made her home a prison as surely as the cell in which he was now waiting. Inside, Eve Guthrie heard them and refused to answer.

'Have you got anything else for us, Dew?' asked *Herald* Andrew, when he had given up knocking.

'No,' said Constable Dewi.

'Aw, come on Dew.'

'No, and that's enough.'

'Well, that's alright then, because we've got more than enough. Get a pic of the house before we leave, Lloydy-boy.'

Flash.

In Eve's front room, through the narrow fissure between the curtains, knives leapt up the walls.

Mr Tanner roamed his empty school. He went into every classroom and trailed his hand over the desktops. Silence was everywhere. He loitered but, eventually, he found his way into Mr Hughes' classroom and stood in the doorway, as he had so many times when it was full of children.

Chalk dust had settled on Mr Hughes' desk. He leaned forward and blew it, swirling, into the air. He sat behind the desk and looked at the rows of children's desks: ink-stained miniatures, carved into, scratched, each with a chair too small for him to sit on. He looked at the paintings and drawings around the walls. The children had written their names unsteadily in big letters at the bottom of each one. He knew them all.

He sat – waiting for what? Until the chalk dust stopped dancing in the light? He closed the door behind him, sending a frisson through the floating dust, and wandered disconsolately down the corridor to the double doors of the hall.

When he pushed them open, he saw Mr Topliss at the far end, painting a window frame, carefully running a brush along the bottom, his tongue poking between his lips, concentrating hard on not getting paint on the glass.

Mr Topliss heard the door creak and looked up. He balanced his brush on top of the paint can and wiped his hands down his overalls. 'It needed doing,' he said. It was something to do because he was running out of jobs and there were no children to keep breaking things. He missed feeling exasperated.

'Perhaps,' said Mr Tanner.

'How is Mr Hughes?'

'Not very clever. I'm going down to the hospital later to see how he is.'

'Let me know, will you, Mr Tanner?'

'I will.'

Mr Topliss shook his head, 'It beggars belief.'

'It does.'

'What could the police want with Mr Hughes?'

'What indeed, Mr Topliss? The accusation itself has led to the most dreadful consequences.'

'Is there more, Mr Tanner, do you think?'

'More?' Mr Tanner took a deep breath and let it out. 'More? Under any other circumstances I would defend the police's actions as motivated by information to which we are not party, but Mr Hughes? I hesitate to use the word irresponsible so I will say inexplicable then; the police have acted inexplicably without revealing the foundation of their suspicions and left the press to do the rest. Let us hope justice will out but, as we stand here, I admit I am at a loss.'

'Amen to that, Mr Tanner but, in my experience, it often needs a helping hand. People make justice, don't they? It doesn't happen on its own.'

'No, it doesn't, how true…' Mr Tanner stopped and held the artless Mr Topliss in a stare as his thoughts ordered themselves and, suddenly, his foggy diversion cleared as if a breeze had sprung up. 'You know, you're *right*, Mr Topliss.'

'Am I?' Mr Topliss asked, surprised and pleased to be of help to the headmaster in something other than handiwork, but not knowing how. It was only one of his sayings – he had lots of them – that he bandied about in conversations, oft repeated, not always relevant and mostly ignored by those who knew he was not a man of hidden depths, an old soldier who had been in North Africa and was now a caretaker ('But we mustn't complain about life's journey').

'Yes, you are,' said Mr Tanner, who was thinking properly again.

'Well, that's good then,' said Mr Topliss, picking up the paint brush and resuming. The tip of his tongue darted out – he might have been one of the children with a crayon: *B r i a n T o p l i s s.*

'Thank you,' said Mr Tanner. 'Keep it up.'

'Thank you, Headmaster,' Mr Topliss replied, without taking his eyes off the paint's gleaming line, inching along the frame.

Mr Tanner had greater purpose as he walked down the corridor and out onto the playground. He chained the school gates behind him (Mr Topliss had other means of entrance and exit). At the end of the street, he saw Ellis, hands in his pockets, slouching in the opposite direction. Mr Tanner looked at his watch. 'Pub,' he said to himself.

'She can't stay like this, Alan,' said Gwen, bending over Jean, motionless in the armchair. 'Jean?' Gwen jogged her shoulder.

Jean didn't move, except to blink.

Aled was banging the plastic table of his high chair in the kitchen and yelling.

'What is the matter with that child?' asked Huw. 'Is Auntie Jean asleep? But her eyes are open.'

'I had to put her to bed last night,' said Alan, 'and get her up and dressed this morning. She hasn't said a single word. She's like a zombie.'

Aled's furious cries rose to a screech.

'He'll have that high chair over if we're not careful.'

Aled banged the wooden arm against the wall and Brenda reached over to hold it.

'He can't sit in Jean's lap all day,' said Gwen. 'I think you should get the doctor back and get him to give her some different pills. She's not eating anything either, is she?'

'*Aled.*' He took no notice. 'Will you call the doctor, Gwen?' Alan went into the kitchen and plucked Aled out of his chair, who struggled and threw his head from side to side and turned puce. Alan took him out the back door and through the alley into Eve's garden, stepping around the holes and broken glass.

Aled's little fists whirled about his head and he bent himself backwards, beside himself, his cries growing hoarse.

The curtains twitched. Alan tapped on the window. 'Eve? It's me.' But Aled was making all the noise he needed to announce himself.

The back door opened. Eve's features were as worn as old tread, her brown hair was lank and her weary eyes resigned to further reproach, but a light glimmered when she saw Aled.

He stopped crying and reached for her. They could hear themselves.

'Eve,' said Alan, 'Jean can't cope. The doctor's given her something and now she can't even look after herself, let alone Aled. She doesn't recognise anyone. Gwen's calling the doctor again.' Alan looked around the garden.

Eve said nothing.

Aled reached for her again.

'Will you take him? You're the closest thing he's got… without his mother. Will you, Eve?'

She took him. Aled snuggled into her. Eve's eyes filled with tears. 'Cariad, cariad, what's all the fuss about?'

'Thank you, Eve.'

She went inside.

When Alan got back, Constable Dewi was waiting for him in the kitchen. 'Detective Jeffries is here.'

'Have they found something?'

'No,' replied Constable Dewi, 'he wants to speak to Jean about Gwyn Roberts.'

'What?' Alan pushed past him.

Jeffries was in the porch. 'I want to speak to your wife,' he said. 'This is a murder investigation.' At the door of a missing child he was tasked to find it was all the licence he needed to do whatever he wanted.

'You *can't*,' said Alan, angrily, 'she's in no fit state to see anybody.'

'I'll be the judge of that.'

'Where is my boy? Why haven't you found *him*?'

'This is a murder investigation,' said Detective Jeffries, again, 'and I'm going to see Mrs Harris.'

'What's the *matter* with you?' demanded Gwen.

Detective Jeffries stepped into the hall. Alan blocked his way.

Brenda said, 'Let him, Alan. He only has to see to know.'

'Oh, *Alan* is it?' said Detective Jeffries.

'Ten seconds,' Alan told him, 'then I want you out of my house,' and he stood aside.

Detective Jeffries looked at Jean, with her head resting to one side against the back of the chair and not acknowledging his presence. He tapped his chin with his pencil. 'How long is she going to be like this? Does she know something you don't want us to know, Harris?' He glanced at Brenda. '*Mr* Harris.'

Alan didn't answer. He clenched and unclenched his hands at his sides.

Constable Dewi put his hand on his shoulder.

'We're waiting for the doctor,' said Gwen.

'Then I'll be back when he's been,' said Detective Jeffries, and passed the doctor in the hall on his way out.

The doctor, in his red waistcoat today, slowly waved his hand before Jean's eyes. There was no response. 'Oh dear, how tight his embrace has become,' he said, as much to himself as them, and stood back. 'We must loosen it a little. I am surprised she has reacted so strongly to what I gave her, but it does vary, some people need more, some less. I will change the prescription, Mr Harris.' He rattled a small, brown bottle in his out-stretched hand, 'I have brought these in anticipation. The same strict rules apply, of course, but don't be overly concerned, it can be a fine balance, to alleviate without impairing the senses too drastically. Do you understand?'

'Yes.'

'Good, well, I'll be back tomorrow afternoon to see how she's getting on. We must hope for glad news in the meantime; more than anything to be found in a bottle of pills. Is there anything else I can do, Mr Harris?'

'No, I don't think so, Doctor.'

He snapped his bag shut. 'I will see you tomorrow afternoon, then, but, should there be any change, you must call me, day or night. Do you understand?'

'Yes, Doctor, thank you.'

'There's no need to thank me,' he smiled at Jean and touched her cheek and left.

The consultant had never considered general practice, the brain was his specialty, but not as the residence of the soul or the seat of emotions; neither was it 'fascinating', it was to be solved, like a puzzle. He was a cold fish: he put on his bedside manner like a white coat and he had gone through many sizes before finding one that was a reasonable fit and effective (as he saw it) in dealing with patients and their relatives in the shortest time possible without provoking hysterical outbursts (which talking about maladies of the brain often did, unfortunately). He had learnt to delegate hysteria to a nurse he always kept close at hand for such times. He got away with it because he accepted a simple truth: he was 'brilliant'. Unlike many of his colleagues, he had yet to start wearing bow ties – he would if they met a purpose but couldn't imagine how they might or what people would think of him if he did (or what he would want them to think). He didn't care what people thought; he did not have the capacity for self-awareness. In his scientific mind, the brain and people were entirely separate.

'Mr Hughes,' he said, addressing Bryn's father and ignoring his mother (the more unpredictable creature). They looked up at him from their chairs next to the low table with its unread magazines on sailing and motorbikes and a dog-eared *National Geographic*. 'It is not possible to make an entirely accurate prognosis of when your son will recover consciousness or whether he has sustained permanent, cognitive damage.'

'I don't understand, Doctor.'

Mr Charles flinched (but not because he had been called 'Doctor').

The nurse sat down next to them and said, 'Mr Charles is saying that Bryn might not be himself when he wakes up.'

'How long for?' asked Bryn's mother.

The nurse looked to Mr Charles for an answer. 'It might be permanent.'

Bryn's mother searched the bare walls for what that might mean.

'It's very difficult to predict, Mrs Hughes,' the nurse interceded, 'he might be himself again quite soon, or it might take some time before he recovers.'

Laura Williams sat with her elbows on her knees and her chin in her hands, as she always did when listening. Her expression was drained and immobile but her father could see shadows passing across her face and he could guess. Whatever the outcome, the best or the worst, he was afraid for his daughter. He reached for her hand. 'Don't let those men do this to you,' he whispered.

She squeezed his hand back. 'I won't,' she said.

'I know what you're saying, Doctor,' said Mr Hughes, 'I understand. But there is a possibility he will make a full recovery?'

It was a question. Mr Charles never speculated in hope, but 'possibility' was sufficient. 'There is a possibility,' he replied.

'He's a teacher, Doctor,' said Mr Hughes, almost boastfully, proud of him.

'Teaching is his life, it is both our lives,' said Laura.

It made no visible impression on Mr Charles who heard it as a fact. He dipped his head, a mannerism he had found, by accident, was a way to end these communications. His white coat swished as he left the waiting room.

The nurse stayed, a middle-aged woman, to absorb their worries and their pointless speculations that involved words like 'could' and 'might'. She sat with them for an hour until they had nothing left to say and their mutual attempts at reassurance had run dry.

Later, when they were in a café in town, Laura's father told her, careful not to repeat what he knew she had already thought, 'You can't hold onto someone who isn't there, who can't be there.'

'I know, dad.'

'I wish your mother was still with us.'

'But she's not.'

Two men came round the corner at the top of the road. One of them stopped to pick something up from a garden border.

As they came closer, Constable Dewi saw it was Ellis with one of his cronies. In his hand was a stone. They stopped outside Eve's house. Ellis Maynard was known to Constable Dewi, their association ran long: they had both been in Mr Tanner's class but, now, he knew him as a policeman knows who to look for when there's been trouble. The paths of their lives could not have diverged further. 'Drop that rock, Ellis,' Constable Dewi ordered him.

Ellis looked at the rock in his hand through his stupor as if surprised to find it there. 'Drop it, Ellis.'

'What if I don't?' he slurred.

'What you say and do next, Maynard, will decide whether you spend the rest of the day in the cells – or worse. Up to you.'

'Come on, Ell,' said the other man, tugging at Ellis' arm. 'Come away.'

Ellis pulled his arm free. 'No, I'm not going anywhere, I can go where I like. You're a copper, aren't you, *Constable* Dewi, so arrest him, then.'

'Who?'

'Brown. I can read, can't I? That's his house so arrest him, or do you want us to sort him out for you, is that it, then?'

'He's already under arrest. Are you sure you can read, Maynard?'

A look of confusion came over Ellis' face. 'We'll sort him out for you, right. Last offer.'

'Drop the rock, Maynard, last warning.'

Ellis looked at the rock in his hand and opened his fingers and let it fall. He swayed again. 'There we are, Constable, all gone.'

'Come on Ell,' urged the other man.

Ellis stumbled backwards.

Brenda came out. 'Ellis bloody Maynard,' she said.

'I bet he had something to do with Bryn Hughes,' said Constable Dewi, watching the two men as they weaved toward the top of the road.

Huw woke beneath the mud and waves and couldn't see or hear. He couldn't move; his body was clamped by the weight pressing down on him, as if he was being held. He fought. It let go and he opened his eyes. He got out of bed and went into his mother's room and slid in next to her.

She stirred in her sleep. 'Huw?'

She was warm. Distantly, as if it was the sea outside, the sound of waves rocked him to sleep. In the alley, the blond haired man looked up at their window and waited.

CHAPTER FIFTEEN

Nyasaland, Papua, Pitcairn Island...

Kenfig Pool reflected the sky and dunes as the early morning light began to flash between the brilliant, green tresses suspended in its crystalline depths. It was so perfectly still, the almost silent dart of a dragonfly could be heard on the far side. The first boat splashed in and ripples billowed across the lake like shouts in church. Another boat. Divers in the blackest black tipped off them backwards and submerged into dense patches of bubbles. The tresses were torn and floated to the surface, littering it, growing dull. The water quickly turned cloudy and brown. The divers could have seen into its deepest parts without going into the water at all. But divers must dive. They searched all day: a line of boats behind the seething, uncouth bubbles. When they reached the far shore and unbuckled themselves, easing the heavy tanks off their shoulders, they had found nothing.

Eve had Aled and she held him, breathing in the smell of his hair, feeling the softness of his cheek, his legs around her waist, his fingers playing with her nose, his raspberries spraying spittle into her eyes. She talked to him as she walked up and down the front room and into the kitchen and back again, in the gloom, behind the drawn curtains. 'Shall I make us something to eat, cariad? Alan should have brought your high chair – rickety old thing, it was Jack's after all – but, never mind, you can sit in a big chair at the kitchen table, like a grown-up boy.' She squinted along the kitchen shelves, trying to see. 'Would you like baked beans? It's one of your favourites. We can both have baked beans. I know I've got some somewhere.' She felt for the light switch on the wall, but hesitated before turning it on. 'It's a bit early for lunch – unless you're hungry now? Cariad?' Aled had gone to sleep. She went back into the front room, suspending her confined circuit, to rock him gently as she stood. 'If Jean's not better, you can stay here. It will be a great help to Alan.'

She heard voices outside and thought the reporters had come back. Then the letterbox clattered open. 'Oh *no*.' She pulled Aled closer and held her breath. He pushed at her in his sleep with his arm. Letters flopped onto the mat. 'Oh, it's the postman,' and breathed, grateful that she was still allowed the privilege of mail. She cradled the venerated child. 'I have lost my husband – no, he has lost me, but it amounts to the same thing.'

When they were all growing up together, Alan and Jean, Geraint – Gwen later – she and Roy, pairing off, why hadn't she seen in him what she saw now – and still hadn't if the police hadn't arrested him? She sighed. 'But I did see.' She had ignored his slyness and believed his excuses; the last to help if someone was in pain – watching them as they suffered, moistening his lips with a flicking tongue. What did he want? Not her, that had ceased soon after they were married when he started working on the railway. 'Is that what you were doing when you were away?' He had asked for marriage and she had encouraged it. It was her choice too, there was no escaping her part in it. 'But there was a good side to you, Roy – that was most of you wasn't it, more good than bad? You must have loved me too, didn't you? All those years, I wasn't in love with a sham, was I?' She heard a car outside. It went slowly past. 'What did you *do*, Roy? Whatever it is, I think they mean to send you to prison for it, *prison*.' No one she had ever known had even visited one or had a reason to.

She hoisted Aled higher on her hip. He rubbed his face with his hands without opening his eyes. She tipped her head back to look at him. He was breathing soundlessly. 'I can't hide in here forever, I will have to know; it can't be avoided.' She shifted Aled again. 'You're getting too heavy for me, cariad.' His head rolled on her shoulder. 'I won't see you again, cariad, probably ever, after this, and you won't remember me. Your mum and dad won't tell you about me.' The happy times before the children were born – not her children – would be lost to hidden memories and never spoken of. 'I will slip out of your life and be gone. I'm sorry, I need to put you down. I wish I could open the curtains to let in some more light.' She tugged at them to make a bigger gap, looking out on the back garden. She nudged the armchair closer to the window where she wouldn't be able to see over the windowsill at the pock-marked destruction and wilted into it with Aled.

Through the remainder of the morning and into the early afternoon, she moved the chair with her foot, without getting up, to follow the shard of light as it made a sundial of the front room, shining as long as the turning world let it, on bric-a-brac and souvenirs: this, and this, remember this? She thought about Jack. She shed tears for him. She was mortally afraid she would never say goodbye (or the last time she had seen him had, unwittingly, been goodbye). Then it was time for lunch and she gently woke Aled and let him play around her feet as she warmed the beans on the stove.

Outside, Huw looked through the fence, but nothing had changed: the curtains were still drawn and there was no sign of Uncle Roy or Auntie Eve. He stamped his foot in frustration, at a loss to understand why Uncle Roy hadn't started on his greenhouse or had left the garden in such a mess (so unlike Uncle Roy who always told him off if he didn't put his toys away). Had they gone on holiday? Why hadn't they told him?

'Hello, Huw,' said the blond man, from the alley.

Huw looked round to see where the voice was coming from. 'Hello. Uncle Roy hasn't started on his greenhouse and the school is still closed so perhaps Mr Tanner has taken a turn for the worse.' People were always having 'Turns', usually 'A bit of' and never for the better. 'And I've got nothing to do except sit in Auntie Jean's kitchen with mummy, except mummy has started to sit in the front room with Auntie Jean lately and I think Auntie Jean is asleep but her eyes are open so she can't be. I've read *The Big Book* so many times, I'm not tired of it, but... can we go to the fair at Trecco?'

'Soon,' smiled the blond man, 'soon, I promise.'

'*Ohhh*.'

'How is your mum?'

'In Auntie Jean's, I just told you.'

'No, Huw, you told me where she was.'

'I didn't mean to be rude.'

'I know you didn't, Huw.'

'Brenda's there and the big policeman outside the front door whose name is Dewi. I've no idea why he's always there. It's a mystery to me.'

'How is Uncle Alan?'

'He's there sometimes, but not all the time. Is this all because Mr Tanner is ill? Do you know if Uncle Roy and Auntie Eve have gone on holiday?'

'I don't think so, Huw.'

'*Please* can we go to Trecco?'

'Soon, Huw. We'll go on all the rides together.'

'What rides?'

'All of them.'

'*All* of them?'

'Yes, *all* of them.'

'When is *soon?* Is it today?'

'Not today.'

'Tomorrow, then?'

'Tomorrow or the day after. We'll be going before you know it.'

'Will we go even if Mr Tanner is better?'

'Yes, Huw, even if Mr Tanner is better.'

Mr Tanner called in at the vicarage.

'Mr Tanner!' exclaimed Reverend Elwiss when he opened the door because it was the first time the headmaster had come to his home, but these were altered times.

'I was going to the hospital to ask after Bryn and to see how Laura is bearing up. Would you like to come with me? There's something I'd like to talk to you about as well.'

'If you give me a moment to fetch my coat,' replied the Reverend, 'I'd be glad to, well, not glad in the circumstances, but, yes I will, of course.' He ducked back inside. 'I'm going down to the hospital with Mr Tanner,' he called to his wife (as if to announce his growing reputation with important personages) and came out putting on his coat.

The hospital was in its permanent state of too hot and too bright, with an obtrusive smell of disinfectant trying to deal with, but not convincingly winning against, the smell of something unpleasant.

Laura was in the waiting room alone. She was holding the *National Geographic* that had been open at the same page for an hour. If asked, she wouldn't have been able to say what the title of the article was let alone what it was about. Incongruously or unknowingly, for a hospital waiting room, it had a picture of a bare-breasted, black woman wearing silver bracelets up to her elbows. She was smiling with very white teeth.

Reverend Elwiss averted his eyes. Mr Tanner eased the magazine from Laura's hands without noticing. 'You weren't reading this, were you?'

She let him take it, still unaware of its contents (Bryn would have laughed and said it was 'educational', if he'd been quick enough to think of it). She was surprised to see them again so soon.

'Where is everyone?' Mr Tanner asked.

She noticed that the waiting room was empty. 'I don't know. I think they might have gone home to get some sleep or get a change of clothes.'

'And what about you, Laura? Have you had any sleep?'

'I might have, I'm not sure.'

'What about something to eat?'

'I'm not hungry.'

'You must eat, Laura.'

'I couldn't.'

Mr Tanner gently clasped her wrist. 'And how is Bryn?'

'The same.' Her lips hardly moved.

'But not any worse? There are some grounds for optimism, then?'

She looked at him. 'But he's not any better either, Mr Tanner. They won't let me sit with him. There's tubes everywhere and they said they don't want me to get in the way. I won't get in the way.'

'Shall I ask them for you, Laura?' Reverend Elwiss sat down next to her. 'Sometimes this has its uses,' and he stuck his finger inside his dog collar and tugged at it.

'Would you?' she asked. 'Please?'

'I'll go and find a nurse.' Moments later, he was back. 'They have to ask the consultant.'

'Oh,' she said, 'oh, do they?'

But Mr Charles was caught on the hop and appeared without a nurse as his lightning rod. He didn't understand religion, he didn't understand why God should exist or for what purpose or why anyone would want him to, but a vicar, he had discovered, wielded curious powers that could summon emotions that, without his escort, he was unequipped to deal with. Mr Charles stood before them.

'Are you Bryn Hughes' consultant?' asked Mr Tanner.

Next to him, the vicar emanated the scientifically unfathomable.

'Yes,' replied Mr Charles.

'Laura,' said Mr Tanner, carefully using her Christian name, 'is Mr Hughes' fiancée.'

Mr Charles' wary expression did not change and he did not, as might have been expected, look at Laura.

Mr Tanner continued, 'She would like, if possible, to sit with him?'

'Would that be possible?' asked Reverend Elwiss, raising his clasped hands to the tip of his nose in a prayer-like way and smiling behind them. 'If that is at all possible, she promises to keep out of the way of the nurses. She only wants to keep him company. She can talk to him about their wedding plans and all the other plans they have for their future. It can only help him in his recovery, do you not think?'

Mr Charles dipped his head. His white coat swished as he turned smartly and left.

'Was that yes, do you think?' asked Reverend Elwiss.

'Let's take it as a yes,' said Mr Tanner, who, as a teacher, recognised instantly why Mr Charles was the way he was: a child bullied and excised, whose abilities might never have been discovered, let alone encouraged. Mr Tanner was surprised, there were few places that could be a greater test for such a man. He cured his patients and paid a hidden price (and wouldn't understand why). Mr Tanner admired his courage but knew he would be impossible to work with. 'Go and see Bryn, Laura, and, if anyone asks, tell them the consultant said it's alright.'

'Thank you,' said Laura, already hurrying out.

'Well done, Vicar,' said Mr Tanner.

'One shouldn't be afraid to wield the power of the Church for a good cause, on occasion,' agreed the Reverend, modestly, but inwardly glowing.

'That's the other thing I wanted to talk to you about.'

'The power of the Church?'

'More or less.'

They found a child's sandal. It had been carefully placed on a clear patch of sand between the marram grass, only a couple of hundred yards from where they had been muddying the waters. It had not been there long, not even a day – it was dry and clean. Leading away from it, were the footprints of a man's boots. The wind and rain had not had a chance to blur them and they were still clearly etched in the sand.

The searchers followed the footprints west, walking carefully on either side. They led to the top of a tall dune next to the one where Sergeant Phillips had been standing only the day before. The grass had been cleared away. A dead rabbit was staked to the sand. The stake had been freshly sharpened and was streaked with blood. It went through the middle of the rabbit's back. It was a pet, white, with floppy ears. Its dead eyes looked west. There were no more footprints, as if its killer had been lifted into the air.

Sergeant Phillips was sent for. He arrived in his big, black car and pulled off the road. He jerked his tunic straight, ran his thumbs over his moustache and put on his peaked cap. Everyone watched as he walked toward them: a procession of one. He looked at the sandal from his unbending height. He followed the footprints until he reached the rabbit. He pouted his moustache and turned to look east. 'Porthcawl,' he said. 'I know his mind. Put the rabbit in a bag and put it in the boot of my car with the sandal.' He watched while they did it. 'East not west,' he told them. 'East to Porthcawl. I know his mind.'

Jean rose into what senses she had left. As the old pills let her go, the new pills supported her climb, but only so far, and there they held her, neither to go up nor down.

She heard voices. They came closer. Detective Jeffries' face swam into view, tapping his chin with his pencil, with his blank notebook in his other hand. Behind him was Alan; next to him was Brenda and closest of all, sitting on a kitchen chair, was Gwen, leaning forward. Jean remembered Aled's weight in her lap, and closed her arms around an empty space. 'Aled?' Jean sprang to her feet and knocked Gwen backwards. Her arms and legs were as rigid as a scarecrow's poles. The sinews in her neck stood out. '*Where are my children? Have you got them? God will punish you.*' She rushed out and fell over the little hedge into Eve's front garden. She pounded the grass with her fists.

Inside, Eve held Aled tight and tried to block his ears.

A big, black car pulled up at the kerb and Sergeant Phillips got out. He smoothed his moustache, yanked his tunic straight and leaned against the bonnet. He observed the scene through half-closed eyes.

Jean threw herself at Eve's front door. It shuddered with a crack of splintering timber. Her fingers made a squeaking noise as they slid down the wood.

Aled heard the bang and jumped. He started to cry. Eve hurried through to the kitchen with him.

Jean lay half on the step and half on the path. Neighbours came out to watch. Brenda and Constable Dewi dragged Jean though the hedge with her feet trailing behind her. They took her out of sight and put her back in the armchair and jammed her knees against the wall with Constable Dewi standing behind her with his arms around her chest.

Detective Jeffries stood back and tapped his pencil on his chin. He went out.

Sergeant Phillips pushed himself upright and said, 'You weren't quick enough, Jeffries, and now you've lost a witness.'

Detective Jeffries gulped.

Sergeant Phillips opened the boot of his car, pulled the bag off the rabbit and held it by its floppy ears. He hooked two fingers into the back of the tiny sandal with his other hand and told Detective Jeffries, 'Fetch him.'

Sergeant Phillips held out the sandal and the rabbit. 'Did your son have a pet rabbit?'

'No,' Alan replied.

'Neither does someone else today, Harris. Did you kill this one up at Roberts' farm too?'

'No.'

'Is this your son's sandal?'

'He was wearing sandals.'

'It is,' said Sergeant Phillips. 'I know it is. I know your mind, Harris. None of your games.'

'Games? My son is missing, there are no *games*.'

'Mr Harris,' said Brenda, trying not to look at Sergeant Phillips, who was still holding out the rabbit in one hand and the sandal in the other, as motionless as justice. 'Come away, your wife needs you.'

'Take this, Colcannon.' Sergeant Phillips tossed the rabbit onto the drive. 'Pick it up.'

Brenda bit her lower lip. Alan bent down. 'No, Alan,' she told him, and picked up the rabbit by its foot. It bumped against her leg. Brenda and Alan stood side by side.

'I will keep the sandal.' Sergeant Phillips got back into his big, black car and was gone.

'Mr Tanner,' exclaimed Doug Protheroe, making his leather chair creak as he leaned back. 'Again? And you have brought moral support, no less.'

'This is Reverend Elwiss,' said Mr Tanner.

'Ah, yes, Reverend Elwiss, I'm pleased to meet you at last. We have spoken on the telephone, have we not? And I do believe we made a modest donation to the church roof fund?'

'You did, that was most kind, Mr Protheroe,' said the Reverend.

'Not at all, we are eager to help. Take a pew – I imagine that's not the first time you've heard that?'

'It's not and, sometimes, people don't know they've said it.'

'So, how can I help you both today?'

'We would like to write an article,' said Mr Tanner, 'jointly, you understand, to appear in your newspaper, if you would be so good as to include it, about the need for calm and how the community should support each other at such a difficult time.'

'Would you, indeed?' said Protheroe, brightening at this unexpected offer. 'I would be delighted to.' He rolled his forefinger over his upper lip. He was already three, four, even five stories ahead. Once they crossed into his world, their secrets would be his: a vicar and a headmaster. His smile, when it came, was spare but triumphal. He let his hand drop to the desk. 'Yes, I would be delighted to accommodate you, naturally – with a picture of the two of you outside the church or the school, preferably the church, a more iconic location – you're not offended, are you, Mr Tanner?'

'Not at all,' said Mr Tanner, 'a school is a building, a church can't be anything else but a church.'

'You have a newspaper man's mind, Mr Tanner.'

'I wouldn't go so far as that, Mr Protheroe,' said Mr Tanner, resisting the flattery, but not wholly successfully. 'I am naught but a teacher.'

'I will arrange for Lloyd to get some shots, some photos of you, then. Just name the time. I'm sure even he can find the church on his own.'

They were amused.

'But, I feel I must warn you, once you put your head above the parapet, you will not be able to duck behind it again. The ink will not go back in the pot.' He smiled broadly: a newspaper man's joke.

Mr Tanner and Reverend Elwiss understood, now they had been inducted.

'We know,' smiled Mr Tanner. He was encouraged. His faith in the press would never be fully restored, but it might be mended, now he had a better understanding of the rules. 'It's a difficult lesson to learn – forgive me – but we must deal with adversity with whatever means are at our disposal – within reason.'

'Of course,' agreed Reverend Elwiss.

'So long as you understand,' said Protheroe. Because, when the feathers flew, he could say, 'I told you so.'

'We quite understand,' said Mr Tanner, feeling determined.

'Good,' said Protheroe, because they didn't.

'You won't change what we write?' asked Mr Tanner, cursorily examining the small print (and failing to heed one of his own maxims: 'A little knowledge is a dangerous thing.')

'No, not substantially,' Protheroe answered. 'I'll probably tidy it up a bit, that's all. We have a certain style, as all newspapers do, the good ones that is, that's why I'm editor. You wouldn't have me out of a job already, would you?'

They all laughed at that.

'Thank you,' said Mr Tanner.

'When can I have it?'

Mr Tanner looked at Reverend Elwiss. 'Tomorrow morning?'

The Reverend nodded.

'Excellent,' said Protheroe. 'Get on with your homework, then, Headmaster.'

Mr Tanner and Reverend Elwiss retired to the vicarage to work on the article. Reverend Elwiss' wife fed them tea and fruit cake.

They worked late into the evening. It was a heartfelt lament for the missing children and the sorrows of their parents: *... for whom all our support is so necessary, even if it cannot, of itself, bring them back. We must wish the police Godspeed in their endeavours to find them... but we, none of us, should be so quick to accuse no matter how desperate, understandably, to find answers and make blame.'*

They ended the article with a more specific, but restrained, admonition to the police who, provided with important information about Bryn Hughes' attackers, should use their best efforts to bring them to book. All in all, as would be expected of these two pillars, it was an appeal to humanity and for it.

Mr Tanner bade Reverend Elwiss, 'Good-night. I will get this down to *The Herald* first thing in the morning.' As he crossed the bridge over the river on his way home, he heard God in the trees, turning over the leaves and faintly dappling the obsidian waters with their pallid undersides.

In the dark, Alan dug another hole for the rabbit in his growing pet cemetery. It was the time of night for a grave robber, not an interment, and he would not leave the rabbit to fester. But, as he shovelled the earth, he wondered why he was doing it. They were only animals and only Sam had any meaning to him. He carried on digging. Out of the corner of his eye, he could see the patch of whiteness on the grass that was the rabbit's remains. 'What child is missing you tonight?' he asked himself, as he dropped it into the hole and filled it back in.

Chapter Sixteen

St Helena, St Kitts and Nevis...

East? Surely *west,* the way of the footprints, toward the fiery eyes? They dare not disobey: but, this time, he was wrong. They thought of their own children: west, surely west? When they looked up to stretch their backs, Porthcawl was in the distance and, then, they would be in every house and garden. The fiery eyes were telling them they were going the wrong way. Even the dogs whined and pulled and wanted to turn round. But, they searched on, grumbling (not too loudly): 'How will we find them like this?'

Jean cried out in her feverish sleep, '*Where are my children?*'

The neighbours heard her up and down the road in the night, the woman in the semi-detached asylum, driven mad, once one of them, oh but for the grace of God, who had been Jean Harris.

When she tried to get up, Alan and Constable Dewi held her down. She fought them. She covered Alan's face in scratches that bled as he tried to shave with shaking hands the following morning.

Brenda called the doctor in the early hours when Alan and Dewi were exhausted and didn't know what else to do.

He had dressed hastily in his yellow waistcoat but he was tieless.

Jean tried to fling herself at him. '*God will punish you.*'

Constable Dewi and Alan held her back and forced her down into the chair. Brenda stood by and tried to talk to her, as if a woman's voice might make a difference, but it didn't.

The doctor was serious and purposeful, his avuncular demeanour put away. 'Whatever she can see, it is not us,' he told them. 'She sees what is in her mind, what she imagines, but it is not real. Poor woman. You know what I'm going to say, don't you?'

'Yes, there's no choice is there? We can't keep fighting her. She'll end up hurting herself.'

'And you,' said the doctor.

Alan felt his face and looked at the blood on his fingers.

'If we were to allow her to continue in this state, she will do herself harm both mentally and physically. The former will take far longer to heal than the latter, I'm afraid. The harm may already have been done.'

Jean dribbled, her eyes wandering.

'Hold her still for me, will you?' The doctor opened his bag and filled a needle with clear fluid from a small bottle. 'I have been in practice too many years, fortunately or unfortunately,' he said, peering at the filling tube. He felt Jean's forehead. She jerked her head. He pulled his hand away. 'Try not to think of her like this, Mr Harris. Hold her now.' He rolled back her sleeve. 'This can't come soon enough for you, can it?' and he eased the needle into her arm.

She tensed, then, fleetingly, like the sun from between the clouds, her expression softened into lucid understanding. She looked at her husband steadily and wistfully and, there she was, younger, fresh, clear eyed, before the journey began, before Jack and Aled, when there was optimism. Just as suddenly, she was gone: her eyes emptied, her face sagged and her head fell forward.

Alan brimmed with tears.

The doctor stood up and squeezed his arm. 'I know,' he said quietly, 'but she has not left us, she needs help and relief.'

An ambulance came, but not a normal one. Two men in blue uniforms lifted Jean into a wheelchair and tied down her wrists and tightened a strap across her chest.

'It's only to keep her safe and secure,' the doctor told Alan.

'Secure, Doctor?'

'Not in that way, Mr Harris, while they get her into the ambulance.'

'Is it?'

Jean was wheeled out and up a ramp. One of the men got into the back and closed the doors.

'Go and see her tomorrow,' the doctor said, 'when you've had some sleep.'

'I'll be see you in the morning,' said Constable Dewi, wearily.

Brenda told him. 'I'll be back first thing, Alan.'

'In the morning,' Alan replied, absently. He went to bed alone in the house, the first time since he'd been married. For a while, he listened to the creaks of the cooling pipes and flexing boards that he had never heard. He didn't know if he slept, perhaps he did, because then it was an October morning, with a chill, and he was awake in the black light of what had happened, sitting on the back step.

Brenda hadn't arrived and Constable Dewi was understandably late, when Gwen came in from the alley.

Huw looked eagerly from his bedroom window and thought, 'Will it be today?'

In the row of beds, the patients had become part of the machines that surrounded them, neither able to function without the other. Some of the tubes vibrated, others sucked and pumped; lights flashed to muted bleeps but failed to keep time with each other. Here, on its frontier, the rhythm of life was discordant.

Laura was unattached. She had been dropped amongst the cogs like a foreign body. If the hospital was shaken, she would rattle around in it until she dropped out. She watched him but there was nothing to watch: his eyes were taped shut, his mouth was partly open and a tube disappeared up his nose. His bruises had reached their most showy lividity, like flowers blooming before they wilt. She had all the time to see them change, the first petal to fall, then the next, until they were dried, brown heads and he was no more. His arms were laid neatly on top of the blankets along his sides and she had to study him to see if he was still breathing. *Bleep* slow *bleep* told her he was, but she felt the drumming of her heart in each hiatus. His parents came and stood behind her.

The nurse said, 'Only one at a time.' She was brusque and there was no need for it.

Laura gave up her chair next to the bed for Bryn's mother and went back to the waiting room with his father where they sat without speaking.

It wasn't long before his mother came in. 'I can't,' she said. 'I can't see him like that. I can't listen to those sounds. I'm terrified of them stopping.'

Laura went back to Bryn with his father, expecting the nurse to shoo one of them out. She wasn't there. He stood looking at his son for some moments. Then he patted her shoulder and said, 'I must go back to my wife, she's not coping very well.' Neither was he. 'Look after him, won't you?'

Bleep… bleep: not her. 'What can I do?'

'Everything,' he replied, 'that the doctors can't – or that nurse. I'm going to take my wife for a walk. We won't be long. I'll see you later. I'll see you later too,' and he kissed Bryn's cheek as he had kissed him goodnight as a boy.

Laura's father arrived. 'How is he?' he asked.

She held up her hands and let them flop down.

'How are you?' She didn't answer.

The nurse said, 'Only *one* of you.'

Laura gripped her knees. 'Why…' she began. The nurse dared her.

'I'll be in the waiting room,' her father said, before Laura said something, knowing she was about to (and wishing she would). He ignored the nurse as he left.

The nurse went back to wherever she was spying on them and Laura went back to watching the bruises and the strain of willing him. She had run out of bargains: she had made a promise to live a blameless life and she had said sorry for everything she could think of. She thought, 'If I stop caring, he will get better; if I want it too much he will be taken away.' But she was battling a power that seemed determined to deny her what she most wanted. 'Am I being selfish? If I promise never to see him again, will you let him wake up?' But it knew she didn't mean it. So she begged. But his imperceptible breathing did not change; it didn't deepen to draw life back into him. *Bleep… bleep.*

'Miss Williams?' said a voice that made her jump.

She turned and there was Detective Jeffries, holding his notebook, tapping his pencil on his chin, eager to make up for his recent failure with Jean Harris.

'When can I speak to him?

'What are you doing here? Have you caught who did it?'

'When can I speak to him?'

'You can't, *look* at him.'

Detective Jeffries tapped his chin. 'What about you, Miss Williams? Is there something you haven't told me?'

'I've got nothing to say to you. This is a hospital. Why aren't you looking for whoever did it?'

'The question is *why* did they do it, Miss Williams?'

'*Why* they did it? *Why*?' She stood up and advanced toward him. 'It doesn't matter *why* they did it. It was because of *you* and that… that *rag* of a newspaper.'

'Do you think so? How well do you know him, Miss Williams?

'*Go*,' she spat, and looked for the nurse.

'No one's going to help you,' said Detective Jeffries, 'and they're no use,' he nodded at the line of beds.

The nurse appeared around a screen. She had heard their voices (or had been waiting to make an entrance). Her expression was furious. 'Are these friends of yours?'

'I'm a detective, and I'm here on police business.'

'I don't care who you are or why you're here. Get *out*.'

Herald Andrew and Lloyd leaned around the door.

Flash.

Bryn was caught in sensational definition. 'Got it,' said Lloyd. Detective Jeffries followed them out through the swinging door. The nurse chased after them. *The Herald* had its picture.

Gwen sat down next to Alan on the doorstep. She shivered. 'Why are you sitting out here? It's freezing.'

'I didn't want to sit inside.'

'Where's Brenda and Dewi?'

'I don't know. On their way, I imagine. There's only me here now, anyway. Aled's still with Eve. I shouldn't have left him with her all night.'

'You didn't have any choice, Alan. I heard. I saw the ambulance. I didn't know whether to come round.'

'What for?' he shook his head. 'There was nothing you could do.'

'Where have they taken her?'

'The same place where they keep the man who told us about the dead sheep. I'm going down there later, perhaps I'll have a chance to say hello. I'll go round and fetch Aled after. I don't want to take him down there. And then what? Will it just be the two of us?'

'Don't say that, Alan.'

'I do not want to think it but it has to be said. Jack will not come home. Jean will not recover until Jack comes home, so she will never recover.'

They thought the same thought. Gwen said it first, 'Not that anything else matters.'

'Not now, more than ever?'

'I'm not his mother, Alan. If Geraint hadn't died there would have been no need.'

Alan raised his head. He could see Gwyn the Milk's fields beyond the alley fence and the farm buildings, bleakly dark, at the top of the slope. He had seen the unchanging landscape since he and Jean had moved in, not long before Roy and Eve, and then Geraint and Gwen after them: peas in a pebble-dashed pod. The landscape had been abandoned, the houses were emptying; the joy had drained away. 'How do you fill in the spaces?' he asked, to her and himself.

'You can't,' she said. 'We can't remove ourselves from our lives and live another one. These are our lives and this is what they are.' She stood up. 'That step really is cold.'

'It is,' he replied, not moving.

She went out by the alley gate and almost drifted past Huw who was waiting for her at the back door.

'Mummy?'

She went upstairs.

'She's upset, Huw,' said the blond man, looking over the fence at him.

'Is she? I don't know why. I wish Jack would come home from the shop. He's been up there for ages.'

'A little while,' said the blond man, 'but not so long.'

Huw put his hands on his hips and frowned, 'Today is tomorrow because it was yesterday when you promised. Can we go now?'

The blond man laughed. 'Today is tomorrow because it was yesterday when I promised? That's a mouthful, Huw.'

'Can we? You promised.'

'And I keep my promises. It will be soon, I *promise*.'

Huw's frown darkened. 'Is soon today or tomorrow?'

'Either or neither, but soon.'

'*Ohhh*. I don't know what that means. I want soon to be now.'

'I know you do, Huw, I know you do.'

The other sandal was lying on its side under a clump of grass. It was wet and the leather was wrinkled and some of the stitching near the buckle had come away. It hadn't been placed there. It had fallen and been lost. If it had been found, it would have been carefully displayed next to the other one. It was east of its partner, east of the dead rabbit and the man's footprints heading west. The searchers who had found it pulled the grass back to fully reveal the small, childless clue.

Sergeant Phillips smoothed his moustache with his thumbs as he towered over it. 'East,' he growled. 'East. I know his mind.'

How could they have doubted him?

'East,' he rumbled. 'He will not escape me with his games. Leave it there.'

As he was walking sedately back to his big, black car, he told Detective Jeffries, who was struggling to keep up on the soft ground and getting his trouser legs soaked to the knees, 'Tell that reporter friend of yours to take a photograph of it and make sure you get the story straight. East *not* west?' He stopped. 'Is that clear?'

Detective Jeffries' foot slipped but he managed to steady himself, half crouched at an angle, his head tilted to cock an eye as if Sergeant Phillips was the threat of bad weather.

'Write it down, Jeffries. Get the story straight. This is your last chance.'

In Detective Jeffries' mind, a pleading, '*But…*' formed, but it did not reach his mouth.

'And when you've done that, bring the shoe to me.'

Sergeant Phillips began walking again, his long, even tread unhindered by the topography and clinging vegetation. He arrived at his big, black car and got in without another word, leaving Detective Jeffries at the roadside, swallowing at the indignity of being abandoned.

Detective Jeffries made notes, as instructed, and slipped the notebook into the inside pocket of his shabby sports jacket. He looked up and down the empty road hoping to see a phone box to call *Herald* Andrew. In vain. He went back down to the searchers, got wetter, and ordered one of them to take him to a phone box.

But his authority was impeached and even the most junior constable made a show of making him wait while a car was fetched.

They found a phone box two miles away. *Herald* Andrew wasn't in. 'Take me back to the station,' he told the young constable. On the way, Detective Jeffries sulked and contemplated what 'last chance' meant, how unfair it was and what Sergeant Phillips might do to him. What could he do? Anything he wanted.

When Detective Jeffries called *Herald* Andrew from the station, he still hadn't returned to the office. He found him and Lloyd in The Red Lion.

'We thought we'd finished for the day,' said *Herald* Andrew.

'He wants you again,' Detective Jeffries told him.

'Back down the hospital?'

Detective Jeffries took out his notebook and told them about the sandal.

'Come on, Lloydy-boy, neck it,' said *Herald* Andrew.

Alan knocked on Eve's back door. The curtain twitched before she opened it.

He had been to see Jean and found her sitting in a shabby lounge in a cavernous, threadbare chair alongside other ancient armchairs, all circled around a television soundlessly displaying the test card. No one spoke. Jean was faraway. Nurses came and went, adjusting cushions (perhaps for his benefit, not the patients – or were they inmates?). Alan held her hands in his. He laid them gently on her thighs but they slipped off and he had to prop them loosely together to keep them in place. He spoke, but she was not there to speak to, so he left.

'Hello, Alan,' said Eve. Aled was peacefully asleep in her arms.

Alan wondered if she had put him to bed at all and cuddled him all night. 'I've come to collect him,' he said.

'No, Alan, he's safe here.'

What did she mean by that? 'He's safe with me,' Alan replied.

'He's sleeping now,' said Eve, 'let's not wake him. Where is Jean?'

'In the hospital.'

'I heard the commotion.'

'I'm sorry.'

'There's nothing to be sorry about, it didn't disturb him. If Jean's in the hospital, wouldn't it be easier for you if Aled stayed with me? It's no trouble, Alan.'

He hesitated. Easier? But would that be for him or should he do the dutiful thing by his youngest child? Or was it a pretence? He could have the house to himself. Gwen? No, Dewi and Brenda would be there. 'I must take him, Eve.'

She half-turned away, shielding the sleeping boy from him. 'He's happy as he is, Alan. It's no trouble, really.'

'Eve?'

'But, if Jean's in hospital?'

What would he do if Aled had another screaming fit? Without even his wife's dumb presence to pacify him, he would have to bring him back to Eve. 'Are you sure you don't mind? I don't like to burden you.'

'It's not a burden, Alan – are you, cariad?' She nuzzled the sleeping boy, with his head against her neck and his thumb hanging from his mouth. 'No, of course you're not.'

'Thank you, Eve.' She closed the door. When he got back, Brenda was in the kitchen and Constable Dewi was out the front. All was as it had been, except they were less.

'Mr Protheroe is a newspaper man,' said Mr Tanner, 'and he must go where the news takes him but there are limits and I believe he knows what they are. I can't believe he is aware of what happened, let alone be a party to it. But there is no possible justification for their actions. It's unconscionable.'

'Utterly reprehensible and deeply shocking,' said Reverend Elwiss.

They were gathered in the waiting room at the hospital. Bryn was alone as they could not all crowd around his bed. 'It was that detective,' said Laura.

'I have already met him,' said Mr Tanner. 'Bryn's parents weren't there, were they?'

'No,' said Laura, 'I was on my own.'

'Well, that's something, at least.'

'But they will see his picture in the newspaper, with all those tubes sticking out of him.'

'We will see none of it in the newspaper,' said Mr Tanner, firmly. 'Reverend Elwiss and I – with Mr Protheroe's agreement – have written an article, about to go to press, that will correct these rumours and gossip and I do not think for a minute that he will print a picture of Bryn on his sick bed next to it, do you Vicar?'

'I agree,' said Reverend Elwiss, 'he is hardly likely to do that.'

'I think he will send those two reporters packing when he learns of this, I really do. But, that detective is a different matter. I think we should speak to his superiors. I was minded to when…' he hadn't told them about Ellis Maynard. 'I think we should, Vicar, you and I, do you think so?'

'Most certainly,' replied Reverend Elwiss, who couldn't help enjoying his growing reputation as someone who should be listened to.

'It is Bryn we should be thinking of,' said Mr Tanner. 'Try and think no more of it, Laura, let Reverend Elwiss and I deal with the matter.'

'Thank you,' said Laura, 'I'm going back to sit with him.'

When the door had closed behind her, Mr Tanner asked her father, 'How is she, in herself?'

'Totally shattered, she loves that boy, but she is stronger than she looks, she takes after her mother in that way. It's heartbreaking to see him like this. The injustice, for him – and her.'

'It is more than unjust,' said the Reverend. There had been many meek and wasted years and he was going to make up for them.

Sergeant Phillips dangled the little sandal from the end of his forefinger. Alan came to the door when Constable Dewi called him. 'Look here,' said Sergeant Phillips, 'do you think I would not find it. East not west. Did you think your games would fool me, Harris? I think not. What happened to your face, did one of the animals fight back?'

Brenda watched from the shade of the hall. Constable Dewi was standing rigidly to attention, glassy-eyed.

'I am close, Harris, close enough for you to feel my breath on your neck. I know your mind, your every thought, your schemes, your plans. I know what you will do next and I will be waiting for you.' He swung the sandal into his hand and gripped it, 'Just like a trap.' He smoothed his moustache with his thumbs, still holding the sandal as if it was a morsel he was about to pop into his mouth. Then he got into his big, black car. It was a moment before he drove away.

Alan went through the house, into the alley and into Eve's garden. 'I must have Aled back,' he told her.

'Please, Alan, a little longer?'

'I must take him back, Eve. I have to look after what I've still got.'

'Alan, please?'

'Eve, he's all I have now.'

'He's all I have too, Alan. Let me come round and look after him? Let me do that?'

'Perhaps, later.' He reached up for Aled who struggled to stay in Eve's arms. Alan took him.

Aled began to scream. He kept looking over the fence as if something was waiting for him in the house. He carried on screaming as Alan took him there.

Eve retreated into her cloistered home with only the slit between the front room curtains to let in the light. She closed them. She could hear Aled through the wall. Roy's painkillers were on the top shelf in the kitchen. They had been there, untouched, since he stopped taking them after hurting his hand at work. The bottle was almost full. She emptied them onto the table. They were red and wasp-yellow. She poured herself a large glass of water and sat down.

Chapter Seventeen

St Lucia, St Vincent, Seychelles…

Now they were certain it was east, they were eager and filled with fresh hope. The line of men and dogs advanced along the shoulder of Rest Bay, a flat and featureless beach that the tides planed smooth where there was nowhere to hide. But they poked into every rock pool and disturbed the crabs and pulled over the round, wet rocks and dug amongst the shingle and into the sandy banks where the common began; into the fields and hedgerows, to the outskirts of the town, inoculating and eradicating and, finally, into the houses and gardens themselves where people lived who did not want to believe what they were looking for could be hidden in their midst or who did it could be one of them.

Sergeant Phillips leaned against the bonnet of his big, black car at the top of the beach car park, empty on this sharp autumnal morning, where he could see the sweep of the bay. His back was to the fiery eyes. 'I am close and my trap is closing. He knows it. He knows he cannot escape.' The dogs whined and barked and strained on their leashes. 'I am close now. I know it.'

'Jeffries?'

'Sir, I am on my way.' Detective Jeffries walked quickly up the shallow hill and tried not to run. But he was out of breath when he got there. 'Sir?'

'What do you want, Jeffries?'

'I heard you calling me.'

'I did not.'

'But, I heard you. I am here now.'

'Why? What use are you?' Sergeant Phillips smoothed his moustache with his thumbs and took off his peaked cap. He paused for a final inspection of his underlings, bent into their task, and then he got into his big, black car and drove sedately along the road above the beach, with the sun flashing on the windscreen, showing the way they must follow.

Detective Jeffries was left like a fence post without wire. He hurried down to the searchers. 'What have you found? Why not? Why aren't you doing your job?'

Not one of them replied; no one looked at him (neither man nor dog).

'We are close. There is no room for mistakes. Do you *understand*?'

The line of searchers moved away from him. They stopped talking to each other.

Detective Jeffries followed. 'There? What's that there?' he pointed at an insignificant tussock. They carried on. 'You've missed that.' He fell behind, even though they moved across the common as slowly as melting dew in the rising sun.

One of the searchers glanced over his shoulder. 'He's gone,' he said. He stood up and the long line stood up too and, soon, they were all talking and swapping cigarettes.

Vicar and Headmaster Condemn Police

There was a picture of Reverend Elwiss and Mr Tanner outside the church, side by side, looking uprightly Victorian. Beneath was a smaller picture of Bryn Hughes on his sickbed, *a possible suspect*. In black and white, his bruises made him appear unwashed.

Mr Tanner and Reverend Elwiss' crafted paean to the essential goodness of mankind, and the people of the town in particular, had been splattered with exclamation marks and adjectives spicy enough to warm the chips they would soon be wrapped around.

When Reverend Elwiss picked the paper off the mat and opened it in happy expectation, he reeled against the wall in shock. His hand searched blindly for the chair next to the hall table and knocked the telephone receiver off its cradle. It swung on its lead and banged against the chair leg. He fumbled with his reading glasses but only managed to balance them lopsidedly on his nose with the arms hanging beneath his ears so that he couldn't focus properly and it was with disbelief that he forced himself to read what he and Mr Tanner were purported to have written. It made no sense. He read it again.

'What is it, dear?' asked his wife, replacing the swinging receiver.

He plucked his glasses off his nose and pushed the paper towards her across the little table. 'There,' he croaked. He rested his head against the wall and closed his eyes. He could feel the pungency in her silence as she read and had to wait as she read it again. Then he held his head in his hands, knowing she had finished it for the second time, and waited for her obvious questions that would make him angrier and more afraid than he already was.

'But you didn't write this, dear.'

'*No*,' he snapped, 'I *didn't*. No, I didn't,' he said, struggling to restrain himself. 'I didn't, that's the point.'

'But it says you did. You and Mr Tanner.'

'We wrote an article – you saw it, you read it, didn't you?'

'Yes, but it wasn't like this, was it?'

'No, it wasn't,' he answered. 'Why are you always so obtuse? I know we wrote it.' He felt a fleeting comfort at 'we'. 'But it's all been changed by that man at *The Herald*. We didn't write it like that, it was nothing like that at all.'

'It doesn't seem to be, dear.'

'*No*, it *wasn't*.'

'I'm sorry, dear, but it's not my fault.'

'I'm sorry, no, it's not. I'm not blaming you.'

'Is he allowed to change it, can he do that?'

'Well, he has. What am I going to do? People will think I wrote it.'

'What does Mr Tanner think?'

'I haven't asked him, how could I? I've only just seen it.'

'Don't upset yourself, dear.'

'*Read* it.'

'I have.'

'I wish Mr Tanner hadn't talked me into it.' A country pastor he would never be: his genteel retirement in Hampshire's leafy lanes, with cricket matches and walks by chalk streams had been irrevocably withdrawn like the best offer he had ever had. 'Why couldn't I have remained anonymous?' he rued. 'It was easy enough. I could have served out my time here. It wouldn't have been so long.' But shadows had already come into his sun-filled dreams: 'Why be a priest if that is all I aspire to, a quiet life? Is this what I am, what I *truly* am?' He shook his head. 'Was that all I was meant to be? Was that my purpose?' He had come upon the injured Bryn Hughes on the proverbial roadside and could not have refused to help. 'Did you guide me there, Lord? Was that part of my… oh, no,' he pressed the ball of his hand into his forehead, 'oh *no*… you were *testing* me, you gave me strength to *test* me. How could I not have seen it? What have I done? All this parading in the newspapers – my *pride*, I have committed the sin of *pride*. Oh Lord, I have failed you and I have received my just deserts. My eyes have been opened.' He felt dizzy as he got to his feet. 'I must pray,' he told his wife.

'In your study, dear?' Where he shared his personal troubles and sought God's advice informally.

'No,' he replied, 'in the church.'

'Oh, to really pray, dear?'

Mr Tanner thought, 'Why didn't I listen to that small voice?' But he was angered and deeply offended by Protheroe's disregard for what they had written. Its meaning had been wilfully misinterpreted. He had turned their sentences and paragraphs inside out; he had deleted words and added others. But Protheroe had been cunning so that he couldn't be accused of making it up: he had transformed a tune of subtle melodies into a cacophony of denunciations, each with a chord of its original refrain and each one accompanied by a crash of cymbals and he had twisted their words to imply that Bryn Hughes had it coming. It was a wink to Ellis and his kind and he and Reverend Ellis would have to explain it or deny they meant it and how could they do that? How cynical and how bereft of honesty and responsibility. All to sell a few more newspapers. Protheroe was beneath contempt and Mr Tanner never felt that about anyone.

He threw the newspaper in the bin but, as he walked to his empty school, he found it difficult not to be furtive. He padlocked the gate behind him and went in. He could hear hammering coming from the boiler room. That's where he was: Mr Tanner wanted to rehearse his explanation with a simple man.

'Hello, Mr Tanner.' Mr Topliss wiped away beads of sweat. 'I read what you and the Reverend said in the paper.'

'We didn't say it, Mr Topliss.'

Mr Topliss frowned. 'But it was in the paper.'

'Yes, it was, but the paper changed what we had written.'

Mr Topliss shook his head. 'Why did you tell them to do that, then?'

'We didn't. They didn't tell us they were going to.'

'Can they do that, then? Why would they do that if you didn't ask them to?'

'To sell more newspapers.'

'But I only ever buy the one or, rather, I only have the one delivered.'

'Yes,' said Mr Tanner, patiently, 'but people who wouldn't normally read *The Herald* might be tempted to buy a copy.'

'Why?'

'Because of the headline – when they see it in the newsagent.'

'Is that why you wrote it, then?'

'No, that wasn't the reason, Mr Topliss.' Mr Tanner sighed. 'What's the matter with the boiler?'

'It's the regulator, or the thermostat, I'm not sure yet.'

'Do you need a hammer for that?'

Mr Topliss looked at the hammer. 'Yes.'

'Well, I'll leave you to it, then, Mr Topliss.'

'Right you are, Headmaster,' and he was hammering again before Mr Tanner had escaped from the boiler house.

He went through the silent hall, smelling faintly of fresh paint as well as its usual mustiness, and into his office. He could still hear the hammering on the other side of the building.

Alan paced the front room clutching a distraught Aled.

'Let Eve have him, Alan,' said Gwen, 'or at least ask her to come round to see to him?'

Alan waited for Aled to come up for breath. 'But he's my child, Gwen. He has to live here. He has to. He has to have *me*.'

'Where's Auntie Jean?' asked Huw.

Aled cried harder and buried his head in his father's shoulder.

'*Ohhh*,' cried Huw, covering his ears with his elbows and stamping off into the kitchen to his usual place against the radiator.

Aled quietened and took some steadier breaths between sobs.

'It won't be forever, Alan,' said Gwen. 'What will you do with him when you go to see Jean?'

Alan looked at her and then at Brenda.

'We can, Alan,' said Gwen, 'of course we can, can't we Brenda?'

Brenda nodded.

'But, for some reason, it's only Eve that seems able to calm him down at the moment. But he'll get over it, I'm sure.'

'He must get used to me on my own,' said Alan, 'he must.'

'He will, Alan, but now, Jean needs you.'

'She doesn't know I exist.'

'It's the medication, Alan, she's still Jean.'

'My wife?'

'Yes, your wife, Alan,' said Gwen, frowning.

'Take him then, will you, and I will go to see my wife.'

He handed a surprised Aled to Gwen, who flung out his arms and legs and hit Gwen on the nose with the back of his head. Her eyes streamed as she struggled to wrap him up. Brenda helped and they forced his arms down and bunched his legs and, between them, enclosed him. Brenda put her hand over his head to stop him banging it against the kitchen door frame as they took him into the garden where there were no walls for his cries to echo off and he couldn't hear himself so loudly and, at last, he settled.

When Alan arrived at the hospital, Detective Jeffries was coming out. His woollen tie, always sorry, was halfway down his chest and the two top buttons of his shirt were missing as if he had wrenched them open.

When he saw Alan, he stopped dead and gritted his teeth. He shook with anger. '*Harris*, I'm going to get you. I don't care how long it takes, I'm going to get you. You're not going to take this away from me, no one is. Do you hear me?' He pushed past Alan, snorting through his nose.

The receptionist asked Alan, 'He said he was a detective. Is he really?'

Alan looked back through the glass door but Detective Jeffries couldn't be seen.

'We didn't let him in.' There was a big male nurse in white standing at the entrance to the wards with his arms folded. 'Honestly, I thought he was a patient.'

Alan went into the shabby lounge. The chairs were still gathered around the silent test card. 'Jean?' but there was not a flicker of recognition.

Reverend Elwiss went before the altar. He thought to prostrate himself, but he knew God wouldn't be fooled by medieval gestures. 'My vanity again,' he breathed. He knelt. Every thought, every deed, had become imbued with ulterior motives; he was riven with unintentional sin. He prayed. 'I will ask you for nothing, Lord. I have no right to ask. I surrender to your judgement.' To live in the world was to sin; to seclude yourself from it was to sin. He tried to clear his mind, to let the word of God resound: whatever penance he decided, so better to hear, to listen, to understand. Nothing came, no rising wind in the trees, no sign at all.

After an hour, Reverend Elwiss got to his feet, and rubbed the pins and needles in his calves. 'Very well,' he said, looking up at the altar, 'whichever way you choose to guide me, Lord, I am your servant.' He bowed.

Flash.

'*What*?' he gasped.

'Vicar,' demanded *Herald* Andrew, notebook poised, 'why do you think the police are failing in their duty?'

'This is the house of God.'

'Yes, it is. Why do you think the police are failing in their duty, Vicar?'

'I don't. That's not what we said.'

'Do you think they'll ever find the missing boys?'

'I pray they will.' But he had not. He had been praying for himself. Inwardly, he groaned.

'Is prayer enough if the police aren't doing their job?'

'But I'm sure they are trying to.'

'Are the police incompetent, then, Vicar?'

'No, that's not what I'm saying at all. Their professional commitment must also be seen in an ethical context, that's…'

'Is ethical the same as moral, Vicar?'

'Moral? Uh, yes, more or less, if one takes account of…'

'Thank you, Vicar. Come on. Lloydy-boy.'

'But I haven't…' Reverend Elwiss turned back to the altar. Awash with shame, he prostrated himself before it, and meant it.

'Listen, Jones,' said Detective Jeffries, 'I've got unfinished business.'

'He's not here,' Constable Dewi told him.

'Don't you think I don't know that? I know where he is every moment of the day.'

'Do you?' asked Constable Dewi, doubtfully.

'No,' he prodded Constable Dewi's shoulder with his finger. 'Yes, no, what I want to know is what *you* know.'

'About what?'

'About what? You're here all the time, what have you heard, Jones, what haven't you told me?'

'Nothing.'

'Yes, *nothing*, no, don't give me that. Yes? You know he's guilty. We both know he is.'

'No, I do not,' said Constable Dewi. 'Does Sergeant Phillips know you're here?'

'I'm his right-hand man, Jones, what do you think? Where's Colcannon?' He went in. Brenda and Gwen were still in the back garden with Aled, who was sucking his thumb and staring but no longer crying. Detective Jeffries came out of the kitchen door. 'Colcannon? *Alan*, is it? Oh, *Alan*, is it? What haven't you told me, Colcannon? All of you? I'll find out so you better tell me. If you don't, then you'll be sorry.'

Constable Dewi leaned down and whispered, acidly, in Detective Jeffries' ear, 'Leave, Jeffries, or I'll report you for drinking on duty.'

Detective Jeffries whirled round. '*Drinking*?' But he rushed past Constable Dewi and Huw sitting against the radiator and out onto the road. He looked to left and right as if he didn't know which way to go. Then he held out his arms and followed them toward the main road where he thought he had parked his car.

Flash.

Mr Tanner was locking the school gates.

'Why are the police failing in their duty, Mr Tanner?'

'I *beg* your pardon?' exclaimed a startled Mr Tanner, dropping the padlock. 'I didn't say that at all.'

'But you think the police arrested the wrong man?'

'Yes, of course I do, they did arrest the wrong man; it was inexplicable. But, let me put the record straight here, if I may? Reverend Elwiss and I did not condemn the police. We did no such thing.'

'Bryn Hughes is innocent, then?'

'Yes, he's innocent,' said Mr Tanner, angrily, 'and he is now in hospital suffering from grievous injuries that resulted from his name – and his picture, I might add...'

'Running away,' interrupted *Herald* Andrew, nudging Lloyd.

'I might *add,* from a picture which you took and your newspaper printed and, yes, he is *totally* innocent.'

'So, that's why you condemned the police, Mr Tanner?'

Mr Tanner took a deep breath. 'We did *not* condemn the police and, if your newspaper did not print such inflammatory articles it would not provoke gossip or incite what can only be described as the actions of a lynch mob.'

'Lynch... mob,' repeated *Herald* Andrew, writing in his notebook. 'Thank you, Headmaster. Come on Lloydy-boy.'

Sergeant Phillips read *The Herald* in his big, black car then he folded it carefully, as he might a map, making sure there were no creases, so that the edges came together with perfect symmetry, wanting to keep it for a purpose more lasting than chip papers. He placed it on the passenger seat, inspected the fingertips of his brown leather gloves for ink stains, tightened them over his knuckles and pouted his moustache. He started the engine and gently pressed the accelerator so that his big, black car glided away with velvety smoothness.

The blond man said, 'Soon, Huw.'

'Is soon today?' asked Huw.

'Tomorrow will be today, very soon, Huw.'

'*Ohhh*, will it? I want it to be *now*.'

'It will soon be now.'

'Can Jack come too, when he comes home from the shop?'

'Yes, he can come, Huw.' To the fair by the sea, with the sound of the waves and the lively music.

'I can hear the sea,' said Huw.

'I know you can,' said the blond man, 'so can I.'

CHAPTER EIGHTEEN

Sierra Leone, Solomon Islands, Somaliland...

The line of searchers assumed the crenelated shape of the houses and gardens, marking each one with an *S* on their maps, until they reached the hotel, redoubtable on its promontory, high above the Bristol Channel, savagely rough today, sending a barrage of waves thumping into the promenade wall and surfing back on themselves in a haze of rainbows. At the end of the promenade was the harbour. 'I am close,' said Sergeant Phillips. 'There is no escape.'

There were days when acres of blank paper taunted him from the desktop, when concocting a drama from a dispute between neighbours about an encroaching tree and births, deaths and marriages were the only news fodder he had. Not lately; not today. He already had the next two front pages prepared. He had them side by side:

Police Immoral Claims Vicar

Over a picture of Reverend Elwiss caught in a seemingly righteous pose before the altar, arms outstretched, when he had been remonstrating with *Herald* Andrew.

Terrified Townsfolk a Lynch Mob Says Headmaster

With a picture of Mr Tanner locking the school gates. All Protheroe had to decide was which to run first.

He spun his chair and rubbed a hole in the dirty window with his finger. The river, swollen with rain, was brown and bowling along. He jiggled his leg, unable to contain himself. Doug Protheroe was at the fulcrum of a story that was attracting interest in the national press. Sales were at record levels. Even at his age, he nursed dreams of Fleet Street and escaping this small, grey town in South Wales.

'Knock, knock,' said *Herald* Andrew, coming in through the always open door. 'You were looking for me, boss?'

Protheroe swivelled his chair round. 'Look at these,' he said, opening his hands to present the headlines.

'Aye, aye,' said *Herald* Andrew, 'the copy's not bad either.'

'But it's the headline that catches the eye that sells the newspaper, Andrew.'

'Right you are, boss, I do the hard work and let you have the credit.'

'It was ever thus, young man. What else have you got for me?'

'Well,' *Herald* Andrew replied, making himself comfortable in the creaky wooden chair, 'what do you want?' he smirked.

'More,' said Protheroe, 'more of the same and keep it coming.'

'More on the vicar and the headmaster? That's easy enough.'

'And?'

'There's the parents, we haven't got much on them yet, not since the appeal, but I'm working on it and more on the girlfriend, fiancée or whatever, and,' he lowered his voice, 'I hear that Mrs Harris has had a breakdown and been taken in.'

'Has she *indeed*?'

'I was going down there with Lloydy later. We'll get some outside shots, at least.'

'Get on with it then.'

'I was, boss, it's only you holding me up.' They both laughed.

The phone rang. 'This is Douglas Protheroe?' He stiffened as if he been told to sit up straight. He held his hand up to stop *Herald* Andrew from leaving and pointed at the receiver. 'Yes, Sergeant Phillips.'

Herald Andrew's eyebrows lifted.

'We can do that… delighted… always… thank you for calling me.' He replaced the receiver with great delicacy as if the voice within had given it a mystical quality. He rested his chin on his thumbs; his eyes had become almost dreamy. The day had got even better (if that was possible). 'That was Sergeant Phillips,' he said.

'I gathered that,' said *Herald* Andrew.

'Get this written before you do anything else,' Protheroe said. Then he told him what.

Mr Tanner held his head up defiantly as he walked up the busy street. He saw Ellis coming towards him on the other side. Mr Tanner stared him down with a furious glower. But, when they were close, Ellis gave him the thumbs up, whether in approval or mockery, Mr Tanner was too taken aback to decide. He watched Ellis, hands in his pockets, trailing smoke from a cigarette dangling from his lips, heading towards The Red Lion with the tired lope that had been insolent during his school days but had become slovenly as life continued to refuse him what he believed was his due.

Not far away, a man winked at Reverend Elwiss as he passed and said, 'Nice one, Vicar.'

Mr Tanner and Reverend Elwiss met outside the main doors of the hospital without having arranged to.

'Reverend Elwiss?'

'Mr Tanner?'

'Why are you here?'

'To offer an explanation, if I can.'

'Yes,' said Mr Tanner, 'I didn't think I would ever find myself doing something like this.'

'Nor I,' replied the Reverend, 'but we must.'

'It was a mistake to offer to write that article. Please accept my apologies for suggesting it.'

'There is no need to apologise, Mr Tanner. I would like to think we are guilty of naivety and misplaced trust but there is more to it, I fear, as I reflect upon it, as I have had to, but it is not for ourselves that we should be concerned.'

'So very true, Vicar. Shall we go in?' Mr Tanner pushed open the heavy doors.

Laura, her father and Bryn's parents were gathered in the waiting room. A copy of *The Herald* was on the table with a corner of the *National Geographic* poking out from under it. Faint hope that they might not have seen it.

'The nurse showed us,' said Laura.

Mr Tanner sat down with Reverend Elwiss next to him. He searched for a preamble. None occurred, so he said, simply, 'It was not what we wrote and it was certainly not what we meant and I – *we* – understand how terribly upsetting it is for you.' He tugged at his earlobe. 'But, what we want to say,' he looked at Reverend Elwiss, who nodded, gravely, 'it was a great mistake to have written it. It doesn't matter what our intentions were, it is what has resulted from it that matters and we want to say how sincerely sorry we are to have placed this additional burden on you at such a difficult time.'

Reverend Elwiss said, 'Words we say now cannot expunge the words that have been printed, indelibly...' he tightened his lips in disgust as his eyes were drawn inexorably to the picture of Mr Tanner and himself outside his church, 'in that… *newspaper*. I am truly sorry and ashamed, yes, ashamed…' he trailed off, remembering his compact before the altar.

'But the picture of Bryn too?' asked his mother, tearfully.

Mr Tanner shook his head. 'I did not believe they would print that. I truly didn't.'

'But he's not your son,' replied Mrs Hughes.

Bryn's father put his arm around his wife. 'It's not Mr Tanner's fault, Susan.'

She slumped a little: the blame was elsewhere.

'It's a sorry business all round, Mr Tanner.'

'It is. I'm not going to search for any more words. Enough has been said, more than enough, it's words that have got us here, and me, a teacher of the English language,' as if words had betrayed him and not the editor of *The Herald*.

'Those boys,' said Laura, quietly. They sat in silence; no one looked at each other.

They stared at *The Herald* until Laura's father drew the *National Geographic* out from under it and covered the picture of Mr Tanner and Reverend Elwiss with the black woman's breasts.

'I would like to ask,' said Reverend Elwiss, when the offensive image had been hidden, 'if there is anything we can do that would be of any help although, I fear, the answer would be that you've already done enough but, I will ask nonetheless: is there anything?'

Mr Hughes smiled, sombrely. 'If Bryn recovers, if those boys are found, there'll be nothing else to ask for.'

Mr Tanner placed his hands on his knees. 'Let us hope so, let us dearly hope so.'

'Let us pray so,' said Reverend Elwiss.

'Bryn is on his own,' said Mrs Hughes.

'No, Mrs Hughes, in God's eyes, we are never alone.'

'No, he's on his own.'

The Reverend looked surprised.

'I mean he's on his own, there's no one sitting with him.'

'Ah.'

'I'll go,' said Laura, and stood up.

Mr Tanner said, 'Reverend Elwiss and I are going to see that detective's superiors to make our views known – although I suspect we will have to explain what we meant, or didn't, by that article before we do, as the police are portrayed as the villains, as it were.'

'I'll stay here,' said Mrs Hughes to Laura. 'Those machines… but tell me the moment there is any change.'

'I will,' Laura answered.

Bryn was looking peaceful, or so she thought. His bruises were not so livid, as if his injuries were receding from the memory, and his breathing seemed more confident. But none of this was perceptible to thc machines. 'Bryn?' she asked.

It was before opening time when Ellis Maynard arrived at The Red Lion. Detective Jeffries was waiting outside. They sized each other up.

'What are you doing here,' demanded Ellis, 'I haven't done anything – what did Dewi Jones say about me?'

'I'm not here for you and I'm not on duty,' said Detective Jeffries.

'What are you here for, then?'

'The same reason as you, Maynard, for a drink. What's it look like?'

Ellis digested his answer. He couldn't. 'Right,' he said.

They waited in awkward silence until, inside, there was the sound of heavy bolts being drawn back.

'After you,' said Detective Jeffries.

Ellis frowned suspiciously but he led the way into the empty pub, full with promise.

'Do you want a pint, then?' asked Detective Jeffries.

That was too much. 'What's your game, Jeffries?'

'Do you want a pint or not, Maynard?'

'I always want a pint.'

They sat on the bar stools and waited for both pints to be poured (to be polite), briefly admired the poetry of their creamy heads, and plunged in their faces and drained them.

'Same again,' said Ellis.

Two more came. They didn't wait to admire this time.

Ellis drank because he did, and would, without stopping, day in day out, until he was dead. He chain smoked. It was unnerving to be drinking with a policeman but, after a few pints, moving on to whisky, he stopped caring.

'There we are,' said Detective Jeffries, who drank to be numb. As he drank, he boasted to Ellis about his time with Sergeant Phillips. He told him a lot of things he shouldn't. Neither of them would remember.

The criminal and the policeman drank together all day until, at 4.20pm (on the dot), drinking-up time done, they staggered out into the failing light with take-outs to keep them going.

'What are we going to do until they open again?'

'Get some chips,' replied Ellis, 'and drink these. Let's take them down by the river.'

'Right you are,' said Detective Jeffries, and they headed to the chip shop and then down to the river where they drank the bottles under the trees like a pair of tramps.

Just before 6pm, in the dark, they emerged from the playing fields into the lights of the town and were outside The Red Lion to hear the bolts coming off the door. At the same bar stools, they resumed.

'Where's Aled?' Gwen asked Alan.

'He's asleep upstairs. He was so exhausted, he went straight off after you left last night and now I'm afraid to wake him.'

'Have you thought anymore about Eve?'

'He's all I have and if I give him to Eve, I'll be giving him away.'

'He's not all you have, Alan.'

'Not you?' he replied, quietly, hearing Brenda filling the kettle in the kitchen.

Gwen looked away.

'He has a mother who does not know him and a brother he will not remember and that leaves me.'

'Huw was a brother he might have had,' she said.

'Was? Perhaps they can still be as close as brothers?'

She sighed. 'We can only hope for that. Jean will come home, soon, Alan, I'm sure.'

'Come home to what? I am afraid there is nothing for her here…'

'Aled will still be here.'

'And we'll go back to living in our houses, yards apart when it might as well be a hundred miles.'

Brenda called, 'Tea.'

'More tea?' said Gwen. 'If we must.'

They went into the kitchen and sat down.

Alan looked at Brenda and asked, 'Why is he persecuting us? I know you hate him.'

Brenda raised the tea to her lips and looked into the cup and didn't answer.

Alan reached across the table and placed two fingers on the rim and pressed it down.

Her eyes followed it. She said, 'I'm here to support you, that's why I'm here, and Dewi, to stop people bothering you and provide information about progress.'

'That isn't an answer.'

'Sergeant Phillips doesn't tell me anymore than he thinks I need to know, which is nothing.'

'Don't we deserve to know?' asked Gwen.

'Yes,' said Brenda, 'you do.' She lifted the mug back up to her mouth, held between both hands, and blew gently into it to cool the tea.

'That's Aled,' said Alan, looking up at the ceiling.

'*Ohhh*,' groaned Huw, from his place by the radiator.

'I mustn't leave him,' said Alan, 'in case he starts up again. I'll take him out to the garden to see if I can get him in a better mood before he does.' When he came back, he was carrying a sleepy Aled.

Huw folded his arms and banged his elbows on his knees. 'When's Jack coming home,' he asked, crossly, thoroughly fed up with the prospect of Aled screaming all day and no one to play with, 'and when's Uncle Roy going to start on his new greenhouse?' Was today tomorrow and would he be able to go to Trecco soon – and why was school still closed? Had Mr Tanner died?

Alan walked up and down the garden path trying to keep Aled entertained. He glanced over the fence. Was Eve watching and hoping he would take Aled to her? But the curtains were still closed; the house no longer seemed lived in. He hadn't seen her leave. Was she still there? There was no sign that she was.

Mr Tanner and Reverend Elwiss approached the police station with trepidation. 'Our penitential progress,' said the

Reverend, 'going from door to door making explanations when it is that newspaper editor who should be explaining.'

'He knew what he was doing and we didn't,' replied Mr Tanner, 'and offering explanations was never going to be part of his plan.'

'What shall we say?' asked Reverend Elwiss.

'I think we should begin by telling Sergeant Phillips that it was not our intention to criticise the police,' answered Mr Tanner. 'We need to make that clear straightaway.'

'Will he believe us?'

Mr Tanner turned to the vicar in surprise, 'Dressed like that?'

'Well, yes, of course,' said Reverend Elwiss, flustered.

'Is there any reason why he shouldn't believe us?'

'No, but we've given him a reason not to listen to us if he doesn't want to.'

'We should have kept a copy of what we wrote. We could have shown him that.'

'Yes,' said Reverend Elwiss, 'that would have been very helpful. I don't suppose Mr Protheroe will give us his?'

'That's hardly likely, Vicar.'

'My first name is Ernest.'

'Is it? Ernest Elwiss, you've got to have your teeth in, haven't you?'

They laughed. It helped.

'I'm Raymond.'

They told the policeman behind the desk why they were there and waited like two nervous schoolboys outside Mr Tanner's office (who sometimes made them wait), staring at the door to the inner sanctum of mystery.

Mr Tanner said, 'We are in the right, here, let's not forget that.'

'Yes, we are, Raymond,' replied Reverend Elwiss, 'we most certainly are. *Stiffen the sinews,*' he added, bravely.

'*Summon up the blood.*'

No one came or went for half an hour. Then he was there, standing in the doorway, running his thumbs over his moustache (gloved, even now), his hat upon his head, his matt black eyes fixed on them from under its peak, his face stone-like, hostilely expressionless, making no effort to greet them or recognise their mutual bond of authority or the assumed trust that would clear up this obvious misunderstanding in no time at all. He was as intimidating as it was possible for a policeman to be. They had come to him, they had to explain why.

Mr Tanner and Reverend Elwiss got to their feet.

Sergeant Phillips didn't move. He filled the doorway like a monolith. It was here, in the police station's public place, where criminals were admitted and old ladies with lost cats could listen, that he was going to make them present their case.

Mr Tanner didn't know what to do with his hands so he clasped them together. They almost sidled up to him until Mr Tanner found himself looking up Sergeant Phillips' nostrils, like two portholes above his raven moustache, his eyes no longer visible under their canopy.

Sergeant Phillips did not incline his head.

Reverend Elwiss copied Mr Tanner with his hands.

Now, they had to find the words. Mr Tanner cleared his throat. 'Sergeant Phillips,' he began, 'I am sure that you will have read the article in *The Herald*?' High above was the silence of an icon. 'It was most unfortunate. When we wrote the article, Reverend Elwiss and I, we did not write it as it appeared. The editor at *The Herald* edited it. He changed it substantially. Its meaning became not what we intended and most certainly not the headline that accompanied it – which we had absolutely nothing to do with. We want to reassure you that under no circumstances would we criticise the police, let alone use incendiary vocabulary such as "condemn".'

'No, we most certainly would not,' said Reverend Elwiss.

'We wanted to explain,' continued Mr Tanner, 'so that there is no misunderstanding and to assure you of our full support.'

They waited for Sergeant Phillips to speak. He did not.

Reverend Elwiss' hand crept to the crucifix around his neck.

'But, that is not the sole reason we are here,' Mr Tanner's voice wavered like a teenage boy. 'Although an explanation for the newspaper article is reason enough. But, no,' Mr Tanner rushed to his point, gabbling, before he failed completely, 'we wish to bring to your attention the behaviour of Detective Jeffries.' He expected Sergeant Phillips to interrupt him. He did not. 'On two occasions, once when I came to him with information about Bryn Hughes' assailant – information, I believe, which could be instrumental in bringing him to book – and, on the second occasion when neither of us was present, he came to the hospital with two men from *The Herald* to take pictures of Mr Hughes on his sickbed.'

'And he was very offensive in his questioning of Laura Williams, Mr Hughes' fiancée, immediately after the attack,' said Reverend Elwiss, feeling the crucifix digging into his palm (stigmata? 'Lord?'), 'which she had just witnessed and was in a state of shock. It was most unnecessary.'

'We believe you should be made aware of Detective Jeffries' behaviour,' ended Mr Tanner.

Sergeant Phillips pouted his moustache. Then he spoke, his words thrumming like a hive, 'Write a formal complaint and I will act.'

Out of the corner of his eye, Mr Tanner saw the policeman behind the desk hold out a form.

Sergeant Phillips turned and the door closed behind him.

Reverend Elwiss was shaking. 'I didn't expect that,' he said, and let go of the cross.

'No,' said Mr Tanner. 'What will he do, I wonder?'

There was nothing to do. Detective Jeffries was already sleeping in the gutter.

At last, the tides washed the black silt away, bathed him clean and left him partly expressed like a china clay mould, a Wedgewood boy in soft relief, waiting…

Chapter Nineteen

South Africa, South-West Africa...

Only to be seen. It is first light and the tide is ebbing, settling the boats onto the harbour mud.

EXCLUSIVE: Sergeant Phillips Takes Charge

Said the headline over a half-page picture of the dark Emperor standing next to his big, black car outside the Harris' house and, beneath, a smaller picture of the tiny sandal, with the grass pulled back, where it had been found. *In an exclusive interview, Sergeant Phillips has told* The Herald *that he is following a number of important lines of enquiry, including the discovery of a child's sandal near Kenfig Pool identified as belonging to missing boy Jack Harris. 'I am close,' he said, 'there is no escape for whoever did this. I want him to know that.'* The Herald *understands that painstaking police-work and expert judgement has led to the latest breakthrough. Sergeant Phillips declined to comment on recent press reports about progress on related cases except to say that enquiries were continuing and it would be counter-productive to release further information.* The Herald *has followed Sergeant Phillips' impressive career in the town for some time and it is the considered opinion of many, including this newspaper, that Bridgend is lucky to have him.*

'Say you did it because we know you did.'

'I didn't, I didn't, I *didn't*.' He heard the sounds of the words but didn't understand what they meant; he smelt stale cigarette smoke and old beer but didn't know what smell was; he saw fractured images of a room and two faces, one whose mouth was moving, the other punctuated with black but he didn't know what sight was.

'What are you crying for?' He heard the sound of crying but didn't know that it was him. Then it was colder.

'Why have the police released you? Are they going to ask you any more questions, Mr Hughes?'

Flash… flash.

'It's over, Bryn, all over and done with. It was wrong, I know, very wrong… what of it… what's a few photos… they'll be chip papers tomorrow… you didn't have anything to run from, Bryn.'

'I do not know how badly you are hurt because I am not a doctor, but you have a choice. It is your choice, Bryn Hughes.'

Bleep… bleep.

'They *must* have proper cause before accusations are made. You can't suspend the rule of law, no matter *what* the circumstances… these events will not defeat us, we will go on, come what may.'

'How will I get over this? How will I ever be able to go into a classroom again?'

'It is your choice, Bryn Hughes, but, remember, you do not make it only for yourself.'

'When they find the boys, Bryn, and catch who did it.'

'While I am still a suspect?'

'No, you're not.'

'And who is to say I'm not? Sergeant Phillips, the papers, the whole town – what else are they supposed to think until they know otherwise?'

'Isn't it for you to say, Bryn Hughes?'

'Bryn, as Mr Tanner said, it's over, that's the end of it. They were wrong, just wrong.'

'I don't think even Mr Tanner can put this right.'

'You will not remember what happened next, Bryn Hughes, and I do not have the power to make you… wait… wait… it is over.' The wind rose in the trees.

'Only *one* at a time.'

'I must go back to my wife, she's not coping very well. Look after him, won't you?'

'What can I do?'

'Laura?'

'Good, Bryn Hughes.'

'Everything the doctors can't – or that nurse. I'm going to take my wife for a walk… We won't be long… I'll see you later too.' He felt his father's kiss on his cheek.

'Dad?'

'Keep trying, Bryn Hughes.'

'Miss Williams? When can I speak to him?'

'What are you doing here? You shouldn't be here.'

'The question is *why* did they do it to him, Miss Williams?'

'Because of what was in the paper, that's why – when he was outside the police station – after all the questions you asked him for no reason, and me, for no reason, that's why.'

'No one's going to help you.'

'Why don't you help yourself, Bryn Hughes?'

Flash… flash.

'Well, Bryn Hughes, what sort of man are you? Will you be a sad footnote? Will you let Laura marry another man? Will you let her bear another man's children? Will you let your parents grieve or make them proud? Will you let Mr Tanner's efforts be for nothing – he fought for you. What is it to be, Bryn Hughes?'

He was offered his life back: he saw the ceiling as the sky and the bright light above his head as the sun. He felt the warmth of the ward as a summer's day and the bleeping of the machines was birdsong.

'Well, Bryn Hughes, well? Make your choice.'

He opened his eyes but another slept with her eyes open, in the armchair of the day room, held there without choice, growing older with no perception of time, gathered with others around the silent television. Periodically, her medication was reduced to enliven her, to see how she was, to find out what was left. '*Where are my children?*' Each time they sent her back. What purpose this served, how she could be saved, no one questioned. It could go on forever because, in the outside world, if the reason remained the same, there was no reason to change anything. After a while, they referred to it as her 'condition'. Every patient had one.

Was it the next day, days after, weeks, months, a year? Ellis Maynard and Detective Jeffries met outside The Red Lion before opening time. Their previous bonhomie was fuzzy, a vague recollection that was renewed in a fug as the day progressed. Then chips and drinking down by the river, back to The Red Lion and the evening was lost. How they got home, how they got to bed? Until they woke up the following day in dirty, stinking clothes, still damp which, in Ellis' case, were not changed.

They said little to each other as they waited for the doors to open. They busied in when they did, desperate to drown the effects and still their shaking hands.

The landlord poured them pints without asking; neither did he make small talk when he poured them their second. He was disdainfully familiar with how it went, so long as they took trouble elsewhere and he cared nothing for whether the man was a policeman or had been, because he knew what he was now and every pub in town had an Ellis, some of them more than one.

Every day, Ellis and Detective Jeffries learnt how to

be best friends. The morning drifted on and they began to slur and, by mid-afternoon, they were draped over each other, swearing undying loyalty with watery eyes and disconnected sentences.

Sometimes, when the landlord got fed up with them sitting at the bar, he banished them to the dark corner behind the piano where, if they didn't try play it, he let them stay. But, he would throw them out the moment they started bothering other customers.

At last orders, they bought some bottles and staggered out as the doors were shut. They were too drunk to be served at the chip shop and the owner threatened to call the police if they didn't leave. Detective Jeffries waved his imagined warrant card but it made no difference so they headed for the river in the darkness.

Under the trees, in what might have been the same spot as every day before, they sat on the top of the steep bank and drank, rolling the bottles off into the water.

Ellis started the argument. There was no reason for it, but it turned into a fight. They wrestled impotently then Ellis picked up a bottle – a full one – and smashed it into Detective Jeffries' face. Then he kicked him off the bank into the river.

Later, Ellis tottered back to The Red Lion with no recollection of what he had done; he hardly remembered Detective Jeffries at all.

The landlord asked, 'Where's your mate, then?'

Ellis swayed over the bar and tried to sort his change.

'Get out, Maynard, I'm not serving you in that state.' After protests, the landlord bundled Ellis through the door.

The police found him on a bench and locked him up for the night to sleep it off. In the morning, they let him out and he was back at The Red Lion before it opened.

The landlord shook his head as he let him in. 'Where's your mate this morning, Maynard?'

'Who?' asked Ellis, proffering the exact change because he knew the prices from the pumps to the top shelf by heart. It was just another anonymous day for Ellis Maynard.

Constable Dewi stood in the doorway of the kitchen. It was a moment before they noticed him.

Alan sensed his presence and looked up, then Gwen and Brenda did too.

Huw craned his neck up his leg and was relieved it wasn't Sergeant Phillips at the top.

'They have found a body.'

'A body?' Huw asked.

Constable Dewi took a deep breath, 'In Porthcawl. Alan, will you come with me and I'll take you there.'

'Yes,' he said, in little more than a whisper. He looked at Gwen and handed Aled to her.

He let out a scream and stuck his thumb in his mouth and stared resentfully at Alan with his head resting under Gwen's chin.

She felt the softness of his hair and his gently warm breath on her skin. He dribbled down her cleavage but she barely noticed and didn't wipe it away.

'Yes,' Alan said, again, and slowly stood up. His limbs ached and he had difficulty in straightening himself. He felt thirty years older, as frail and sick as his father before he died. 'Will you stay here?' he asked Brenda.

'I'll be here when you get back, Alan,' but what was the point of reassurances? She had been there mostly for the women because the men pretended not to need her. It lessened her task but did not dismiss it. She was glad Constable Dewi had given the news; she had never done this before (and neither had he, there were others who had, and she wondered why they had been chosen: no doubt Sergeant Phillips' decision) and she never wanted to do it again.

'Shall we go, Dewi?' said Alan, like glass bending in a warping, greenhouse frame.

They left without another word and the remaining emptiness filled with the dreadful strain of waiting that was worse than the unbearable strain of not knowing because the verdict would be final: who?

Constable Dewi didn't drive fast, it was the latter of life and death, and he only used the blue lights and the siren once to get through the traffic at the roundabout on the bypass and then they turned left onto the Porthcawl road that led directly into the town centre.

They did not speak. They emerged onto the promenade and drove along it to the harbour. Constable Dewi parked the car, unable to get close because of the other police cars clustered around the slipway where an ambulance had been reversed up. Both its back doors were open. A stretcher lay on the concrete just before the slope began. The harbour was mirror calm but its waters were murky.

'Do you want me to come with you, Alan?' asked Constable Dewi.

'Yes.'

Everyone turned to look at them, then they turned away, thinking of themselves and the families they still had.

Next to the stretcher, there was a small bundle wrapped in a grey blanket, shaped like a pupa.

Two ambulance men stood near.

A policeman knelt. He was fighting away tears.

Alan knelt next to him and nodded and the policeman drew back the blanket.

Sergeant Phillips' big, black car murmured along the promenade and stopped.

Everyone looked, except Alan, who was leaning back on his hands, awed by the serenity of innocence.

Sergeant Phillips yanked his tunic straight and ran his thumbs down his moustache. He tightened his gloves over his knuckles. He walked slowly to the top of the slipway.

His shadow fell across the child and, then, Alan looked up at him.

The policeman let the blanket fall. He smoothed its edges. It became a bundle again.

Sergeant Phillips went back to his big, black car. He got in. It seemed to float up the promenade before turning off in the direction of the train station.

'Alan,' said Constable Dewi, 'there is nothing more. Shall we go?'

'Yes.'

They drove back to Bridgend in a different silence because now they knew and others must be told. Alan went into the kitchen with Constable Dewi behind him.

Gwen was still holding Aled. He hadn't moved. A long rivulet of dribble ran down between her breasts and the top of her dress was wet. 'Is it Huw?'

'Yes.'

'I knew it would be.'

'Tomorrow is today and soon is now, Huw,' said the blond man over the fence.

Huw jumped off the back step and ran into the alley. 'Is it? Can we go to Trecco now, can we?'

The blond man held out his hand and Huw took it. 'Yes, we can.' Huw skipped alongside him. 'If you're Buttons, Huw, what shall we call your dog?'

'Have I got a dog, *have* I?'

'Yes you do.'

'I haven't thought of a name.'

'What about Sam?'

'But that's Mr Harris' dog's name.'

'It's a good name for a dog, though, isn't it?'

'Yes, it is, but there can't be two Sams.'

'There's only one, Huw, but as long as you agree it's a good name?'

'I do.'

'That's settled then.'

'Arrest him, Prosser,' ordered Sergeant Phillips.

Detective Prosser, Sergeant Phillips' latest familiar, pulled Alan's hands behind his back and put him in handcuffs.

'Did you think you could escape me, Harris? I know your mind.'

'Alan?' Gwen's face was chalk. 'Alan?'

'No, Gwen, *no*. Why are you doing this?' he demanded of Sergeant Phillips.

'Because you're guilty,' said Detective Prosser.

'Where is my *son*?'

'Mine, what of mine?' Gwen pleaded, 'he's gone.'

'Gwen?' Alan cried, as Detective Prosser took him outside.

Flash.

The news moved on. Protheroe discarded the unused headlines and made up a banner replacement.

CHILD'S BODY FOUND

It said who, where and how before rushing breathlessly on to yet more praise for... *Sergeant Phillips... Sergeant Phillips... Sergeant Phillips.*

Chapter Twenty

Straits Settlements, Swaziland, Tanganyika...

He listened for the clacking sound of the van's old engine and the groaning of its suspension as it rolled in the potholes but it did not come back. He saw a movement, and pressed himself against the wall: half a cat, black and white, a sketch but, unmistakeably, a cat. It lifted onto its paws and arched its back, absorbing silence into its softness. It came towards him and rubbed itself back and fore on his bare shins and flexed its cheek against his knee and purred. Even in the darkness, there was a highlight in its liquid eyes that regarded him judgementally.

Rain suddenly pattered on the roof like a handful of chippings and quickly set in, becoming louder and constant. Drips fell on him and became a stream. He shuffled to one side. The cat was in the dry, but it stopped purring and curled up at his feet and went to sleep.

He tried to see if there was anyone else. 'Hello?' he whispered, but there was no reply to be heard over the drumming rain. 'Hello?' He stared into the darkness, at shapes that could be a man's head and shoulders, a face, two huge hands. They grew larger, closer, looming, becoming a man, a ghost, a ghoul. He waved his arms. It was beyond his reach, waiting there: a nose, a mouth, breath. 'Who are you?' The rain became a frenzy. He couldn't be heard. He would not say it louder. It might answer. The rain died back. He stared at the shapes. They changed: two men, one crouching. They changed again. One man standing: that was his head. The rain slowed and stopped. He listened. It was quiet except for a few drips falling wetly onto the sacks and sharply between them onto the wooden floor.

Light came budding through knotholes and gaps in the planks and the hairline cracks in the corner of the roof. It made a board of snakes and ladders, which his uncles at the shop had taught him, and chess too, which they never let him win (but he was getting better) and draughts, which was easy and sometimes he did win.

His dim world was a hut or a shed. Sacks, the shapes were heaped sacks. There were more sacks strewn on the floor, like the ones in the van, reeking of diesel and sourness. The planks smelt of tar. His father and Uncle Roy had creosoted the fence together, each from their own side, talking and laughing as he watched in Uncle Roy's garden with Huw. Auntie Eve brought them squash and ruffled their hair as she always did. It was a hot afternoon in the school holidays, their first (how grown up they had felt).

The heap of sacks did not move. The man beneath did not throw them aside. Jack stood up slowly, sliding up the wall, with his hands flat against it. The planks were oily smooth.

The cat sprang away, immediately awake, landed, and was instantly still as if it was a practised trick. It raised a paw and licked it leisurely, stretched and slinked to another dry spot and kneaded a sack before curling up again, but not to sleep: to watch and calculate.

Jack's eyes stung with tiredness. More light. He crept over to the pile of sacks and carefully lifted up the top one, then the next, peeling them back, until he could see bare boards. He sat down on them. He saw two doors on rails. He jumped up and rushed to open them. They wouldn't. Chains rattled on the other side. He looked up, searching for a catch or a handle. A dog barked. The cat stiffened. '*Sam*?' It barked again, further away. '*Grandpa*?' He tried to get his fingers in the crack between the doors. '*Grandpa*?' There were no more barks. He sank down with his legs under him, small, and fell forward onto his hands. Tiredness crushed him to sleep.

He slept with the buses grinding up Trebanog hill outside, safe inside beneath his auntie's satin eiderdown; the white beaches of Ceylon, 'Uncle Idris?' In the morning, the fire began to crackle and the butter was on the black hearth.

He woke up late in the afternoon, to the smell of diesel from the rough sacks, and rolled onto his back.

Alphonsi's ice cream. To be in the café with its red benches and Mr Alphonsi smoking and talking to Grandpa. Grandpa, dad, Uncle Roy, Mr Tanner, Gwyn the Milk, his uncles, his protectors, those who made his world and permitted entry. This hut did not have their permission to be in his life.

He heard the van. He ran at the wall. He ran at it again: at the doors, at the other wall. He bounced from one side to the other. The walls threw him back. He lay amongst the sacks and turned on his side, waiting for the doors to be slid apart. He couldn't hear the van. It had stopped outside. He waited for the chains to rattle, for a crack of widening light to appear between the doors. He waited. They stayed shut.

He felt for the loose plank. It bent outwards, enough to see the grass. It was stiff and he couldn't hold it open. He looked for something to lever it with. There was nothing. He lay on his back and banged it with his heels and the balls of his feet, swapping legs. It shuddered but would not give, snapping back into place. He kept at it until he was sweating. He took off his jumper.

The cat nuzzled it as if it liked the warmth and smell of him.

His legs were tired. He took off a sandal and put his hand into it to give his feet a rest. He hit it over and over, jarring his arm. He changed hands. The plank began to bend outwards from further up. He stopped and pushed at the plank with his shoulder. His feet scrabbled on the wooden floor. It bent more. There was a sudden crack and the plank fell out from top to bottom and thumped onto the grass. He tried to squeeze through sideways. He got stuck with one half outside, feeling the cooler air and the endless space; he could breathe it with his head sideways. He scraped his face. It let him go and he fell onto the grass and sand.

He looked back through the gap. He could see his jumper, with the cat curled up on it, and his sandal, but he couldn't reach them. He left them. His sock was already soaking wet.

He peeped around the side of the hut: it was an old railway car, he had seen them in the marshalling yards with Grandpa. There was no sign of the van. A farm track stretched away across fields. He ran as fast as he could in the opposite direction toward the dunes.

The cat came to the gap in the planks and looked out and sniffed. It went back to his warm jumper.

He sank in the sand and lost his sock. He was out of breath when he reached the top. From there, he could see the foaming rocks and the barren span of Sker, the fiery eyes beyond and, on the breeze, the faint smell of sulphur; in the other direction was Pink Bay, the beginning of Rest Bay and Porthcawl, too far.

He ran down the other side, big leaps and fell and got a mouthful of wet sand. At the bottom, between the dunes and hidden from sight, he wandered amongst the brambles and scrub, with one bare foot, with the marram grass whipping at his legs, the thorns spiking and tearing at him, tiring, so he waded on the dunes' steep sides. He left a trail of footprints not much bigger than a bird's. He limped. He saw no one. The dunes were as endless as a desert.

It grew dark quickly and started to rain again. He crawled under a scrappy bush, drew up his knees, wrapped his arms around them and rested his head. The rain came in and ran down his back and through his hair. The wind moaned in the dunes as if they were tunnels and stung his legs with sand.

The sky over the dunes was lit with flashing blue lights. He watched them from his hiding place, afraid to come out, terrified of being mischiefed. After a while, the blue lights grew less and his head nodded back onto his arms resting on his knees as the rain ran over him and the sand was wet and scratchy between his toes: this once happy place, with Grandpa and Sam. The Seychelles' warm seas, *Perf. Wmk. 10 Cents.*

Eve Guthrie bustled out with her face set and determined, through her broken garden, tarnished with flourishing weeds like an old bomb site, into the alley and into Alan and Jean's house. She didn't knock and would not have thought to and would not have waited to be asked in (not the inhuman Jean banging at her front door).

Gwen sat with Aled in the kitchen. Dirty tea mugs were still on the table, cold and unused.

Brenda was on the other side. They had not spoken for some time. Brenda was doing her best to let Gwen be alone without leaving. She watched clouds through the window. Aled was a remnant they had no answer for, but must, soon, and here was Eve. Brenda jumped as she came in.

Eve's eyes fixed on Aled and softened with relief and a faint smile. 'Cariad,' she said. 'Give him to me, Gwen.'

'Eve?' asked Brenda.

Eve stood at the head of the table with her hands on her hips.

Aled wriggled and leaned from Gwen toward her.

'Let me have him,' said Eve, 'please.' But it was a command.

Gwen frowned. 'He's been sitting quietly.'

'No, Gwen, let me have him. You have enough to bear.' She took him and he came to her eagerly. 'Cariad, cariad,' she cooed, and closed her eyes.

He snuggled his head into her shoulder.

She swayed with him.

His blue eyes looked into her face as if she was the Madonna.

'Cariad, cariad.' She turned to leave.

'Where are you going?' asked Gwen.

'I'm taking you home, aren't I cariad?'

'This is his home,' said Brenda.

Eve turned back to face them. She pulled Aled tighter. 'Home is where your family is.' She tickled him under the chin.

Brenda stood up. 'Eve?'

'Who else is going to look after him? Gwen? You, Brenda? It's because of the police that he's on his own.'

'He's not on his own,' said Gwen, but her protest was relenting.

Brenda sat down.

'You see,' said Eve, 'no one gave this little one a thought, did they? Except me. I saw them take Alan away. I heard. I'm so sorry, Gwen. Poor, poor Huw. I loved him like my own, I did.'

Gwen said, 'I know you did.'

Eve closed the back door behind her. She went home and left her back door open. She went into every room and opened the curtains and windows. Finally, she opened the front door. The crisp autumn air filled the house. 'No more of it, cariad,' she told him, 'hiding in here.' She took deep breaths. 'Shall I make us something to eat? Would you like that?'

Standing next to the stove, the upper half of her body was warm – she held him in one arm as she stirred the saucepan – and her lower half was cold. The plates were cold too as she took them down and the food steamed as she ladled it out. She sat Aled on her lap to feed him.

The front door slammed shut in the growing draught blowing through as if it had run out of patience.

'That's it, that's enough, all gone,' she sighed.

The house was cleansed and all her wasted years went with it and she would not have it tainted for whoever lived in it next. But it wasn't a catharsis. Living with lies would have been better than this; secrets did not have to out. She and Roy might still be living there, Aled still with Alan and Jean and Jack next door, Gwen and Huw (but Geraint, no, not part of it, bless him, remembering the gentle boy from school).

There was no need for this coruscating truth. But the bottle of painkillers had gone on the fire. She had an unfounded suspicion that Roy had kept them for himself and had been unable to get to them before he was arrested – or had he left them for her? Could she believe that of him too? None of it need have happened. Evil, like death, had come amongst them. Eve wasn't religious, but that's how she felt.

She closed the back door and all the windows. 'I won't draw the curtains again, but we wouldn't want you to catch cold would we?'

But Gwen had no fresh air she wanted to let in, nothing to be cleansed, everything to be remembered but nothing left. She packed a bag, not caring what or how many clothes she put into it. In Huw's room *The Big Book* was on his desk. On the inside cover, she had written, *To Huw, all my love, Mummy, Christmas 1965.* She turned the pages slowly. Huw was in every photograph, where he had imagined himself to be, at the centre of the stage, indisputably a star, admired and loved, as a boy, as a young man, as a man, in the spotlight, his preordained life laid out, his future history, even as the ailing King, remembering battles, retreats and victories and comrades lost, with honour always and, as the lights went down, she could hear the applause for him. In *The Big Book,* Huw lived on in the life he was born to have. She was so certain of what he would have been it made her proud. She placed *The Big Book* on top of the clothes in the suitcase (she and Geraint's for their honeymoon and Huw nine months later – *nine* months, she had laughed with Jean). She had to place it lengthwise to get it in and it creased the clothes (so what?).

She picked up the silver frame from the sideboard. That was all it was, the photograph was blank: as Huw lived on, Geraint had left. What remained of him moved with the tortured geology of the South Wales coalfield, twisting and bending with the seams, beckoned by restless continents until he became coal itself, burning in someone's grate in a distant, distant future. She put the frame back on the sideboard.

He was gone.

Gwen carried the suitcase to the bus stop with all she wanted in it, going back to Carmarthen without the husband she had come to Bridgend to marry, without the son she had borne him, without the brothers and sisters that might have followed. There had been purpose to it: a moment in time filled with joy.

Constable Dewi and Brenda saw her go. 'What do we do now?' he asked. 'There's nothing for us to do.'

'Go back to the station,' she replied.

'What will he say if we leave?'

'What will he say if we stay?'

'I'll make sure the back door is locked,' he said. He put the dirty mugs in the sink but he didn't wash them.

'Let's walk,' she said. They walked side by side along the pavement toward the town, the last of the police to leave the once happy street, leaving two empty houses, soon to be a third.

At the entrance to Gwyn the Milk's farm, there was a new sign. It said *New Homes Coming Soon.* It was as if Gwyn had planned it all along but not lived to see it (a glitch) and not wanted to run it into old age before getting someone in to help him, perhaps to take it over completely. That someone might have been Jack: it had been the germ of an idea in Gwyn's mind.

Bryn Hughes was moved to another ward where there were two visitors' chairs and the nurses didn't mind if more were pulled up around his bed (but strict visiting times were still enforced).

He was sitting up, weary of being suddenly accessible by everyone because everyone came (understanding the harridan's method too late or he would have asked to remain there): his parents, Mr Tanner, Reverend Elwiss, Laura's father, Laura, others. He rested his head against the pillow and smiled. If he said nothing, they talked amongst themselves and then he didn't listen.

Slowly, he was recovering; there were no more anxious silences and unspoken but obviously expressed fears. Mostly, he was asked how much longer he was going to be in hospital. 'A couple of weeks and then rest at home for longer.'

'When are you going to be back in school, then?'

'I don't know.' He didn't, but he wasn't thinking about how long, so that was all he would say.

'But you are going back, aren't you, Bryn?' his father asked, doubting his son's dedication for the first time.

'I think so, Dad.'

'It will be a great loss if you don't.'

Bryn lived with his father's pride and understood it: how many times had he heard, 'My boy's a teacher,' (how Welsh) whenever he had a chance to say it, to anyone he had an excuse to say it to. In his father's face was a mix of disappointment at the prospect of losing his greatest achievement and concern that his son might have lost his purpose in life, and anger that it might have been taken – driven – out of him. 'I need a bit of time to get my thoughts straight, that's all.'

'But you are going back? Mr Tanner needs you.'

'Does he? I shouldn't let him down then, should I?'

'That's it, Bryn, you take your time, then. I'm sure there's no rush.' So long as there was no *if*. His father was relieved and showed it.

Bryn said no more.

Laura told him, 'They've arrested Alan Harris.'

'*Arrested?* What for?'

'The boys, Gwyn the Milk, both, I don't know. They won't say for certain.' she said, quietly.

His head came off the pillow. He winced. 'Arres… ted?' He lowered his head slowly back down. 'No, that's not right. Are they sure?'

'They arrested him before.'

'They arrested *me*.'

'It's what everyone's saying.'

'What are they saying?'

'That he's been arrested in connection with the murder of Gwyn Roberts. That's all, but what can we do about it? They've found someone to blame whether it's true or not.'

His bruises had faded to the colours of light filtered through stained glass. 'Is it possible?'

'They're not saying for certain, but they might as well be.'

'No one will believe it.'

'I think they will, Bryn, they believed it about you; it put you here, because they will want to believe their children are safe again.'

'When they might not be?'

She shrugged. 'They have someone to accuse.'

'My dad keeps asking me when I'm going back. I don't know if I can.'

'Are you?'

It was his turn to shrug. '*Ow*, I don't know. Should I?'

'If you want to, Bryn.'

'What about you, Laura?'

'I'll do whatever you want to do.'

'Mr Tanner's been in asking me too.'

'They're opening the school again on Monday.'

'I know. If I go back, I think a lot of them will still suspect me…'

'They've caught him, someone, guilty or not …'

'But if I don't they will still suspect me.'

'That's it,' she said, as the bell for the end of visiting time rang. 'I've got to go.' She stood up and kissed him.

He clutched her hand. 'See you tomorrow.'

She smiled, 'You will.'

Shivering and cold, he dreamed of the lost boys, the stolen boys.

Huw was waiting for him in the sunlight of Porthcawl Harbour, sitting on the seawall, dangling his legs and banging his heels. 'Jack, Jack,' he called and jumped up, laughing, and skipped toward him. 'We've been to Trecco, we have, we have, and I went on every ride, *every* ride, I did, really.' His eyes sparkled. 'And you can come too. Do you want to?'

They walked along the promenade. Huw chattered about the big dipper and the dodgems and something called a whirligig that Jack hadn't seen. They made their way through the town with shoppers mingling around them.

A little boy in a pushchair cried when they went past and reached for his mother. They left the town and had to walk on the verge.

On the golf course, balls flew over their heads and bounced on the fairway. No one shouted, '*Fore*.'

Through the dunes, past the tower of stones. Kenfig Pool: '*Look*, Jack,' cried Huw.

Beautiful girls, with hair of brilliant green tresses, smiled up at them from beneath water as clear as dawn air.

'I knew it.'

A dog barked and moorhens exploded out of the reeds and left churning paths before they settled out of reach and the lake's ruffled surface calmed and became tranquil again.

Jack opened his eyes. The rain had stopped. He came out from under the useless bush, numb and dizzy. The skin on his hands was white and wrinkled. He slowly climbed a dune on all fours. He looked over: more dunes, the grey sea. He stumbled down the other side. An arm reached around his chest and lifted him up. 'Found you,' said a voice. His other sandal, heavy and sodden, fell off.

Chapter Twenty-one

Tokelau Islands, Tonga, Trans-Jordan…

Eve carried Aled from one room to another, upstairs first: bedrooms, bathroom, box room, landing. She looked out at the garden, filled with shadows and the sickly light from a sliver of moon. 'No one's going to mend it now, are they, cariad?' She kissed the top of Aled's head to comfort them both. Downstairs: front room, hall, kitchen. She had dusted and put everything away that had a place to be put; she made the house show-home neat, desirable, if not new, wistfully thinking of the houses to be built on Gwyn's farm, 'Which I shall not see.'

She packed a suitcase. 'That's that,' she said, 'we won't take too much, I don't need much, and some of it's yours anyway, isn't it, cariad? We can't go next door to fetch anymore, can we? So what we've got here is all we've got. It's enough.'

She left her best clothes in the wardrobe and the big chest of drawers on the landing. 'We can buy some more in good time.' With the clothes, she left memories: the dress she always wore for Christmas; the light summer dress with the flower pattern for trips to the Gower when the sun shone; the hat she wore with the green ribbon; those shoes, 'I can't take them – but they were expensive, then, Roy used to… Roy,' she stopped herself, 'the blue cardigan, oh, that scarf, I haven't worn that for I don't know how long,' in the immutable past.

She carried the suitcase downstairs and turned off the upstairs lights at the switch in the hall. 'It's nearly time to go, cariad. The taxi will be here soon.'

It was not long before she saw headlights coming up the road through the bay window and opened the front door. She turned, looking into the front room and up the yawning stairs. She turned off the hall light.

'Good morning,' she whispered to the taxi driver, because the neighbours still slept.

He took her suitcase and put it in the boot.

She got into the back of the taxi with Aled on her lap. 'Goodbye,' she mouthed to the house, colourless in the half-light and gritted her teeth to constrain herself, but a tear still escaped to tickle Aled's neck.

He rubbed where it had fallen.

'The station,' she told the driver. 'We're off to London.'

'London? I've never been there – I'd like to, mind, to see the sights.'

'We haven't been either, but I've got relatives there.' She hadn't.

'Are you going for long?'

'I'm not sure yet.' She was. 'We'll see when we get there, won't we, cariad?'

'It's a big place.'

'Yes.'

At the station, she bought tickets and crossed over the footbridge to the eastbound platform: west was home, east was forbidding. 'We're going on a train, cariad. Won't that be fun?' She talked to him until the train arrived.

The platform guard helped her with the suitcase. The carriage doors slammed shut. The guard blew his whistle, the train lurched.

Cardiff and Wales were quickly done, then under the Severn Estuary to Bristol: England, foreign land, Wiltshire, Berkshire, racing further away from what was familiar.

London began long before they arrived at Paddington. The train pierced its crowding, urban heart like a stiletto. Finally, they arrived at the long platforms and the lines of trains waiting, leaving and arriving. She had taken some comfort from the cosiness of the compartment, a temporary home but, now, the timetable was demanding she leave. 'We have to find somewhere else, cariad.'

No one helped her with her suitcase. Everyone rushed and had somewhere to go. No one spoke. But it was full of noise: traffic, car horns, sirens, all of them angry.

She handed in their tickets and went through the concourse and out of the station, clutching Aled tight.

Across the road was a junkshop with an old pushchair in the window.

She bought Aled breakfast and tea and toast for herself in a grubby café next door and watched the city all morning with Aled in his pushchair, sucking his thumb, as his aunties and uncles came down from the valleys in their ancient car to fetch him from Bridgend.

Idris had a key for Alan and Jean's house. Inside, it was cold.

'He'll be next door with Eve,' said Nesta. The five of them waited on the path as she knocked on the front door.

'She must have taken him out,' said Delia, looking up at the empty windows. 'Let's go back in and wait.'

They waited until lunchtime.

'Where's that police constable and police woman?' asked Nesta.

'Gone,' said Idris. 'What reason did they have to stay?'

'Aled,' said Nesta.

'Surely they will have made arrangements for him until we got here?'

'With Eve?'

'Where is she then?'

'Perhaps we should go to the police station and find out,' suggested Emlyn, 'do you think Nesta?'

'Yes,' Nesta replied, 'I was about to say that.'

At the police station, Constable Dewi and Brenda were found. 'We left him with Eve Brown,' Brenda told them.

'She's not there,' Nesta said.

'She *must* be,' said Brenda, with rising panic. 'Where else would he be?' She looked at Constable Dewi.

'We'll come back with you,' he said. Eve could not be found.

'I took her to the station,' the taxi driver told Constable Dewi. 'She said she was going to London. She said she had relatives there.'

'Perhaps she's gone for the day, or even overnight?' suggested Howell.

'Why would she do that without telling anyone?' asked Idris.

'She'll be back soon, surely?' said Emlyn.

They stayed in Alan and Jean's house but Eve did not return.

'What do we do now?' asked Idris.

'Go back to the shop,' said Nesta.

'The shop? But what about Aled – and Jean?'

'Somebody's got to be there, it won't open on its own. Delia and I will stay here.'

'To wait for news?'

'Yes, to wait for news. Betty can come over to make your tea.'

'We'll manage,' said Idris, bravely.

'You can't open a tin, let alone cook what's inside it. Tell Betty I asked if she wouldn't mind, I know she won't.'

Howell drove. The ancient van made hard work of the climb up to Trebanog and Howell had to put it into first gear and stand on the brakes as it came over the top of the mountain. 'I'll let you out by the Beinon and put the van away round the back,' he said.

Idris turned the *Closed* sign to *Open* and put on his brown shop coat. Emlyn did the same and then Howell when he came in from the garage. The three of them stood behind the counter waiting for customers.

The shop door opened just as Eve and Aled were boarding a train for Devon. She didn't care where, the first reasonable-sized town where they could catch a bus to the north coast.

She told Aled, 'You are Alan Guthrie now, cariad,' an echo of the father he would not remember, or his mother, wandering in a strange land, or his brother. 'I am your mother, Alan, you'll be safe with me.'

That evening, she sat with her purloined son, looking across the Bristol Channel to the South Wales coast, sunlit and so close she could almost reach out to touch it, but her life there had gone and, what remained to be salvaged, she had given up for the precious boy. 'We must turn our attention to practical matters now, cariad, mustn't we? We can't live on a park bench, can we?'

'How's the new job going, then?' asked *Herald* Andrew.

'Well, you know…' replied Detective Prosser, uncertain of what his answer should be.

'We'll see you right, won't we, Lloydy?'

Lloyd nodded.

'We were a big help to Detective Jeffries, a *big* help, and,' he looked one way then the other in the approved conspiratorial manner and lowered his voice, 'to Sergeant Phillips.' He tapped his nose with his finger, an almost comical gesture, 'If you take my meaning?'

'Sergeant Phillips? Really?'

'Yes.'

'What do you mean, you'll see me right?'

'Information: you tell us, we tell you, all to mutual advantage. You tell us, we print it; we get the story, you get your name in lights, all very career advancing and it puts you in tight with you know who, and a bottle of whisky at Christmas, that sort of thing.'

'And who needs to know about this.'

'No one, well, *he* does, but a lot of the time, *all* of the time, he'll be telling you what he wants us to know. That's the way it worked with Jeffries, and very well it worked too. But I wouldn't try any freelancing, if I were you.'

'I see.'

'That's good, so we're alright then? And about Jeffries, have you found him yet?'

Detective Prosser considered the bargain (and Sergeant Phillips' good opinion). 'We're interviewing the last two people to see him before he disappeared.' It was made.

'Who's that?' asked *Herald* Andrew, taking out his notebook.

'Someone called Ellis Maynard and the landlord of The Red Lion.'

Herald Andrew put his notebook away. 'No need to write that down. We know Maynard and Jeffries was always in The Red Lion, wasn't he Lloydy?'

'Yes,' said Lloyd.

'The last people to see him? Well, well.'

At the police station, home from home, Ellis Maynard answered the questions Detective Prosser put to him truthfully even if what he said was not the truth.

'What did you do after you left The Red Lion, Mr Maynard?' It was the last and only time Detective Prosser called him 'Mr'.

'I don't know, went for some chips, probably.'

'Why probably?'

'That's what I usually do.'

'Is it? And then what?'

'Went down to the river, probably.'

'To do what?'

'Eat them.'

'And then what?'

'Went back to The Red Lion, probably.'

'Was Mr Jeffries with you?'

Ellis scratched his head and dandruff floated down to join the rest on his shoulders. 'I don't know, but he might have been. He was on some days but I don't know which day you're talking about, do I?'

'The day Mr Jeffries disappeared.'

'What day was that, then? He might have fallen in the river for all I know.' Ellis Maynard left the police station without a charge, a warning or a night in the cells.

Flash.

'Ellis?'

'What?'

'Can we have a photo of you down The Red Lion?'

'What for?'

'You were the last person to see Jeffries before he disappeared.'

'Was I?'

'There's a drink in it for you,'

Flash.

Ellis leaning against the bar holding a pint with his crooked grin and missing teeth and the landlord behind clutching two beer pumps.

'Famous at last, Ellis,' *Herald* Andrew told him.

'Can I have another pint?'

Missing Detective Had A Drink Problem

Police, led by newly appointed Detective Prosser at Bridgend Police Station, are following a number of lines of enquiry, including a thorough search of the River Ogmore where, it is believed, former detective Darren Jeffries may have fallen in after a day of heavy drinking at The Red Lion public house in the town.

A body was never found because, after a week, Sergeant

Phillips called off the search. He said, 'It's a waste of police time. He's gone off somewhere and I am not his keeper.'

Mr Tanner was early to school on Monday. Mr Topliss had already unchained the gates and they were open wide and welcoming. During its closure, the school had been painted and what could be polished had been and, now, it awaited the children to return it to its former state.

Mr Topliss made his final inspection with mixed feelings at what he knew was to come but looked forward, secretly, with relief, to the melee and the noise (and repairing it again) even as he grumbled.

Mr Tanner walked down the expectant corridors with his hands clasped behind his back, as he always did, seeking solace in old habits. There was very little on this first day. The school had to reopen but there was no feeling of 'at least that's over': it was too grim, too searing and the interregnum would remain as an eddy around a submerged rock in the town's past that history and memory could not avoid – not spoken of but there. Mr Tanner did not know what he would say to the mothers bringing their children or if he should say anything at all.

A young man came into the hall. He looked lost.

'Can I help you?' asked Mr Tanner, as kindly as he could, suspecting – knowing – who he was.

'I'm Paul Rees. Are you Mr Tanner?' Their new supply teacher until Bryn Hughes returned and his first proper job since completing teacher training.

'I am and I'm pleased to meet you, Mr Rees.' (Mr? Master?) Mr Tanner would not have wished so difficult a morning on a grizzled veteran of battles with delinquents (and these were good children, mostly), but it was unavoidable or the school would not have been able to open at all. 'Welcome.'

'Thank you, Mr Tanner.' Paul Rees' suit hung off him, his collar was too big, his sleeves too long. His clothes were new, still with their wrapping creases because his mother had only recently bought them before sending him forth to his digs in the town last evening, her kiss lingering on his cheek.

Mr Tanner could not ease his introduction. He remembered his first day as a teacher and how nervous he had been, but he had been able to find his feet gradually, not so this youth. 'I know you understand the circumstances of your appointment.'

'Yes,' squeaked Mr Rees.

'These have been very difficult times.'

'Yes, I can imagine.'

'No, you cannot,' thought Mr Tanner. 'The children may ask you about what's happened and it will have been kept from them as much as is humanly possible so do not try to enlighten them.'

'What do I say if they do?'

'Tell them that Mr Tanner – *me* – has been unwell, flu perhaps, but is fit and raring to go now, everything is back to normal – normal is the watchword.'

'I'll say that,' said Mr Rees.

'And, when they ask who you are, tell them you're here until Mr Hughes comes back from a holiday... holiday,' Mr Tanner repeated to himself, shaking his head. 'I'll show you to your classroom and then we should wait by the gates for the children to arrive.'

Bryn Hughes' classroom was as it had been, the chalk dust had settled, the opening door disturbed it once more.

'If the mothers ask any questions – I'm not sure they will – refer them to me, would you?'

There were no police cars or policewomen outside the school.

Laura Williams arrived.

'Hello,' said Mr Tanner, relieved and pleased to see her.

'I'm sorry,' she said, 'I had to call in at the hospital.'

'How is he?'

'Home in a week, hopefully, fingers crossed.'

'Oh, that is good news,' said Mr Tanner, glancing at Paul Rees, standing next to him, pale and wide-eyed. 'This is Mr Rees, our new supply teacher. Miss Williams,' he said, presenting her.

Paul Rees held out a trembling hand.

Mothers began appearing with their children. No child was alone and would never be again: they used to walk to and from school alone or with their friends, free to roam before they went home and then it was only hunger that called them, or the dark.

The children chattered and laughed, unaware of what had been taken away. The sound of their voices was a restoration of the past but presaged a future woven with suspicion.

Their mothers were expressionlessly harrowed, their eyes leaden.

Mr Tanner did his best to smile at all of them, but the effort strained his face muscles and his cheeriness became a rictus, like an aged clown, still made up and alone in his trailer long after the show is over.

When Mr Tanner looked out of a classroom window an hour later, some of the mothers were waiting outside the gates, not trusting the school to send their children home safe. They waited all day.

Miss Williams called the register with names deleted. She stumbled when she came to where they had been. The register acquired a rhythm after a while, chanted like the times table, but it never would if three fours were not twelve or two nines were not eighteen; numbers exist, they cannot be ceased.

Assembly. *The Lord's Prayer* in Welsh. Nothing more. Amen, *Amen* they chorused.

Back to class. Mr Rees was alone in his for the first time. The children watched and judged him silently, unerringly, probing for weakness.

At lunchtime, when they were in the playground, Mr Tanner asked, 'Laura, are you and Bryn coming back when he's better?'

Laura didn't answer straightaway. She fiddled with her engagement ring. Eventually, she said, 'Yes, but we did talk about it.'

'I know,' said Mr Tanner. 'I talked to Bryn's father, that's why I asked. I would understand if you wanted to leave, to get away, as it were, but I would very much like both of you to continue at the school. We must continue, if we can, and not let things fall apart. That is our test.'

'Thank you, Mr Tanner. We do want to come back – to stay, rather – both of us.'

'That's good. I'm so glad.'

'If we left,' she went on, 'we would be abandoning the memory of those boys. We have to stay for their sakes, for as long as you will have us.'

Mr Tanner squeezed her arm in as demonstrative a way as a headmaster could. The chirruping of the children was all around them. It was an emotional moment before he answered. 'I will not be here forever, Laura, and, then, who knows, perhaps you and Bryn can run the school together?' He cleared his throat.

'Bryn should be headmaster,' she said.

Mr Tanner laughed, the first time since the dreadful business began. 'Well, that's a plan then, Miss Williams.'

Chapter Twenty-Two

Trinidad and Tobago, Uganda...

Reverend Elwiss stood looking at the vicarage for some minutes with one hand resting on the gate. It was an imposing Victorian house with a heavy black door and a lion's head brass knocker, big windows on either side, also with black frames, one his study, the other the drawing room. All the rooms had high ceilings and a restrained airiness. A garden path ran between colourful but formal borders up to the doorsteps, two of them: vicars looked down on callers. A gardener came once a week to mow the lawns and do the weeding. The house was shaded by yew trees with the church on one side and a quiet, unsurfaced road on the other. A small, slate sign on the wall said *Vicarage* and that was all it could be and, if it became anything else, it could not believably be called anything else even if it was whitewashed, the door and window frames painted pink and the yew trees felled.

To be the vicar there was to behave in an expected way and that was what Reverend Elwiss had tried so hard to do. He had succeeded in convincing almost no one except those who wanted – or needed, for reasons of their own – to play the part of loyal churchgoers alongside him: sanctimonious or, for some of the older ones, habit. True believers dwindled or made their peace silently and alone in the church when it was empty or somewhere else entirely.

He thought, 'How much grander it is than all the other houses nearby. What am I without it,' he turned to look at the squat Anglo-Saxon tower between the yews, 'and the church? What am I without these buildings and a dog collar? That's the measure of me.' He walked up the path to the door as the vicar in residence.

In his study, he brooded. 'I won't talk to you here again – no, I won't talk to *Him* here again.'

His wife came in with a cup of tea and a slice of fruit cake.

'Thank you, but no,' he held up his hand to refuse them.

She put them down on the desk. 'There are more important things you can deny yourself, dear,' she told him.

'No, I just don't want any cake.'

'Yes, you do.'

He took a bite and his teeth sank through it, too soft to chew. She did make very good fruit cake; she was a very good vicar's wife – vicarage, church and wife, a Church of

England trinity. He forgot to remind himself he loved her for more than fruit cake and what she was expected to be.

'You know me too well,' he said, patronising her through sticky crumbs. He sipped his tea and washed his mouth free of them. He took another bite.

She sat in the leather chair and crossed her legs, draping her floral dress over her knees.

He was surprised: it was time for her to leave, the study was his alone.

She waited while he finished the cake.

'Headlines be damned,' he suddenly exclaimed, his thoughts bursting forth.

'*Please*, dear.'

But she had ensconced herself in his domain where he was free, privately, to express himself. 'No, I'm sorry, but it needs to be said, headlines be *damned*.'

'What of them?'

He rubbed his chin and licked the corners of his mouth. 'I am marked and my imperfections are known – even if they're not the correct ones. I am now known to be imperfect.'

She raised her eyebrows. 'You, dear? Is that a bad thing?'

'No, you miss my point.'

'Do I? I'm sorry.'

'I mean I'm glad of it, I'm glad they know.'

'The man behind the vicar?'

'Yes, I...' he stopped and frowned.

She looked back at him, steadily, with compassion, amusement too, but not a trace of mockery.

It was a familiar expression and now, he understood, uncomfortably, what it meant: was it *true*, after all this time, that this was what she really thought of him? 'How long have you thought like that?' he asked before he could stop himself.

'Thought like what?'

Her gentle revelation, but his self-revelation, overwhelmed him (lately, they were coming thick and fast) as if it had leapt out from behind the curtains and shouted, '*Boo*.' How could he not have known that's where it had been hiding – with a foot sticking out? She had put up with his impatience and dismissiveness of her, pretended his trite utterances were pearls of wisdom and laughed at his weak jokes and, all along, she had known he was trying to be someone he was not. He had not known himself and, if not for these terrible events, he might never have come to his senses – or had the courage to do so – and, here she was – suddenly, to him – an intelligent and perceptive woman disguised as a vicar's wife with tea and cake.

'Yes,' he said, 'it is a burden lifted,' trying and failing to disguise his embarrassment, and adding, hurriedly, in mitigation, 'but I would have gladly borne it if things had not transpired as they did,' and remained a pompous fool, a charlatan, and she would have remained ever tolerant, ever loyal to him, understanding what she did, a sacrifice greater than his. He was shamed and daunted by her: who was this woman he had married (who loved him as he had neglected to show the same to her)?

He shook his head, 'They might snigger at me or be offended by what I say but at least they might actually listen.' He would never be the Hampshire Priest – might he visit? (No, he might not). 'Yes, headlines be damned.'

He didn't want to say any more, but she did not get up to leave; his viva voce was not finished.

'My – *our* – life,' he corrected himself as her smile grew more apparent, 'is here.'

She nodded.

'I can go down the pub, I can say what I want to say – within reason – my sermons don't have to be so holy. This awful business has released me. I have learnt, no, been *taught* that you cannot be a priest and not a man; you cannot be one without the other. That is *my* test. I was afraid to frighten the horses.'

'Or the sheep, dear?'

'Sheep?'

'We are in Wales.'

'Yes, we are, but anyone can frighten sheep – the lion lies down with the lamb? Oh, enough of that stuff.'

She smiled plainly and cleared away the plate and the cup and saucer. 'More cake, another cup of tea, dear?' she asked.

'Thank you, no, really, no more. I've made a good friend,' he said, as she was turning to leave him be, 'a good one, I think, someone who doesn't see me only as a vicar.'

'Mr Tanner?'

'Yes,' and *you*: what he should have said but was not yet brave enough. 'I think I'll go for a walk down by the river and then call in at the church for a while.'

The leaves were coming off the trees, coating the water and tumbling over the grass. He hummed no hymns as he walked and pulled his coat tight around his neck. 'Hello,' he said, to a man walking a little dog. The man smiled back, two men out walking, greeting each other.

He entered the church and thought of the camera flashes and *Herald* Andrew's rude interruption – he had every right to interrupt: why was a vicar's communion with God not to be interrupted? Because he was a vicar?

He bowed to the altar and tried to mean it – he did, but he wanted to feel spontaneous sincerity in his obeisance. 'I have a mountain to climb,' he thought, 'a mountain. I know you are with me always, Lord, but, from now on, I will only formally address you in church, except in matters where I need your guidance for the sake of others, as with Bryn, even if, foolishly, I wilfully misinterpreted what you told me. I know you know this, Lord, but I am trying to understand.' He sat down heavily in the front pew. 'Perhaps it should be my wife here, before you, and not me.'

Sergeant Phillips held open the door of his big, black car. 'Get in Harris,' he told him.

Alan held up his handcuffed wrists.

'You're a dangerous man, Harris, get in.'

Alan did as he was told.

Sergeant Phillips slid into the driver's seat and placed his peaked cap on the passenger seat.

'Where are we going?' Alan asked. He saw Sergeant Phillips looking at him in the mirror, but there was no answer. 'Isn't anyone coming with us?'

Sergeant Phillips started the engine and the car came soundlessly alive with only the slightest vibration to indicate it had.

'Where are you taking me?'

Sergeant Phillips put the car into gear and they pulled out of the police station. He drove down the hill and turned left.

Shoppers stopped to see them pass.

Alan tried to hide his face.

'Keep your head up, Harris.' Sergeant Phillips drove funereally slow up Cardigan Street.

Other cars started to queue behind them, but they didn't flash their lights or sound their horns.

Everyone they passed bent to look at Alan's white face through the car window.

'Keep your head up, Harris,' Sergeant Philips told him again.

Alan closed his eyes.

'Open your eyes, Harris.'

Mr Tanner was on his way to school.

Alan pretended he hadn't seen him.

At the top of Cardigan Street, Sergeant Phillips stopped. Behind them, a big queue stretched all the way back to the police station.

Herald Andrew and Lloyd stepped from a doorway.

Flash.

Startled, Alan turned his head to look.

Flash.

Sergeant Phillips drove more quickly now because there were no shops and less people. It wasn't far to Gwyn's farm where they turned under the big sign advertising new homes and up the track to the milking shed.

'Why are we here?' asked Alan.

Sergeant Phillips opened the door. 'In there,' he told him.

The milking shed was dark and cold. Under the window, Sam's blood was a black stain on the concrete, but no one would have known what it was: fresh or old, dried cow's muck or urine, a calf's birth.

'I know your mind, Harris.' Sergeant Phillips' voice came from a darkened theatre behind him. 'I can hear your words before you say them; I know which one is a lie and which is the truth.'

'I have told you the truth,' said Alan.

'Do not turn round; look at the blood, Harris. Is it the dog's or is it Gwyn Roberts'?'

'It is the dog's.'

'I know the games you play before you play them, putting a lie before a truth to make it seem like the truth. Do not turn round, look at the blood, Harris.'

'I *am* telling the truth.'

'Whose blood is it, Harris?'

'It's the dog's. It's where I found him.'

'I can see into your mind, I can see everything that happens there. I can see now, Harris.'

'I don't think you can see anything.'

'I see the man who killed Gwyn Roberts. I see the man who is looking at his blood, who knows how it got there.'

'It's the *dog's*.'

Through the cobwebbed window, Alan looked down the slope of the field to the fence where he had buried Sam and his house beyond it. Next door was Aled with Eve. He had asked to see him. Sergeant Phillips wouldn't let him. 'Gwyn Roberts was my friend, why would I kill him?'

'Dead men cannot prove they are innocent. Do not turn round, Harris.'

'Why would he have to prove it?'

'You see, Harris? A lie before the truth.'

'Another boy went missing after Gwyn was dead.'

'And a cat, a rabbit and a dog, your father's dog. You could not stop yourself.'

'I did not kill anyone or anything.'

'You killed Gwyn Roberts and your father's dog here. I caught you.'

'The dog was already dead.'

'Did the dog have a name, Harris?'

'Yes.'

'Your father's dog but you can't say its name?'

'Sam.'

'You killed your father's dog with your own spade.'

'Someone took it.'

'Gwyn Roberts was dead.'

'Someone else did it.'

'Someone else?'

'It wasn't me. Why would I use my own spade?'

'I told you, Harris, a truth before a lie. Turn round. Walk in front of me.'

They went back to Sergeant Phillips' big, black car.

'Are we going back to the police station?'

But Sergeant Phillips turned toward the bypass and up onto Stormy Down.

The fiery eyes awoke in the distance, rising above Port Talbot to see; through the quarry and the lanes and out onto the road next to the dunes.

Sergeant Phillips parked next to the box-car.

Vehicle tracks and footprints were everywhere, but it was deserted now.

Sergeant Phillips got out and pulled the doors apart. It was as it had been: sacks strewn on the floor and piled in the corner. But the loose plank had been put back, as if it had never happened. 'Stand in the doorway,' Sergeant Phillips told him, and he took off the handcuffs. 'Do you want to run away, Harris? Go, then. Don't turn round. Don't look, go.'

Not far away was the pillar of stones, like a cross on a hill and, beyond that, Kenfig Pool, the cool waters of Galilee.

A gap opened in the clouds and the sun came through. A happy place where he had walked with his father and Jack with his grandfather, and Sam, running ahead, barking at nothing for the excitement of it. 'I don't want to run away. Why should I run? From what?'

'Justice, Harris. Me. Step inside.'

'I don't want to.'

'It was here, wasn't it? Step inside, Harris.'

Alan took two steps.

'Stop. Stand there.'

Alan breathed what Jack had breathed: dank and mouldy but, now, too, faintly, the cat's mortal odour as if they had opened a grave, and tar. He reached to touch the smooth planks and remembered creosoting the garden fence with Roy as Jack and Huw watched and drank orange squash. 'Why are we here?' He heard another car pull up.

'Don't turn round.'

Flash.

In the darkness of the hut, Alan raised his hands to shield his eyes.

Flash.

Caught in the act.

'Don't turn round.'

Alan heard the other car leave.

'You should have run away, Harris.' Sergeant Phillips put the handcuffs back on.

He drove slowly down the promenade so all those strolling there could see.

The tide was out and the black mud of the harbour was exposed with fishing boats listing in its succulent embrace.

'Stand at the top of the slipway and don't move.' Sergeant Phillips leaned against the bonnet of the car, ran his gloved thumbs over his moustache and folded his arms.

Alan stood in his chains looking out at the rolling sea beyond the harbour entrance toward the sunlit coast of Devon. 'This will be over,' he whispered to himself as a crowd gathered to gawp. If there were camera flashes, it was too bright to see them.

'I know your mind, Harris. I know every thought. You cannot swim in handcuffs. Get back in the car.'

The crowd made way, whispering.

Sergeant Phillips stopped the car at an entrance to a field near Pencoed. Nearby was a wood.

'Why are we here?'

'You know, Harris: three boys.'

'But how do you know he was here? Has he been found?'

'Get back in the car.'

In the corridor to the cells at the police station, they met Brenda coming out of the interview room.

'Where are the animals, Colcannon?' demanded Sergeant Phillips. 'Get them.'

'I don't know where they are, Sir.'

'I do,' said Alan, 'I buried them but I will not tell you where. They are at peace.'

Bryn Hughes came back to school. His father brought him and dropped him off at the school gates. 'I'll pick you up in an hour,' he told him.

Bryn was late for class, it was nearly 10am, but he hadn't come to teach or be taught. He was glad to be back, anticipating a return to his old life. *Old?* Its interruption had come just as he was beginning it, a cruel stutter that was nearly its end.

He hobbled on sticks across the playground to the main doors and into the hall where Mr Topliss was studying a broken window and sucking his teeth.

'Well, well,' he said, when he saw Bryn, 'you're a sight for sore eyes.'

'I'm still sore enough for both your eyes, Mr Topliss.'

'Never mind me, Mr Hughes, you're the one who's been in the wars. How are you?'

'You're the old soldier, you tell me?'

Mr Topliss laughed. 'It's good to see you back, one old soldier to another.'

'I'm not quite ready to teach. I don't think I'm up to coping with the little horrors just yet, they'd run rings around me. I've just come back for a visit.'

'Soon though, Mr Hughes?'

'I hope so.'

'Mr Tanner's in with Form Three, but I don't think he'll mind the interruption, not with Form Three, anyway.'

'No, I don't suppose he will. I'll go and interrupt him, then.' Bryn looked through the glass porthole at Mr Tanner who was standing before the class with a book in his hand. Bryn watched for a moment then tapped on the glass.

'Bryn,' exclaimed Mr Tanner, delightedly, 'or is it Mr Hughes?'

'Not quite yet,' Bryn replied, struggling to steady himself on his sticks to shake Mr Tanner's hand.

Mr Tanner turned back to his class, 'Now read quietly until I get back.' He wagged a finger at them. 'Not a peep, is that understood? Let's go to my office,' he said to Bryn.

A boy was standing outside the next classroom, trying to look the other way.

'Thomas,' said Mr Tanner, with mock exasperation (which, from the boy's reaction, was convincing enough), 'not again? Go and ask Miss Williams to come to my office and then you can go back into class and I don't want to see you standing out here when I get back, is that clear?'

'Yes, Sir,' said Thomas, and ran off before Mr Tanner could ask why he had been sent out.

'*Walk*,' barked Mr Tanner.

Bryn settled himself into the chair in Mr Tanner's office and rested his sticks against his knee. 'How is my replacement doing?' he asked.

'Improving, I think. Why don't you go and see for yourself?'

'I'm not sure he'd appreciate that.'

'It will do him good.'

Laura came in. She bent to kiss Bryn but stopped herself.

Mr Tanner smiled. 'Sit,' he said. 'So, Bryn, when can we have you back in harness?'

'A couple of weeks, I hope.'

'That's good. Excellent, in fact. And Laura tells me you're planning the big day for the spring?'

'If all goes to plan.'

'It will,' said Laura. 'I'm not going to let him wriggle out of it now. We're going to ask Reverend Elwiss to marry us.'

'Are you? I'm sure he'd be delighted.'

'We owe him a great deal, Mr Tanner,' said Bryn. 'We owe you a great deal too.'

'Oh, not a bit of it.'

'Yes, we do,' said Laura.

'I'm just glad you're on the mend, Bryn, both to come back and teach and marry Laura.'

Bryn sat in the corner of Paul Rees' classroom and envied his animated manner, unhindered by crutches, even though he was obviously nervous at Bryn's presence. But, soon, the children stopped looking curiously at Bryn and turned all their attention to Mr Rees. 'Good for you,' Bryn thought, 'you're going to make a good teacher.' His father was waiting.

On his way out, Mr Tanner caught up with him. 'Have you heard any more about Alan Harris?'

'No, nothing.'

'So you don't know if he's been charged with anything yet?'

'No, I don't. I can't believe he's got anything to do with it, but if not him then who? Is who did it still at large?'

'God forbid,' said Mr Tanner, 'but I saw him in Sergeant Phillips' car this morning going up Cardigan Street.' He shook his head, 'It was as if he was being paraded around the town. They used to do that to convicted criminals on the way to the scaffold.'

Chapter Twenty-Three

Virgin Islands, Western Samoa...

'Find him and do not come back until you have him for me.'

Detective Prosser half crouched before Sergeant Phillips who didn't look at him and spoke as if he wasn't there.

Detective Prosser's voice shook, 'I will do my best, Sir.'

'Your best,' said Sergeant Phillips, 'will be your last if it does not do what I have told you.'

'Yes, Sir, it will be better than... no, I will...'

'Do as you're told. Repeat it.'

'I will get him back for you.' Detective Prosser wiped the saliva from his lower lip.

'Speak to that reporter. Tell him with *certainty*.' The 'c' sound hissed between the gathering rumbles, still faraway but coming closer and, beneath the horizon, lightning flashed. 'You are that certainty, Prosser.'

'I'll tell him straightaway.'

'Straightaway what?'

'Sir.'

'Certainty, Sir, I will use the word.'

Sergeant Phillips' eyes swept over him like nightfall. 'A word? It's not a word.'

'It's what I must do with certainty.'

'Must?'

'Will, Sir.'

'By the end of the week you will bring him to me.'

Detective Prosser gulped. 'By the end of the week?' he croaked, and cleared his throat, 'by the end of the week, yes, Sir?'

Sergeant Phillips turned and walked away down the corridor.

Detective Prosser swayed and reached for the wall to steady himself. Sweat ran down his temple.

Child Missing Believed Kidnapped

Sergeant Phillips is certain of his return within days...

In the morning, Eve sat with Aled on the bench high above the sea as the sun came up, cold, with frost on the grass, and lit the distant coast and Alan, in his chains at the top of the slipway, looked directly into the face of his youngest son.

But the weather closed in: a front grew from the west and wrapped around the sun and doused South Wales in rain and mist. When it reached them, Eve pulled Aled's head under her chin and unfolded the pushchair with her free arm and foot. She placed him in it and wrapped a plastic mac around him.

He looked up at her from under the transparent plastic which made his blue eyes even bigger.

She thought her heart would break in his gaze of trust: how would she explain it to him when, one day, she must – or keep an unredeemed lie? Would she say, 'I am not your real mother and your name is not Alan, it's Aled and you were born over there.'

There was nowhere to go so she pushed him along the path to the road where they sheltered under the awning of a kiosk, closed for the winter. The rain drifted over the sea in curtains and dripped from the roof.

When she asked the woman who owned the B and B about work she was told, 'It's all seasonal,' as if it was an obvious fact, 'everything's closed now. There's nobody here.'

'When does the season start?'

'Easter. You're the only guest I've got. We hardly get anyone this time of year.'

'My husband died,' Eve said, 'there were too many memories, we wanted a fresh beginning, didn't we, cariad?'

'I'm not sure coming here at this time of year gives you the best chance of that. Couldn't you have waited a few months?'

'I've always liked this part of the world,' Eve replied.

'Yes,' said the woman, 'in the summer.'

'We wanted a clean break, we couldn't pick our moment; it wasn't like that.'

'No, of course not,' said the woman, 'I'm sorry.'

Eve didn't stay for any more questions. 'I'm going to take him for a walk,' she said, unsettled by the woman's enquiries and afraid to stay at the B and B even if it meant hiding in her bedroom all day.

'Shall we see if the café is open, cariad?' It wasn't. The village was almost deserted.

A policeman on his beat, with nothing else to do except be curious, saw them walking up the high street (a few tourist shops – closed – a newsagent and the café). He nodded.

Eve gave him a quick smile in return and turned down a side alley as if she knew where she was going. When she looked back, he wasn't following them.

They waited at a bus stop. A bus came. Eve shook her head and it left.

An hour later, when the café opened, she fed Aled scrambled eggs and eked out two cups of tea until past lunchtime.

The rain stopped. She put Aled back in his pushchair and walked up the high street and out onto the cliff path.

She brushed the rain off the bench and sat down. South Wales was still lost in the murk.

Eve thought, 'Perhaps it wasn't such a good plan.' It had barely been a plan at all, only an impulse because she wanted this boy when all else had been lost. 'Why not Devon?' she had asked herself, remembering green, rolling fields and yellow beaches in the sun. She had little money and not once did she think everything might be closed. 'I can work in a pub, I did that for a while, years ago.' And what about Aled when she was working? The thought occurred but it was troublesome to her desires and she didn't think of it anymore.

The days were shortening quickly in late October and it was getting dark. She went back to the B and B.

The woman said, 'Did you have a nice day?' with surprise in her voice because she couldn't imagine what Eve had found to do with a little boy in a pushchair in the rain on the margins of winter.

'We had a lovely day,' said Eve.

'Oh,' said the woman, and frowned.

In her room, Eve sat with Aled on the bed and tried not to think of tomorrow because it would be more of the same. It was impossible but she told Aled, 'Something will turn up, cariad, I'm sure.'

In the morning, another bleak day, she sat on the bench and looked to her home somewhere beyond the grey shroud. She didn't take Aled out of his pushchair, wrapped warm in a shawl and the plastic mac.

The policeman was walking towards them.

Eve watched him out of the corner of her eye.

He walked purposefully with an aim in mind, not the watchful amble of his beat. 'Good morning,' he said, 'it's rather bracing weather to be out walking with your child?'

'The sea air will do him good and we won't be out for long.'

'I'm sure it will,' said the policeman. 'Are you visiting someone here?'

'No, we've just come for a break. My husband died. I wanted to get away.'

'Oh, I'm sorry to hear that.' He bent down and inspected Aled, 'The boy's father? And what's your name?'

'Alan,' said Eve.

'And you are?' he smiled.

'Mrs Guthrie.'

'Well, good morning Mrs Guthrie. Let's hope the sun makes an appearance during your stay.' He touched the peak of his helmet with his forefinger and continued up the path.

'Thank you,' said Eve. She watched until he was out of sight, then she pushed Aled in the opposite direction.

She told the woman at the B and B, 'I've had an offer of some work.'

The woman frowned. 'Here? Have you?'

'No, not here,' Eve replied, trying to smile. 'I telephoned a friend. But it means I have to leave immediately.'

'What sort of work is it in such a rush?'

'Oh, you know,' said Eve, unable to think of an answer, 'temporary work, but she needs someone as soon as possible.' She lifted Aled out of his pushchair. 'Excuse me, but I must go and pack.'

There was nothing to pack and, within minutes, she was gone from the B and B and waiting at the bus stop.

'We'll catch a train, cariad.' Where? 'But not back to London.'

When she got to the station, there were only local trains to catch for the rest of the day.

She bought Aled a ham roll and looked for another B and B. There were lots of them, all with a *Vacancy* sign in the window.

In her room was an electric fire with two bars. She sat on the floor and turned both of them on. She stared at their brightening orange glow as they heated up.

Close to the warmth, Aled went to sleep with his head in her lap.

Eventually, she dozed off too with her head resting against the bed.

She woke with a start to banging at the door, not polite knocking, but the thumping of the flat of a heavy hand.

'Mrs Brown?' said a man's voice. 'Open the door, we know you're in there.' Aled stirred. Eve didn't reply. There was more thumping. 'Mrs Brown, open the door, *now*.'

'My name is Guthrie and I'm in bed. What do you want?'

'I've got the pass key,' said a woman.

'Eve, open the door, Eve.' It was Brenda.

Eve didn't move. She heard the key in the lock. The door opened.

Brenda came in. 'What were you thinking, Eve?'

'I just had to take him, to keep him safe.'

'Enough of that,' said Detective Prosser, 'you don't need to talk to her. Get up,' he told Eve.

She was stiff and tired, too slow.

He grabbed her arm and pulled her roughly to her feet. 'Hold your hands out,' and he put her in handcuffs.

'There's no need for that,' said Brenda.

'I want her properly trussed up,' he gloated, with a triumphant smile that almost turned into a laugh. 'Get the child, Colcannon.'

Suddenly woken up, Aled was frightened.

'Shut it up,' Detective Prosser told Brenda.

'He won't. He wants his mother.'

'She's not his mother,' Detective Prosser scowled at Brenda. He pushed Eve out of the room with one hand in the small of her back and the other gripping her arm.

In the car, Aled wriggled and bucked. Brenda had to lower him between Eve's handcuffed wrists and he subsided to slowing sobs and silence.

'Everyone is looking for him,' said Brenda.

'Everyone couldn't keep him safe,' said Eve. 'I had to make sure.'

'His relatives want him back, Eve,' said Brenda. 'They will keep him safe.'

'They're old,' said Eve.

'Not all of them.'

'They are, and Jean can't look after him, can she?'

'She might get better. How will she even have the chance to get better without Aled?'

'She won't get better.'

'You don't know that, Eve, it's not your decision to make, is it?'

'I did what was best for Aled.'

'How? You've got nowhere to go, nowhere to live, no job, hiding in a strange place where you don't know anyone.'

All true and the consequences inevitable, but Eve insisted, 'He won't be safe, I can keep him safe.'

'I expect he'll go and live with his aunties and uncles in the Rhondda.'

'But they're *old*. What future is that for a little boy?'

'That's not up to us, Eve.'

It was a long journey home. When they turned into the police station, Brenda said, 'I've got to take him now.' She had to prise Aled away.

He clung to Eve with fingers like hooks. He screamed.

Eve could still hear him as she was led away to the familiar place. She cried. Brenda cried too, trying to hide it. Eve's life was in ruins but she didn't care for herself. Her last hope struggled in Brenda's arms.

'Give him to me, Colcannon,' Detective Prosser demanded.

Sergeant Phillips ran his thumbs down his moustache.

Detective Prosser held Aled out like a big, wriggling fish. 'I've got him, Sir.'

Sergeant Phillips yanked his tunic straight and said nothing as he left.

Detective Prosser almost threw Aled at Brenda, 'Take him, *take* him,' and he hurried after Sergeant Phillips. 'But I got him, Sir, and it's only Thursday.'

Sergeant Phillips Finds Kidnapped Boy

Over a picture of him outside the police station standing next to his big, black car.

Mr Tanner sat in the empty classroom and reflected on his bachelor's life and the girl he had wanted to marry a long time ago when he was in his twenties. She had married another and it had broken his heart and he would not have it broken again. He had lost all appetite for the chase. Laura reminded him of her and Bryn of himself. They didn't look similar, they weren't similar as people, but their circumstances had been the same: she had been a teacher in the same school when they were both starting out. After a year, they became engaged. He had asked the vicar. They were where Laura and Bryn were now, with marriage hastening toward them and a date set. But there had been no real trial for Mr Tanner and his betrothed, no testing of their feelings for each other; what might have been for better or worse, forsaking all others, because a boy from her past came home from his posting in the RAF and it was as if he had never been away (every time a Vulcan flew over he was reminded). 'If I had married her,' thought Mr Tanner, 'and he had come home after, wouldn't that have been worse?' It was thin consolation. He had been left with no one to talk to except his own resounding thoughts in countless empty classrooms after the school day was done. He had wanted to talk to someone and he dearly missed what he had never had. 'Out of a clear blue sky, both the welcome and the dreaded. What a close run thing it has been. *One* day, Ellis Maynard – but the proof? And that detective has gone missing.' He tapped his fingers on the desk. 'It's as if events are being manipulated, but for what purpose?' He sighed, 'It is the inexplicability of events, the persistence of the unforeseen, but will everyone pay for their crimes in the end? Ah, but should we forgive? Should we, *can* we, can there be forgiveness? It's a question for the Reverend. I wonder if he's read Hardy?' The door opened and he turned to see who it was. 'I'm just going, Mr Topliss.'

'Right you are, Headmaster, I'll lock up then.'

'I'll get out of your way.' Mr Tanner got to his feet. He thought, 'I have spent my life amongst chalk dust, I have breathed it like the dust of the pit... that's a bit over the top, one cannot hew the childish mind like coal – perhaps I should be made into a piece of chalk when I die, then I can carry on, at least as long as it lasts. I might make quite a lot of pieces of chalk.

'I am *not* responsible for what Ellis Maynard became.'

He thought about stopping off for a glass of whisky at The Red Lion on the way home but remembered that was where Ellis Maynard drank. He looked at his watch, 'Anyway, they're not open yet.'

As he walked by the river, Ellis Maynard was drinking in the trees below the bank. Mr Tanner did not see him.

The bulldozer clanked and rattled its way up the farm track. A low loader followed with a crane on its back, its mast horizontal and quiescent. The low loader swung round and reversed to the edge of the yard between the buildings. The slurry on the concrete had dried crisp. The crane inched down the ramps and its mast came up holding a chain attached to a wrecking ball.

The low loader, skinny after its birthing, pulled out onto the road and left the crane and bulldozer to do their work.

The two drivers talked for some minutes, laughing and pointing, before getting into their cabs.

They roared, coughing gouts of blue smoke and, at their mercy, was Gwyn the Milk's unremarkable legacy: some empty buildings and the bony remains of milking equipment.

The crane heaved the wrecking ball off the ground. Its first swing was lazy, as if it was testing the weight, but it went through the end wall of the milking shed and disappeared inside as the roof fell about its chain. The crane pulled the ball free and swung it again. The bottom half of the wall collapsed. The limbs within were revealed for the first time in fifty years, their clothes torn off, humiliated and tarnished in their nakedness. The remainder of the roof collapsed. Grey dust rolled out over the field.

The bulldozer busied itself about the crane, pushing the stones into piles. Not long and the milking shed was gone.

The crane turned its attention to Gwyn's house and positioned itself to swing the wrecking ball.

The bulldozer waited, huffing to itself.

The crane swung and laid bare Gwyn's bedroom and the kitchen beneath with its first, slow swipe. The crumbling stones sounded like slops being emptied into the street. Rags of striped wallpaper hung from what was left of the walls.

Next, the parlour and the living room; the second bedroom; the dining room beneath; the bathroom, tipping out a cast-iron bath, end over end; the scullery, smashing a deep, porcelain sink; the third bedroom, smaller, once intimate (the children's before the line ceased). Pieces of glass flashed from a splintering frames.

The back wall: daylight. Two more swings and the side walls fell like sentries. Gwyn's farm became a hole in the view, unseen for generations.

The crane was done, its chain hung limp and the driver opened his cab door, stretched out his legs, and began eating his brawn sandwiches and drinking his flask of coffee, watching the bulldozer tracking over the rubble, tidying up.

The low loader came back, carrying a scraper, long and lean and yellow. It changed places with the crane.

The scraper planed the fields, shaving off the grass and topsoil to make them level. When it got stuck, the bulldozer gave it a push.

All day and the next, the scraper worked until all of Gwyn's fields were bare earth.

Near the fence behind Alan's house, the graves were too shallow.

The bulldozer grubbed out the hedges and made bonfires of them.

A digger came with tipper trucks and filled them with rubble. Gwyn's farm was taken away.

Surveyors with plans divided the fields into squares with cord and wooden pegs, a surprising number of them for a small farm; if they had gardens, there would be no space for greenhouses or vegetable plots.

Footings were dug. Bricks and breeze blocks were laid, plasterboard for the rooms. They grew into the artist's impression on the billboard and the advert in *The Herald* (for a while, until they were lived in and their impermanence became apparent). The hole in the view was filled: there was no view.

CHAPTER TWENTY-FOUR

Zanzibar.

'He's been found.' It was to Jack's face that Jean opened her eyes in the day room next to the black and white test card, dusty and flickering on the television. There he was.

'Are you a memory?'

He frowned. 'A memory of what, Mum?'

'A memory of you, my memory of you. Please don't be.'

'No, I don't think so. Am I, Dad?'

There was Alan, standing behind him with a hand resting on his shoulder and his other arm holding Aled. 'And look who else we've brought to see you?'

'I've got your jumper,' Jean murmured. She touched him, she felt him and he did not evaporate. 'Where have you been?'

'In a shed, with a cat. It was dark.'

'How did you find him?' she asked Alan.

'I kept telling them. I knew he had to be there somewhere, in the dunes, and he was.'

‘I was,’ said Jack. ‘Can we go home now?’

‘Yes, we can,’ said Alan, ‘at last.’

‘At last,’ said Jean, ‘I can breathe. Help me up.’

Alan put his arm under hers and a nurse did the same on the other side. Jean’s knees almost gave way and they had to stop her from falling until the dizziness passed.

‘How long have I been in that chair?’

‘A while,’ said Alan.

‘I remember the doctor with the yellow waistcoat.’

‘Do you?’

‘Yes, but that’s all. I think we should throw that old jumper away, Jack, and buy you a new one and, if that’s you smelling, I think you need a bath.’

‘We came straight here,’ Alan said. ‘There will be plenty of time for baths.’

‘Yes, there will. You and Aled. You can share one.’

They did. Aunties and uncles crowded at the door as they played in the suds and laughed.

‘It never happened, but it did, and now we’re all back together.’

The aunties and uncles squeezed into their ancient van and waved through the window and Howell beeped the horn as they left to go back to the shop.

The four of them sat in the front room in silence, Jean cuddling Jack and Aled with Alan. They didn’t talk about what happened or ask Jack any questions. Alan put Aled to bed and he went straight to sleep and his thumb slipped out of his mouth onto the pillow. He told Jack,

'If you want to stay up late, you can, go to bed when you want to.'

'I want to go to bed,' said Jack, 'I'm tired.' He looked at his mother. 'Will you sit with me until I go to sleep?'

She stroked his hair as his eyes closed. 'Let's go to Rest Bay tomorrow,' she said.

It was windy and Jack lifted his coat above his head and ran with it like a sail. Rest Bay was wide and long. Jack could run forever, into the days and years to come that might have been denied: he ran back to his first memories.

Jean had come here when she was Jack's age, every day in the summer holidays, and swum in the sea or walked as far as Pink Bay and back: the girl with the golden hair and the beautiful smile. Then they always went for ice cream at Alphonsi's. She had the happiest of childhoods, in the sunlit days between the wars. 'It must never change,' she told herself. 'We deserve to be happy as children. We must have those days to remember.' She could see Jack at the edge of the sea, a long way out. Lines of breakers came piling in. She watched them rise and pause at their highest, towering over the small figure of her son, tip and down they came with a white thump and the next, queuing up and rearing, unceasing ranks.

Jack ran back with the wind blowing him sideways. He veered and lifted his coat again and he was swept up the beach almost faster than his feet could keep up.

Jean couldn't laugh; she wouldn't take her eyes off him.

Jack ran and ran and, when he stopped, he was tiny in the vastness but now he had to walk back with the wind and the sand biting at his face.

The tide came in quickly across the flat beach, once it had decided to. Jack dug a hole with his spade and made a sandcastle. The hissing tongue came closer with each advance. The sandcastle melted.

Jean called, 'Jack?'

The waves had reached the rocks almost before he had time to climb up. Not long, and the water was deep and a swell heaved. Jack went up on the grass.

Jean saw the fiery eyes burning over Port Talbot along the lonely coast and shivered.

'Ice creams?' Alan asked.

Mr Alphonsi was in his usual place, smoking and drinking his tiny cup of coffee. When they came in, he jumped up and spread his arms wide, 'Wonderful, all of you, at last. God be praised, but I never thought I'd see it. Sit, sit with me. Emma?' he called to his daughter-in-law who came rushing out of the kitchen to hug Jack and Aled. 'Ice cream for these boys, lots of ice cream and not a penny will you pay. It will always be free ice cream for these boys – and not a word will I hear against it,' he added as Alan made to protest.

Jean told herself, 'The world is not full of bad men,' but who could she trust?

They slid onto the red benches.

Emma came back with two huge bowls of ice cream (four scoops) and squirted chocolate and raspberry sauce over them.

Soon, Aled had it all over his face. Jean tried to wipe it off with a paper napkin but she gave up and left him to finish. Aled was two saucer eyes and a mask of red, brown and white smears.

Mr Alphonsi admired and winked and smoked.

Emma brought coffees and another expresso.

Other customers they knew said, 'Hello,' softly, reverently, at the miracle, at the possibility they had given up on because all such things ended badly, endings unspoken of, as they waited for news, or no news which was the same.

But Jean couldn't help her suspicion: was it you, or you? In her changed and fragile world there was a need for vigilance as never before: and how delicate her mind that had been sent into madness by the anguish. Jean had no words to describe it to herself or anyone, she didn't want to try. She vibrated like a tuning fork to her emotions; she was in shock and would remain so; fear would never leave her, but the relief was overwhelming.

'Finished, boys?' asked Mr Alphonsi. 'More?'

Jack shook his head and leaned back on the bench, bursting with the fabulous, legendary ice cream. 'I'm stuffed,' he said.

'What do you say, Jack?' asked his mother, a mother again.

'Thank you,' said Jack.

Jean said, 'I don't want to go home over Stormy Down.'

'Then we won't,' Alan said. He drove slowly through the town and out over shallow hills, through trees and fields where they could not be seen by the fiery eyes watching for their escape: they who could have told all but would not speak.

Alan wouldn't let Jack go into the front garden as the Vulcan went over.

Jack saw it through the bay window, a black triangle pent with immense power and noise, whose wings didn't flash in the afternoon sun as it banked east.

In the kitchen, its frigid air made warm, they sat round the small table with Aled in his high chair and ate sausage and mash with tomato sauce – failing to finish it all after so much ice cream, but it was teatime and must be observed like before.

Jean said, 'I didn't believe it would be.'

'No,' said Alan, quietly. 'No school for a while, Jack.'

'It's Sunday tomorrow, why don't we go up to the shop?' because Sunday was the day they always did.

'Yes, please,' said Jack.

He lay on the landing with Idris and turned the pages of the stamp album under the mountain that filled the window.

Jean watched them from the top of the back stairs with Nesta.

'When I'm gone,' Idris told Jack, 'this will be yours.'

'Where are you going, Idris, you silly man?' laughed Nesta. 'Don't listen to him, Jack.'

'Is she smiling?' asked Delia, holding Jean's hand. 'You know, I think she is.' The test card flickered. 'Do they ever switch that television off?'

A nurse overheard her and turned it off. 'Sometimes they like to watch it so we keep it switched on.'

'You know, I think you're right,' said Nesta, 'she is smiling.'

'Definitely,' said Emlyn. 'Well, well. Is it a sign, do you think?'

Aled was collected from the police station as if he were lost property: he was, the baffled child.

Brenda handed him over to the crowding relations, pale with relief.

'Can we see, Alan?' Delia asked.

'No,' said Sergeant Phillips.

'Can I take Aled to see him?' Brenda asked.

'No.'

'Is Eve here,' Delia asked. 'Can we see her?'

'No.' He left them at the front desk without another word.

Aled screamed.

Alan could hear him from his cell and could do nothing. He pressed his face to the cold metal door and clutched at the grille. No one would tell him. Sergeant Phillips forbade it.

Nesta carried Aled out to the van. She said, 'But we are old.' They would do anything for him, but they were old and anything would not last. 'He needs his brother.'

'He needs his father and mother,' said Howell, from the front, 'but I cannot find it in my heart to blame Eve so very much. I think she did it for love.'

'Did she?' asked Delia.

'There's too much of everything,' said Idris. 'Everything is up in the air, where will it land?'

'Will it be resolved?' asked Howell. 'Will justice prevail?'

'We must do all we can,' said Idris.

'What is that?' asked Emlyn. No one replied.

The Herald: a picture of Alan in Sergeant Phillips' big, black car, ghostly white through the window, with the blaze from the flash reflecting back off the glass. It was as if he had already been cast into the flames.

Father of Missing Boy Charged with Murder of Gwyn Roberts

Alan Harris has been charged with the murder of Gwyn Roberts of Blackbrook Farm. Sergeant Phillips said the murder, 'Was a distraction from Harris' true purpose.' He went on to say that, 'Significant progress,' was being made in the case of the missing three boys, of which, the body of one, Huw Evans, 6, was discovered in Porthcawl Harbour. The search for Jack Harris, 6, the son of Alan Harris, and Rhodri Mitchell, 7, continues. Sergeant Phillips told The Herald *that he expects charges to be brought in the next few days but wouldn't comment further.*

Eve turned to see Aled's uncles and aunties already getting up to leave the court. On the bus on the way home, she thought, 'I am being made to go back to where I don't want to be. There's no escape.' She was hollowed out and the painkillers had gone on the fire.

It is within my power to impose a stiff sentence. You stole the boy away and attempted to cover your tracks in doing so. You did not volunteer his return, you had to be sought out and brought back and, if not for the commendable work of the police, he may still have not been found.

She was exhausted when she got to the house. 'I didn't want to see this place again. I didn't think I would.'

The emptiness of the two houses on either side was filled with the memory of children's laughter: she kept listening but could not hear it.

In mitigation, I am aware that you had a relationship with the boy's family that went back to your own childhood.

Her grief was not less for the children she had wanted but never had. Jack, Huw and Aled had almost quelled the ache.

I take account, also, of the tragic context in which your actions took place.

Now, she echoed like an empty oil drum to the sound of her lonely voice, her thoughts as loud as her voice, she couldn't tell them apart: 'This is what happened to Jean.'

She slept in the chair in the front room where she had nursed Aled to sleep, craving the faintest smell of him.

You believed you were offering him protection but, in so doing, you denied his blood relations that right and expectation and caused them considerable anguish.

In the morning, she surveyed her wrecked garden and went out and, without stopping to think why, began picking up the broken window frames from Roy's greenhouse and stacking them against the fence. Wearing his gardening gloves, so big she had to push her fingers deep onto them to pick up the pieces of shattered glass amongst the weeds. Methodically, she filled in some of the holes.

I believe you are a decent woman who has suffered in turn.

She worked all day without stopping and, by the evening, it was tidier but still not a garden.

She slept in the chair: if she went to bed she would never get out of it – tempting, though it was, to waste away there.

I am not, therefore, inclined to hand down a custodial sentence but, under the strict terms of your probation, you are to have no further contact with the boy for a period of two years and then only with express permission of his parents or legal guardians. Seek forgiveness from them.

The next day, she was in the garden again, making herself tired. At the end of the day, she went upstairs for the first time to wash and change.

The houses in Gwyn's fields were taking shape. She would have new neighbours who must not know who she was or the part she had played.

Should you not obey the terms of your probation and find yourself before me again, you may be certain of prison.

She would hide herself away.

But, for now, Eve Brown, you are free to go.

'I didn't think we'd see this day,' said Bryn's father.

'Let's be glad we have,' replied Mr Tanner, as they stood before the church doors, watching the guests arrive. It was a spring day, with showers forecast but none yet, and the sun was sharp.

'But here we are and I give thanks for it.'

Mr Tanner smiled, 'You're in the right place for it.'

Mr Hughes nudged him and leaned closer to his ear, 'Don't tell the Reverend but I'm not very God fearing, to be honest.'

'Perish the thought that I would divulge your secret. Do you cross your fingers in church?'

Mr Hughes laughed, 'Not quite.'

Mrs Hughes adjusted her husband's buttonhole carnation nervously. 'Shouldn't we go in? Everyone's arriving. We ought to be inside.'

'I suppose we should.'

'After you,' said Mr Tanner.

Reverend Elwiss was standing with his back to the altar at the top of the aisle, resplendently gleaming, with his hands gently gripped in front of him, slowly rising and lowering himself on his toes in anticipation. When he saw Mr Tanner, he beamed.

Mr Tanner raised his eyebrows in response and took his place on the groom's side (he had been in a quandary, but Laura had insisted).

There was a small choir of children fidgeting next to the organ, all in their school uniforms, being glared at by the elderly Mrs Wright (she who had seen off four vicars) playing a subdued, preliminary accompaniment to the filling church. When Mr Tanner entered, the children immediately behaved.

'This is a day your mum should have seen,' said Laura's father in the back of the car as they journeyed to the church.

'Yes, Dad, she should.'

'I'll be thinking about her all the time. I won't be able to help it but, if I think about her too much during my speech, I don't think I'll be able to get through it.'

'You will get through it, you know you will.'

'I'm not looking forward to it, I can tell you; I hate public speaking.'

'Try standing up in front of a classroom every day.'

'There is that,' he said. 'It's not quite the same though. It's not too late, you know?'

'For what?'

'To change your mind.'

'Dad.'

'I'm joking.'

Laura and her father waited at the door to the church with the sun shining on her dress and through her veil.

Mrs Wright struck up with gusto.

Reverend Elwiss raised his hands and the congregation stood.

Bryn Hughes pushed himself up more slowly with the arm of the pew. He was wan and thin and walked with a slight limp that would disappear in time, but the hearing in his left ear would never fully recover (and he had already developed a habit of turning it to noisy classrooms – Laura teased him, 'You're like Nelson looking through his telescope with his blind eye.').

He took a step forward with his brother at his side, but he didn't turn to look at her until she was next to him. Then he smiled.

Reverend Elwiss bent down and whispered, 'You look lovely, Laura. Are you ready? I'll say a few words and then we'll begin the service proper.' He stood up straight and looked over their heads and motioned to the congregation to sit, which they did with a rustling of uncooperative dresses and the creaking of wooden pews.

'Good morning,' he began. 'A happy day, finally, a joyous occasion to be celebrated and more so after the ordeal Bryn and Laura have endured, along with their family and friends.' There were murmurs of agreement. 'We all face our trials and the trials faced by this wonderful young couple have been greater than most and, yet, here they are. Sometimes, we are forced by inexplicable circumstances to question our fellow man and to question ourselves. But, if we are to make sense of the trials that enter our lives, it is by believing in and supporting each other as Bryn and Laura have done. So, look away from the flaws that we can see too easily and believe that we are good people at heart. We must not stop believing because if we do, we lose all – love, friendship and our community

– and it is on days like today that the proof of our belief is there for all to see, for even as the shadows loom, they will recede. Bryn, Laura, you are testament to our enduring faith in each other.' He smiled. 'Shall we begin?'

'Fine words,' listened Sergeant Phillips, as the breakers boomed against the seawall.

He ran the outside of his thumbs down his moustache and took off his gloves, carefully placing them, one on top of the other, on the dashboard. He reached into his breast pocket and took out a half crown and two shillings. He stroked the half crown in the palm of his hand and circled the two shillings around it and his eyes rose to look at the people walking on the promenade and the congregation filing out of the church, alive with colour and gaiety, led by the bride pristine and her minted groom. Slowly, his fingers closed over the coins and he held his fist like an orb above his knee.

He smiled a scythe. He said, 'I know their minds,' but his lips did not move.

He slid the coins back into his pocket, buttoned it and smoothed down the flap. Sergeant Phillips drew on his gloves and flexed his calfskin muscles tight over the bones.

High in the sky, there were two puffs of white smoke and two bangs: the maroons.

Flash

Births, Deaths and Marriages.
Sir and Miss become Mr and Mrs.

Acknowledgments

Chapter 8, Page 114: Extract from *The Buried City of Kenfig* – Thomas Gray, 1909

With special thanks to Judy, who read it chapter by chapter, and to Tracy and Debbie for telling me what they thought and to Gill, whom I plagued for the right answers and to Shahidur who told me, ‘Even if only one person reads it, that’s better than no one.’

And to my Uncle Dilwyn, whose stamp album it was, and now is mine – as he promised it would be, ‘When I am gone,’ on that rain-filled day in the Rhondda beneath the mountains when I was a boy and didn’t understand what he meant.

R David

April 2020

Printed in Great Britain
by Amazon

48787549R00222